KEEPER

THE BOOK OF AON

Rachel,
Enjoy the
adventure! Happy
Reading!

Kate H

K. M. Higginbotham

Printed in the United States of America

First Edition, 2016

ISBN-13: 978-1535091398
ISBN-10: 1535091398

To my parents, for their unconditional love and support, and Haley, who watched Aon grow from the ground up.

KEEPER

THE BOOK OF AON

one

I've always liked books. As a kid with a less than perfect life, they became saviors, my getaways in bad situations and comforters when I had no one to turn to. I could imagine myself in any world as any character and ignore the pain of reality. My books held my hand and offered a shoulder for me to cry on when my few real friends didn't live up to the job.

I really shouldn't complain about my life. I've seen worse. I've lived worse. What I've seen in the real world is nothing compared to what I've seen in places less tangent.

But first, let me back up to the beginning. None of this will make sense if I keep rambling.

It all started the night after the big storm, on the slick deserted streets. I was exhausted from a double shift at the diner and hours of studying for a history exam in the library. It seems like a lot for a twenty-year-old who's still barely getting used to college, but a girl's got to pass her exams if she wants to do anything with her life. Or at least, that's what my professors tell me.

Shivering and yawning, I couldn't wait to get home and collapse. I became so wrapped up in my own thoughts that I didn't hear the sound of rapid footsteps splashing down the sidewalk right behind me.

It's funny how fast a situation can change. One minute, a stranger comes barreling down the sidewalk behind me, and the next, I'm walking with him like an old friend.

Still, for some reason, something seemed off about the young boy standing next to me. Was it his tattered clothes? Or the alley he'd been sitting in? Maybe the muddled British accent that seemed totally out of place in our small all-American town?

No, I decided. *It's the journal he's holding onto like it's a lifeline.*

After almost being knocked over into a puddle, I'd seen him sprint into an alley. It scared me a little, truth be told, seeing someone so young by himself on the streets in the dark, but I convinced him to walk with me on the contrastingly *very well lit* sidewalk. Seeing him alone unnerved me; I couldn't leave him there.

Covered head to toe in mud and soaking wet to the bone, he joined me without question. His curly dark chestnut hair dripped water onto his face, and his green eyes sparkled under the droplets hung on his lashes.

"What did you say your name is again?" I asked him. We walked side by side down the sidewalk. "Edward?"

"Ed," he corrected me. "What's yours?"

"Elizabeth," I responded. "Elizabeth Knight." I stuck my icy hands into the pockets of my rain jacket. Coldness hung in the air tonight; Edward didn't seem to notice.

"Ed, how old are you?"

"Thirteen."

"And you're out here on your own? Do you have a place to stay tonight?"

"No." He shrugged it off, a seemingly unimportant fact to him.

"Don't you have *anyone* you can stay with?"

"Nope," he answered simply.

I frowned, scratching my head. "Well, I can't leave you out here on the streets by yourself. It's dangerous."

He didn't say anything. He just folded his arms around the leather journal he carried and continued walking.

"Where are you from, Ed?" I asked. "How did you get here?"

"It's a long story."

"I think I can keep up."

He sighed. "To be honest, I don't really know. It all happened so quickly. I was running from the Night Rider—"

"Night Rider?" *What an odd name.*

"Never mind," he mumbled, shaking his head. "I was running from... someone, and this Book brought me here—"

"You aren't making any sense." I took in the image of his wet clothes and dirty face. Where would he stay? I couldn't leave him on the street. I'd never live it down.

"Do you have anywhere to go?"

He shook his head. "I'll find somewhere, though. I'm fine."

"Yes, I can see that," I muttered.

"I don't appreciate the sarcasm."

"Listen," I said with a sigh, making my decision,

"since you have no place to stay, do you want to stay with me? Just for tonight? We can figure something out about your family tomorrow."

He seemed to want to protest, but perked up when something like a crash echoed through the streets. His jade eyes went wide and he froze where he stood, petrified with fear.

How has he survived out here so far if he's scared of a little noise? It was probably just an alley cat.

"Yeah," he said without question. "Thank you."

It was late by the time we got to my apartment. As soon as I opened the door, I scrambled to find dry towels to wrap him in; he wouldn't show it, but he had to be freezing.

"You can sleep on the couch." I pointed to the living room. "Have you had anything to eat? Do you want some food?"

"No, I'm fine."

I frowned. When was the last time he'd eaten? "Are you sure?"

Nodding, he flashed me a reassuring smile. "Positive. Thank you, though."

He laid his journal out next to him on the couch. He twiddled his thumbs, watching me carefully.

"Do you need to dry that off?" I gestured to it. The beautiful dark leather cover shone, spotted with caramel patches where the color had worn down. An embossed scroll pattern weaved around the perimeter of the cover and crossed over the spine.

"It's dry," he answered.

"That's impossible. It's been raining all day."

"It's dry, I promise. Don't worry about it."

There's no way.

My hand reached for the Book, jerking back when

Ed's hands shot out to grab it before me.

"Okay then," I relented, stepping back. He gripped the binding protectively in his hands. "So, are you good here?"

"Great."

"You're sure?"

"Go to bed, Elizabeth." He waved me off. "I'm fine here. Good night."

With a wary glance at Ed, I padded back to my room and hoped that I hadn't let a thief or a murderer into my apartment. No one else lived there but me; I'd only have myself for protection.

Really, Liz? You're smarter than that. He's a thirteen-year-old kid, not some creepy middle-aged psychopath.

Sleep came easily to me, but it didn't stay like I hoped it would. I woke up around 3 AM, feeling overheated and parched, drenched in sweat from the nightmares that invaded my dreams.

They were always the same, the nightmares, though I couldn't tell you what they were about. Sometimes, I didn't even remember. I always tried my best to ignore them.

I changed to dry clothes and tied my hair up on the top of my head before I padded into the kitchen for a glass of water.

I jumped when I noticed Ed asleep on the couch, having forgotten he was there. The journal that he had carried so protectively only hours earlier had fallen, and the pages lay sprawled on the floor.

Maybe it wouldn't hurt to read a little bit of it. Maybe it will tell me something about him.

Convincing myself that everything would be fine, I forced my hand to grasp the leather binding before retreating to my room and curling up under the duvet.

He won't miss it for an hour. It'll be like it was never gone.

Curiously, I flipped through the worn and slightly brittle pages. They smelled faintly of dust, lavender, and grass. Every few pages the handwriting would change, and I'd find a different name, as if someone had picked up where one had left off. Darren, Maximilian, Josephine, and a few other names flashed before my eyes as the pages flipped.

Maybe this is his family.

Flipping back to the first page, I found a name written in the middle in a large, curly script: Alice Dayton.

Paying little attention to the name, I turned the page and read.

Once upon a time, in a beautiful world far away, there lived a colorful kingdom called Aon. The capital city, Devereux, lay at the center of the land, a city on a hill. Surrounded by villages, cities, and quiet countryside and bordered by acres of colorful, peaceful woods and simple cottages, where the few forest-dwellers made their homes, the land was envied by surrounding kingdoms.

Is this a storybook? I wondered. *Is Ed a writer?*

The king and queen were loved, and the villages were peaceful places filled with compassionate people. Aon was on good terms with every diplomat and kingdom in the world; the citizens never feared danger. Everything was perfect.

Until the long-lived peace came to a startling end.

One day, a stranger rode into the capital city. His horse and cloaks were as black as the night, so the people dubbed him the name Night Rider.

The Night Rider rode to the castle and threatened the monarchs, speaking of his power at the great cost of tragedy. He threatened to make Aon suffer if he wasn't given the crown.

Night Rider, I thought. *It sounds familiar.*

The king laughed in the face of the Rider and banished him beyond the forests of Aon. Grudgingly, the Night Rider promised he would return the moment the king was dead. He disappeared and never returned, leaving the kingdom forever… or so they thought.

True to his word, the moment the king drew his last breath, the Night Rider stepped foot in Aon once again.

The words started to swim before my eyes, and soon, I gave in and fell asleep. Exhausted, I let my mind wander back into the land of dreams, hopeful that tonight's dreams would be different than the dreams of years past.

two

I've never really been one to take kindly to being woken up, especially when I'm suffering from a lack of sleep. Waking up to a life or death situation, though... Now *that's* a different story.

"Oh, now you've done it," someone mumbled, shaking my shoulders. "Get up, we have to move!"

I squinted as Ed's freckled face came into focus. "What's wrong? Did someone break in?"

"Elizabeth, we aren't in your apartment anymore. Come on, get up! We have to move before they find us!"

Speechless, I looked around. He was right.

This was *definitely not* my apartment.

The thick grass tickled my neck where I laid under the canopy of towering trees. The sun streamed down and cast a bright yellow light around us. Ed loomed over me, his book in one hand.

My first thought: This had to be a dream.

That's impossible. You've dreamt the same thing over and over again for ten years.

"Liz, if you don't get up, I'm leaving you. I'm pretty sure you don't want to meet the men hunting us on horses."

At that, I shot up and grabbed his hand, taking off into the woods. The hoof beats got louder, and Ed's grip on the Book got tighter.

"Who is *that?*" I asked as we sprinted through the trees. He stopped me, pointing up.

"Later, Liz! Start climbing!"

In a flash, Ed was at the base of one of the large trees, climbing up each branch, one by one. I followed suit, gripping a knot in the trunk to pull myself closer to the lowest branch. I'd never really done a lot of climbing, not since I was younger; the branches felt familiar in my grip, though, so I went with the feeling and soon scaled the tree right behind Ed.

I reached the top just as the men on horses came into view. I was thankful that the foliage concealed us—I didn't like the idea of having an arrow shot towards my head. Ed signaled at me to be silent as they trampled the ground below us, and I tried my best to quiet my heaving breaths.

Just when I thought they were gone, Ed cursed under his breath. He grabbed my hand, silently telling me to stay still as he pointed below us.

On the ground below our tree, a horse as black as night carried a faceless rider. The horse came to a halt as the rider scanned the area around him through the cover of his cloak. I held my breath. I didn't know *who*, or... *what* this thing was, but I didn't want to find out.

Ed suddenly pushed himself higher into the tree, dragging me behind him. Now, we could see this rider, but he seemingly had no view of us.

The rider perked up at the faint noise of us moving. He glanced up, staring in our direction for what seemed like forever, before he snapped the reins and galloped away.

Ed and I let out simultaneous sighs of relief.

"Who was that?" I asked quietly, as if he could still hear us. I didn't notice my body shaking until I looked down at my hands.

"How did he follow us?" Edward asked, mumbling to himself. "That's impossible."

"Edward?"

"It's all ruined. He's going to spoil everything," he said, ignoring me. "What am I going to do?"

"*Edward!*"

He whipped his head around. "What?"

"Would you mind telling me who that was?" I asked. "When my life is put at risk, I find it convenient to know the reason why."

"You could call him a terrorist," he answered, avoiding my gaze. "He's after the crown of Aon, and so far, he's stopped at nothing to get it."

"Does he have a name?"

"No," Ed said. "We call him the Night Rider, but we don't know who's under the cloak."

"How appropriate," I muttered, beginning the descent. I grasped the branches firmly, making sure I wouldn't lose my grip. The shaking still hadn't stopped, and the bark pressed into my hands as they hit the tree over and over.

Ed shot me a deadly glare at my remark. "He's terrorized our cities, our villagers, and our kingdom. He rides during the day and attacks at night. He's just recently become more active, striking without hesitation.

No matter what we try, we can't get rid of him. He's *killed* people, Elizabeth."

I grimaced.

A murderer? How long have I been here again?

How did I even end up here?

"Hey, Ed?" I asked, warily taking in my surroundings as the adrenaline from all the excitement faded. He raised an eyebrow.

"Where exactly are we?"

"Well, we're rather close to Devereux, I believe."

"No, I mean… Where am I? How did I get here?"

A wide grin broke out on his face. "How much do you remember about last night?"

"Everything. I mean, everything until I fell asleep… reading your journal…"

He chuckled. "Welcome to Aon, Elizabeth."

I glanced around. The bright colors, the autumn breeze, and the bright blue sky all pieced together what could certainly pass as the fictional world.

Ed did say that the man on the horse was called the Night Rider. I read that last night, didn't I?

Was that what he was running from last night?

"But where are the forest-dwellers?" I asked. "And the capital city? And the villages and fields?"

"We're only on the outskirts of Aon," he cut me off. "They're here, just further in towards the city."

"This is the most real a dream has ever felt," I marveled. "How is this possible? I've never dreamed up a place like this before."

"Elizabeth, this isn't a dream." Edward shook his head, a frown apparent on his face.

"That's exactly what someone in a dream would say," I pointed out.

"You can't get hurt in dreams, can you?" He climbed

a branch lower before springing from the tree towards the ground. He cried out as he hit the dirt, rolling onto his back and holding his ankle.

"See?" He winced as he shifted his weight. "Not a dream."

"Are you insane?" I watched him struggle on his hurt ankle. "Are you okay?"

"No," he said. "Let's go, and I will be."

It's my dream, not his, I reasoned to myself, *so of course he can get hurt.*

Maybe I shouldn't tell him that—he did just jump out of a tree for me.

I slid to the bottom branch before dropping down next to him, holding his ankle in my hand. After making sure it wasn't broken, I stood up and pulled him with me. His arm came around my shoulder as he used me as a crutch.

"Where are we going?"

"There's a cottage around here somewhere. I recognize the area. My friend's mother was a forest-dweller, and he should be taking care of her home today. Also," he glanced at my clothes, "you can't go around wearing *that*. You need to change if you're going to blend in."

I eyed my shorts and faded t-shirt. Unfortunately, I didn't normally sleep with shoes on, so my socks ended up being the only barrier between the ground and my feet.

"You're probably right," I said sheepishly.

"Mm," he said in agreement. Together, we limped through the woods until the trees turned from oak to aspen and the grass became spotted with wildflowers. Oddly enough, there were no rocks on the ground. I was thankful that my feet were spared from anything that could put a hole in my foot.

Dream or not, I don't think that'd be pleasant.

Soon, a small cottage could be seen in the distance. It was something you'd see in a movie, with piles of wood waiting to be chopped and a small garden growing on the far side of the walls.

The smile on Ed's face grew as he let go of me to hobble towards the house. A boy stood outside, washing his face in a barrel of water that stood against the cobblestone wall.

"Joey!"

The boy perked up, smiling as we came into view. Tall and dark headed, he held a resemblance to Ed. I wondered if they were related.

He flashed an uncertain glance at me, his eyes traveling up and down my figure before he dried his face on his sleeve. Suddenly, I felt extremely self-conscious of my appearance. I tugged my shorts down a little further on my thighs.

Ed launched himself into Joey, hugging him tightly.

Joey returned the hug and then stepped back to study him. His expression changed from happy to solemn. "You know you've put the kingdom into complete and utter chaos. You didn't tell me where you were going, and you didn't leave a note. I've been worried sick, Ed. And what happened to your ankle?"

"I jumped from a tree," he stated.

"Do I need to ask why?" Joey said. "Well, when you get back to the city we'll have Alec patch up your ankle. In the meantime, I'll make a splint for it, okay?"

He nodded. "All right."

Joey seemed to remember I was still there, and gave Ed a suspicious glance before approaching me. Ed grinned.

"I'm Joey." He held out his hand. I noticed that he had a faint accent that I couldn't recognize, similar to Ed's. Was it British? Irish? Maybe a mix of both? "You are?"

Joey was strikingly similar to a younger version of Fitzwilliam Darcy. He had dark, tousled hair and striking ice blue eyes. He was tall and muscular, sporting a vest under a jacket, a cravat, and tight pants tucked into riding boots. He couldn't have been but a year or two older than me, so I suppose *boy* isn't the right way to put it.

"Elizabeth Knight." I extended my hand for a handshake. Instead, Joey took my hand, flipped it over, and kissed the top, taking me by surprise.

"Well, Elizabeth," he said with a fleeting glimpse at my appearance, "you look like you're not from around here."

"I'm not." I tossed a glance at Ed. He shrugged, as if to say *just go with it.*

"I think I might be able to find something for you to wear." Joey eyed me, scrutinizing my rumpled t-shirt and faded shorts. "You need to look like a villager, at least for a little while."

"You might want to start with a pair of shoes," Edward said, flashing an amused grin at my dirt-covered socks. I narrowed my eyes at him.

"Good idea." Joey smirked, crossing his arms across his chest.

Edward nudged my shoulder. "I'm going inside for a while. Elizabeth?"

"I'm fine out here, actually," I said with a sudden burst of confidence. I wanted to learn more about this place, and this man seemed more willing than Ed.

Ed shrugged before opening the door and

disappearing inside.

"You're an Outsider," Joey said, as soon as Ed disappeared from view. He shrugged out of his coat and vest then untied his cravat to reveal a simple white shirt.

"Is that a question?"

"No." He chuckled, reaching for the axe stuck in a tree stump to my right. "No, it's a statement. You'd have to be a fool to think that you fit in around here. Lucky for you, you have to be a little smarter to put two and two together and realize you're from *that* world. Outsiders can be hard to uncover, sometimes. Not many people can do it."

"And you can?" I snapped. If he aimed to make a good impression, he failed. I was annoyed already. *So much for asking him about this place.*

"And you have *names* for people from my world?"

"Yes, I can, and yes, we do have a name for you. You're an Outsider."

I remained silent as he chopped wood pieces from the large pile next to the stump.

"Are you *smirking* at me?" I asked, noticing the corners of his lips turned up.

"What? Who would do such a thing?" He grinned mischievously, turning his face away.

"You are!" I pointed at him. "You're smirking at me!"

"What's wrong with that? I *am* allowed to have emotions."

"You're making me feel stupid! Stop it!"

"You don't need me for that, love," he said, throwing a piece of rotted wood to the side, "you've got that all on your own."

Did he just call me 'love'?

He laughed. I ground my teeth.

"Whatever. Just let me know when your maturity level decides to pick up. Obviously, you can't handle having Outsiders around. Ed is more mature than this, and he's a kid!"

His mouth had dropped open, and he closed it with a glare. "I can handle Outsiders, just not the exceptionally annoying ones."

Feeling smug, I allowed my lips to twist into a smile. "You're one to talk. I'm sure every Outsider you've met thought you were just as bad, if not worse."

He scoffed. "As if. You're just unnaturally unbearable."

"Do you just *have* to come up with an answer for everything?"

"You started it!"

"I didn't start it, but I can end it," I threatened.

"Whatever." After a final glare, he gripped the axe and paced away from me towards the thick woods, murmuring to himself. I shook my head in frustration, stomping to the house to join Ed.

The cottage was small, but simple. A circular mirror hung between two lanterns on the wall and a crocheted lace doily rested in the center of the table. It was decorated with a modest dining set on top of plain and beautifully preserved wood, which offset the room perfectly. In the fireplace burned a blaze that lent cozy warmth to the room. Open windows let in the fragrant, fall air, and I could detect the subtle scent of lavender and grass—the same smells that perfumed Edward's book.

"What did you do to him?" he asked with a laugh as I pulled up a chair. "I've never seen him this angry… And I'm not quite sure if leaving a madman with an axe by himself in the woods is a good idea."

"I didn't do anything!" I defended. "It's his fault!"

"Whoa, it's okay. I'm not attacking you."

I took a deep breath. Joey had brought out the worst in me in less than ten minutes. "Sorry."

"Don't worry about it. Tea?" He carefully moved a steaming kettle from the fire to the table.

"No, thank you," I replied. As he poured a glass for himself, I used the opportunity to try to pry information from him and figure out what was going on. "Ed," I said, watching him prepare his tea, "mind explaining to me how we got here?"

"Sure," he said nonchalantly. "The Book brought us here."

I frowned. "The Book?"

"We call it the Book of Aon, but it's more like a journal than anything. Basically, you read the story, fall asleep, and the Book brings you here while you're unconscious."

It was then I noticed the journal—or the Book, or whatever—lying on the table, the light from the window giving the worn down leather a muted shine. "So, you're telling me that this little notebook has the power to transport people to another dimension?"

"Almost. That's probably as close to an explanation as you'll get. The key here is to try not to think about it too much, or you'll probably go insane."

"Did I bring you here with me?" I asked, ignoring his comment and turning back to face him.

"No, I woke up after you took the Book." He eyed me. "And I read the first part and went to sleep as soon as I found it by your bedside. I couldn't let you get far without me."

"Why did you follow me here?"

His face read '*What do you think?*' before he answered.

"Do you honestly think you could've survived the first ten minutes without me here?"

"Never mind, you're right." I remembered the panic of the chase and the fear that I'd felt. I never would have survived that without Edward. "By the way, how do you know anything about this place?"

Another look.

"Stop," I said. "Your face will stick like that."

"Liz, this is where I'm from. I *live* here."

I dropped my head into my hands. "Never mind, I feel like an idiot. Keep giving me that look, I deserve it."

He laughed. "Don't worry about it. Wonderful kingdom, Aon is," he said with fondness. "I was born in the capital city."

"It's beautiful so far. You know, minus being chased by the horsemen. Speaking of which," I said curiously, "why were they after us?"

"The young prince is missing," he replied easily, staring down into his teacup and stirring absentmindedly with his spoon. "They assumed that we knew something about it."

"Does this prince have a name?"

His response came sharp and short. "I'll let you know when I remember it."

I gave him an uneasy glance. "Why would they assume we knew anything?"

He shrugged, and gave me no more answer on the subject. "I should take you to Yula when we get to the capital city—she'll have answers to all of your questions."

"Who's Yula?"

Ed sighed. "You ask so many questions."

I wanted to press him further but stopped when I spotted Joey pacing across the grass with a large bundle of wood in his hands and the axe balanced on the top. He dropped the wood onto the top of the already large stack of logs before dusting the dirt off his hands. The sound echoed through the woods. He seemed conflicted for a moment as he surveyed the area around him but stiffened when he caught my eye through the window.

He hastened up the steps into the cottage, a small, rectangular wooden splint in his hand.

"Ed," he said calmly, avoiding my eye as he washed his hands in a basin of water, "I have business to attend to in the country, but I'll take you as far as the outskirts of town. I'll wrap your ankle, then will you go ready the horses?" He dried his hands and then pulled something white from his pocket.

Ed nodded politely, adjusting his chair for Joey to reach his leg. Joey knelt next to him with gauze and a square of soft fabric. He wrapped the boy's ankle with care and attached the wooden splint. When he finished, Ed smiled at me and limped out of the cottage with the Book in hand.

"Come with me," Joey said when we were alone. "I think I have something here that will fit you." He washed and dried his hands again on a rag draped over the edge of the basin and rolled his sleeves back down to his wrists from his elbows.

His boots made loud thumps against the wood-planked floor as I followed him into another room where a small bed stood against the wall with a thin quilt draped over it. A rocking chair occupied the space in the corner, and a heavy wooden chest sat against the wall next to the door.

Joey knelt next to the chest and lifted the lid.

Inside, blankets almost overflowed the chest. As he sifted through the fabric, he spoke quietly.

"Forgive me for how I've acted," he apologized. "You've only just arrived and I've already left a bad impression."

My jaw dropped open slightly. *He felt the need to apologize?*

"No worries," I replied, closing my mouth, "I acted the same way. I'm sorry."

He flashed a crooked smile. "We're even, then."

"You could say that."

At last, he pulled out several items and laid them on the bed.

"These were my mother's. You seem to be about her size. Let me know if they don't fit, though, and I'll see what I can do."

His mother's?

Based on what Joey wore himself, I guessed I would stand out a little by wearing shorts, socks, and a t-shirt, so I decided not to argue.

"Thank you," I said, catching his arm as he passed me. "For everything."

He glanced down at my hand on his arm. "My pleasure." He bowed and then left the room, closing the door behind him.

Bowing. Slightly odd, but I could get used to it.

Hesitantly, I approached the bundle of fabric that lay on the bed. I picked up one article of clothing, only to let it drop when I realized what it was.

A corset?

I'm supposed to wear a corset?

I heard horses whinny outside and decided to suck it up. It took a few minutes of awkward positioning, but I figured out how to put it on. I left it loose so that I could breathe.

Next came a pale blue dress made of linen, quarter

sleeve length that flowed all the way down below my ankles. I surprised myself at how much I liked it. Hardly a girly-girl growing up, I avoided dresses as much as I could—not that I could afford many anyway—but this one felt different. It flowed from my waist and hugged the right places. Faded and worn, it smelled of dust and pine, and I could tell it hadn't been pulled from that chest in a long time. It had character.

I ignored the stockings, avoiding them as soon as I saw them. I did, however, very much like the boots. I was even more surprised that they fit me rather well, despite my feet sliding around in them a bit. My hair bun from last night had come down, and I combed through the waved strands with my fingers.

When I returned to the kitchen, Joey sat at the table. He didn't say anything for a few seconds.

"What?" I asked.

He cleared his throat, shaking his head. "Nothing. Do the clothes fit you okay?"

"Yeah, great. Thank you."

"You're welcome. Are you ready to go? Ed has the horses ready."

"Yeah, let's go. I'm curious to see more of this place."

He seemed amused as he opened the door for me and let me go out first.

Two hours later, we rode through the forest side by side. Joey and I talked quietly to each other as Ed took the lead, weaving through trees for fun.

"So, how do you know Ed?" I asked. "Are you related?"

"He's my half-brother." His eyes briefly flicked in my direction. "We share the same father."

"That explains why you two are so similar. He has

the same color hair and the same nose as you."

"So I've been told," he responded, a ghost of a smile on his lips. "What about you? Have any siblings?"

"None. I'm an only child."

"Your parents never thought about giving you someone to play with?"

"I don't know," I answered. "They died when I was four."

His mouth dropped open. "Oh, I'm sorry."

"Don't be. It was a really long time ago."

"What happened to them?" he asked cautiously. "If you don't mind my asking, that is."

"They died in a house fire. I was at the neighbor's house when it happened. I lived in a girl's home until I was eighteen. I've been on my own ever since."

"Surely your parents had relatives."

"Neither of my parents had siblings, and my grandparents were too old to care for me. They died not long after my parents did."

"Well, that's something I can understand," Joey said, offering a smile. "Neither of my parents had siblings either. When they died, Ed and I depended on each other."

"I'm glad you two had each other. I'm sure it made it easier."

"Did you get lonely?"

"It's something I learned to live with. I just kept myself busy and it was easier to manage. Like college, for example—I worked my butt off in school to make sure I'd get a full scholarship to college, and I work double shifts to pay for my apartment. It's hard to focus on loneliness when you have a list of things to do, you know?"

He didn't answer.

"It's not all bad, though; they left me a little money in my inheritance, and I got some money from the insurance company from when the house burned that they've been holding for me. It's enough to keep me comfortable, when you add the money I get from working at the diner."

"You said that you're in school. What do you want to be?"

"I don't know," I said. "I'm still undecided. I'm trying to make it through one class at a time before I decide my major, though. I have exams to study for; that's what I was doing before I found Ed."

"How *did* you find Ed?"

"It's a long story."

"We've got time," he replied.

"I'll start at the beginning," I said, brushing my hair out of my face. I recounted everything, from beginning up until running into Joey. The sun started setting, and by the time I finished, the moon lit up the sky.

"We should set up the camp for the night." His gaze traveled up to the stars that dotted the sky. "I'll start a fire."

He stopped his horse, jumping down and tying the reins to a tree. I did the same, helping Ed down as he jogged off into the woods for firewood.

"I love sleeping out here," Ed said as we tied up our horses. "I love how big the sky feels when you can lie down and look up at it."

"It is amazing, isn't it?" I agreed.

"Joey prefers sleeping in the trees. He says he likes being high up, but he never does it when it's just me and him."

"Why not?"

"He's afraid something bad will happen to me. He

won't let me do most things without him coming with me nowadays."

"The Night Rider?" I asked, piecing it together.

"Yes," he said, "the Night Rider."

Joey came back with a bundle of wood, dropping it in front of us, and then he stooped over to light the fire. In no time, a crackling flame engulfed the large stack of wood, and the warm smell of burning pine and smoke filled the air.

"I'm going to go get more for the rest of the night," he said, turning around.

"I'll help," I offered. He glanced over his shoulder, casting a wary glimpse at Ed.

"I'll be fine, Joey," Ed said. "It's five minutes."

Joey's eyes shifted between Ed and me before he continued into the woods, me at his heels.

"You can gather rocks," he said. "We'll need them so the fire doesn't spread."

"On it." I picked up a large rock. I carried it back to camp, dropping it on the edge of the fire before heading back into the woods to gather more.

In no time, Joey had a large stack of wood at camp and rocks surrounding the flames to keep them in one place.

"Ed," said Joey as he finished stacking the wood, "you're going to go straight to the castle tomorrow, right?"

I caught Ed's eyes flicking in my direction.

I decided to wait to ask Ed about it later. From the expression he gave me, I guessed he wasn't telling me something.

Ed lay on his back on the ground when I crouched next to him. Joey jogged past us and started to climb a large tree a few feet from where his brother lay.

"How many stars do you think there are?" Ed asked me.

"Probably more than there are people in the world."

"You're probably right." He grew quiet, but after a moment of comfortable silence, he spoke again. "I think everyone has his own star."

I smiled to myself. "You think?"

"Yeah." He grinned. "I think some stars shine brighter than others on purpose. The brightest ones are the people we remember; they're the ones who were secretly great."

"Not all of them are secret, though," I said, lying down next to him on the ground and sharing the view of the night sky. "Some of them are so obviously great that you can't help but stare."

"Like that one." He pointed up into the sky. My eyes focused on the biggest, brightest star, almost directly above us.

"Yes, like that one. Who do you think that one is?"

It was peacefully quiet for a moment, and then he answered. "I think it's my mother."

"Your mother?"

"Everyone tells me she was the kindest woman to walk the earth."

"You never met her?"

"Yes, but I was too young to remember much. I barely remember her. All I have are portraits to go by, and those are never perfectly accurate. I wish I knew what she looked like, down to the last freckle and the sparkle in her eyes. I want to know what her voice sounded like, what she smelled like, and what made her smile."

I frowned. "I'm sorry."

"Don't worry about it." He waved me off. "I just like

to think that she can see me, you know?"

I already admired Ed so much in so little time. He was so young, but he'd already come to terms with his feelings. "So, you think that star is hers?"

He let out a short laugh, a faint smile resting on his lips. "Yeah, that one is hers."

I smiled, appreciating Ed's imagination. It was a nice thought, to think we still had a way to see the ones we lost.

"Goodnight, Liz," Ed said after a long silence.

I looked over at him.

"Goodnight, Ed."

He closed his eyes, crossing his arms across his chest as he settled in. Only a few minutes passed before I heard his soft snores fill the hushed forest air.

three

Morning came fast. I woke up, expecting to see my apartment, but instead, I found a smoldering fire and a young boy standing over me.

"Wake up, Elizabeth."

I sat up, rubbing my eyes. It was early; I could feel it in the air. The dew still glinted on the grass, and the frigid air sprouted chill bumps on my arms.

Ed grinned as he watched me yawn. "Still tired, eh?"

"Just a little." I got up and brushed the dirt and grass from my dress. "So, what're we doing now?"

"Riding." He limped over to the horses and untied his, and I did the same. "Joey left earlier this morning. He wanted to get back by tomorrow morning, so he went on ahead."

"He left *earlier?*"

He laughed. "Time doesn't seem to have an effect on him. Some days he'll wake up at four in the morning to start his day, and some days he'll wake up at eleven."

"Lovely," I mumbled. "So, if he left, I assume we're close?"

"Close enough. It'll probably take us three or four hours to make it to the capital."

"That's not that bad. Let's get a move on; I want to see this grand city of yours." Eagerly, I helped Ed onto his horse and then mounted mine.

Just like Ed predicted, I started to see the top of a tall building over the trees within the third hour of riding. Ed pointed up to it.

"That's the castle," he said, "but that's nothing compared to the entire city." After only a few more minutes of riding, Ed led us out to the edge of a short drop off where we could see everything clearly.

"*This is it?*" I asked, mouth wide open as the sparkling city came into view.

"Yep. Welcome to Devereux, the heart of Aon."

We stood just inside the gates of the city where I took it all in. In the distance, I could see the castle, grand where it rose on top of a hill. There was no dull space below the castle; the lively kingdom had splashes of color all over. Planting fields, houses, manors, chateaus, stables, and even a large marketplace fit in together perfectly like puzzle pieces. Shades of brown, red, green, grey, gold, and silver all rested against an impossibly blue sky.

"It's beautiful," I breathed. I couldn't believe my eyes; I'd never seen anything so big or beautiful.

"It's even better up close. Would you like to see?"

I nodded, still staring in awe up at the castle. Seeing the castle reminded me of something as we continued up the cobblestone road into the city.

"Ed," I asked, remembering Joey's instruction, "what

did Joey mean by telling you to go to the castle yesterday?"

He stopped, thinking for a moment before he spoke. I could tell he chose his words carefully.

"Remember how I told you the young prince was missing?" he asked. "And how the guards are conducting the search for him?"

My blank expression slowly changed to shock as his words processed in my head.

"Ed, you didn't," I said in realization. "*Please* tell me you aren't."

"I would gladly tell you that," he answered, "but that would be lying."

"Ed, that isn't funny! You mean to tell me the reason those guards were chasing after us in the first place is because they thought I *kidnapped* you?"

He smiled mischievously. "Probably."

I groaned. "No, no, no! Ed, why didn't you tell me?"

"Because I thought you'd freak out! I'm sorry! I wanted to see my brother first, not get dragged back to the castle! Besides, I'm not even sure if I *want* to be the prince!"

I tapped my horse's side with my boot so he would begin to gallop.

"Elizabeth, where are you going?" Ed asked, catching up to me on his horse.

"To find some guards and explain. You're going back to the castle right this instant. I don't want them to find us first. I might end up with an arrow in my head."

"Don't you want to see the city first?" he pleaded. "The minute we get back they'll ask me all sorts of questions about where I've been, and I'll never be let out again. Sometimes that castle is as good as a jail, you know."

"Too bad. You should've thought of that before."

I galloped ahead of him, turning on random streets, searching for guards. About five minutes later, I finally spotted a patrol group stopped for a break at a pub.

"Guards!" I yelled just as Ed paused next to me. They turned, and seeing Ed beside me, they mounted their horses and galloped towards us.

Ed held his head in his hands. "Now you've done it."

"Please don't say that again," I mumbled.

The guards reached us, turning the heads of many townsfolk. Instead of approaching Ed, like I hoped they would, they surrounded me.

"Off your horse!" one of them yelled. "Hands in the air!"

"Guys, she's with me," Ed argued. "Release her."

"Not a chance, Your Highness," another said. "We'll have to speak to your brother before we let her anywhere near you."

"News flash, I've been near him for the past forty-eight hours." I dismounted before approaching them with my hands up.

"Quiet!" the guard yelled, prodding my back with his boot.

"Hey!" Ed yelled. "That was unnecessary!"

"Take her in!" the guard said, ignoring Ed. Two guards held my arms and threw me on the back of one of their horses, tying my hands behind my back. I prayed that I wouldn't fall off while we journeyed up the large hill toward the castle.

Ed rode in the lead with my escorts and me behind him. One guard rode closer to Ed, no doubt making sure he wouldn't run off. The guard I rode with spoke to me quietly over his shoulder.

"Don't worry. If you're innocent you have nothing to worry about. Joseph is a very fair man."

"Thank you," I said, glad someone finally talked to me with kindness. "I've already met him, actually."

"Oh!" he exclaimed. "Then you *really* don't have anything to worry about."

"Well, we haven't gotten along very well so far."

He just laughed.

I peered over his shoulder. "You know, you seem to be the nice one out of all of you. What's your name?"

"Cyneward," he answered.

"That's interesting. I've never heard anything like it."

"It's definitely one of a kind. It literally means 'royal guard.' It was given to me by my father, who also protected this same line of royals."

"So, you were basically born to work for the royal family?" He nodded.

"That must have been tough for you."

"You learn to accept your fate and make the best of it. I try to be fair in whatever I'm involved in so that I'm remembered for being kind and fair, not mean and inexcusably shallow just because I was forced into my job." Cyneward sounded incredibly wise, and I wondered if he had decided all of that on his own, or if he learned it growing up.

"Good goals to have," I commented.

"Thank you… I'm sorry, what is your name?"

"Elizabeth. You can call me Liz, though."

"Nice to meet you, Elizabeth."

I smiled. "Nice to meet you, Cyneward."

I hadn't even noticed when we started to ride uphill, so it surprised me when the castle gates came into view so soon. They opened upon our arrival, and the horses carried us up to the large wooden doors.

Before Cyneward or Ed could dismount, one of the men pulled me off of the horse. Since my hands were bound behind my back, I fell straight on my face into the dirt.

"Ouch," I moaned against the ground. "What was that for?"

I can't feel pain in dreams? That must be wrong. I clearly felt that.

"Get up, girl," he snarled. "It's to the dungeons for you."

"Don't you think that's a little extreme?" Ed asked. "Remember, I *do* have more power than my brother, as *crown prince*. You should be taking orders from me."

"Not until you're a little older, sire," the guard stated plainly. "And she's a criminal, Princeling. Let us handle her. There are some things you're too young to make judgments on."

"I *will* be speaking to my brother about this." He narrowed his eyes at the man. He pulled me up and kept a firm hand on my shoulder.

Ed dismounted with the help of a guard, handing the reins of his horse to him, but not before he pulled a leather pouch out of his saddlebag.

"Of course, Your Highness." The man pushed me towards the door as the rest of the guards tended the horses. Cyneward and Ed followed close behind, the little prince leaning against the guard for support.

I gasped as soon as we entered the palace. The entrance was beautiful, with high, painted ceilings and beautiful arches. I didn't have much time to admire it before the guard shoved me again. He led me through rooms that I could barely get a glimpse of before he'd push me another time and I'd stumble and almost hit the floor.

We came to a discreet wooden door positioned under a staircase after journeying through several hallways. Barred from the outside, the darkness seemed to pulsate within.

"In you go." He opened the door. I shot him a deadly glare before taking a step inside.

A stone staircase spiraled down from where I stood, only a torch here and there to light the path. I hesitantly took it step-by-step, careful not to fall. The sound of our footsteps and breathing echoed against the stone walls. The guard didn't dare push me here; he knew that it would cause more damage if I fell here than anywhere else, and he probably didn't want to be responsible for my death.

When we arrived at the bottom, I wrinkled my nose. A putrid stench hung in the air. The only light came from torches bolted to the walls, and the amount of cells seemed to go on forever. The guard led me to the nearest empty one and threw me inside, locking the door behind me with the keys that hung on the wall. He left without a word, leaving Ed and Cyneward standing in front of my cell and me slumped on the floor.

All the other prisoners in the dungeons seemed to be asleep, for no sound came from any other cells. I guessed they had lost concept of time down there; no outside light could enter the dungeon from the looks of it.

I almost couldn't contain the anger I felt as I shot a glare at Edward. "Ed, explain to me how I've been here for less than seventy-two hours and I'm already in jail."

"Because apparently," he said, unfazed by my deathly stare, "our guards have forgotten who is in charge around here."

"But Prince Edward, your brother—"

He held a hand up to Cyneward. "Whether I am of age to be king or not, I'm still of higher rank than my brother. I'm a prince, and my orders are to be followed first and foremost."

"I'm so terribly sorry this happened," Cyneward said, turning to me. "It's ridiculous that they don't know anything about you but they threw you in the dungeons anyway. I'd open it for you, but I'm not allowed to have the keys to the cellblocks. I'm only on protection detail."

"This is outrageous." Ed gritted his teeth. "I mean, look at this place. It's meant for the worst criminals in the kingdom, not defenseless girls from other worlds." He paced in front of the bars, and then turned to Cyneward. "When Joey gets back, we're promoting you."

"Thank you, sire, but... other worlds?" Cyneward asked. "You don't mean—"

"Yes," Ed cut him off. "Elizabeth brought the Book back this time. I don't think Yula will ask for it, either; I have a hunch that she'll let Liz keep it."

"Wow, that's amazing—"

"Ed, I don't have the Book." I gripped the bars with my hands. "You have it."

I had totally forgotten about the Book since we left the cottage.

"I meant that you're the Keeper of the Book of Aon," he corrected. "You're right, I do have it, but you should be the one holding onto it." He held up the leather pouch.

"Do I want to know what a keeper is?" I asked, eyeing the pouch skeptically.

"Not *a* keeper, *the* Keeper. Your job, while you're here, is to hold onto the Book of Aon and keep it safe. You hold the fate of the entire world in your hands when you have this, and it isn't given to just anybody. In fact, Yula hasn't given any Outsiders the privilege of being the Keeper yet. If she agrees with me, you'll be the first."

"Who is Yula and why would she give it to me?"

"Yula is the author of the Book of Aon," Cyneward explained. "She created the base for the entire world, and other Outsiders like you added to it to make it what it is today."

"You'll meet her eventually. First, we need to get you out of here."

"Maybe if you tell them that she's the Keeper, then they'll let her free!" Cyneward exclaimed.

"You might be right, Cyneward." Ed considered the suggestion. "We still have to wait for my brother to return, though." He turned to me. "I'm so sorry, Liz, but you're going to have to stay here until Joey gets back. He should return tomorrow morning, or late tonight if we're lucky."

"I'll survive," I said lamely. He smiled apologetically before he started the walk up the narrow staircase. Cyneward followed close behind him.

I let out a long sigh, observing the damp, dark dungeon. It was silent. I could hear only the breathing of the other cellmates, apart from my own, and my heartbeat. The thick, humid air made breathing a chore.

I turned away from the bars, inspecting my home for the night.

A battered, thin mattress rested on a rickety metal bed frame. The uneven legs caused it to rock back and forth as I sat down and pulled my knees to my chest. As soon as my weight shifted from my feet to the frame, it let out a loud creak. I winced—I could feel every bar and spring pierce through the mattress.

This sure feels real. Probably the most real dream I've ever had. Are details like this common in dreams? If they are, I wouldn't know.

There were holes in the cobblestone walls near the ground, most likely where rats had dug through the mortar. I silently prayed that I didn't have any encounters with mice during the night.

Finally, I grew tired and laid down on the mattress, trying to position myself in the least painful position possible. It took me what felt like forever to fall asleep, but I was grateful when I did.

I woke up to the clamor of footsteps and a loud conversation some hours later. I hoped that I had slept through the entire night and this wasn't just another prisoner caught in the night. I let out a sigh of relief as I caught a glimpse of Ed, Joey, and Cyneward being escorted by the same guard that had brought me down there. Ed had a crutch under his arm and the leather pouch in his hand.

"Elizabeth, I'm so sorry these idiots put you down here." Joey shook his head, clearly annoyed.

The guard cast a hard glare at Joey. "She's a criminal, *sir.*"

"She's a guest, *sir,*" Joey mocked. "And aren't you supposed to follow orders? I've asked you once already to release her. I won't ask again."

"Threats won't sway me, sir. I see no proof of her innocence."

"She's the Keeper of the Book of Aon," Ed cut in. The guard shifted his glare from Joseph to the boy, rolling his eyes.

"She came with the Book? Then prove it. Where is it, girl?"

I pointed to Ed. "He has it."

Ed held the leather pouch, untying the lace and

withdrawing the leather journal. He handed it to me through the bars.

"Here, Liz," he said, finding a quill and a small vile of ink in the bag, "write in it."

"What do I write?" I questioned, confused. I still had no clue what I was supposed to do with this Book.

"Something simple. Whatever you write will come true, I promise."

I eyed the journal, unsure before I flipped to the next clean page. I thought for a moment before scribbling something down into the first line.

They all watched me closely as I blew on the ink before closing the Book and handing it back to Ed.

Joey opened his mouth to say something but closed it as a thin string of light started forming around my neck. The guard's eyes went wide and his mouth dropped open as a clear, teardrop shaped stone appeared at the nape of my neck, fastened around a silver chain.

"Told you so," Ed murmured towards the guard. He cleared his throat awkwardly before unlocking my cell.

"Please madam," he said, "enjoy your stay with us."

"And you," Joey said, taking the keys from the guard, "enjoy unemployment."

Too eager to see the surface again after hours in darkness, I followed at the guard's heels back to the exit. Ed stopped me before I could follow the guard back up the staircase. He handed the pouch back to me. "Keep it. You'll need it more than I will while you're here."

"Ed, what is this thing?" The capabilities of the Book scared me. I wasn't sure I wanted the responsibility of something so dangerous.

"The same thing you've had since you met me in the street. I told you, this book is special. I'll explain everything clearly to you tomorrow, okay? Right now, let's get you in a real bed."

When I followed Ed, Cyneward, and Joseph back up to the first floor of the castle, I realized that the night hadn't yet changed to day.

Wasn't Joey supposed to be back tomorrow? Why is he back a day early?

Before I could ask him where he had gone and why he had returned so soon, he called out orders to maids that came to assist us. I didn't see any of the castle; within minutes, I had said goodnight to all of them, and I was taken up to a room on the second floor, bathed, dressed, and put straight to bed by women I had never seen before. I fell asleep as soon as my head hit the pillow.

four

The sun streamed through the window and onto my face, the warmth waking me up from my deep sleep. Squinting, I opened my eyes to a middle-aged maid sweeping back the white curtains. It took a moment for me to notice that everything in the room was a pristine white: the comforter, the sheets, the pillows, the rug, and even the nightgown I wore.

"Good morning," the maid greeted. "How'd you sleep?"

"Great." I stretched my arms. I felt a weight on my chest and glanced down to find the teardrop stone around my neck—a pleasant reminder of the not-so-pleasant evening in the dungeons.

"Good," she said, opening the door. Another maid came in with a cart of food. "Are you ready for breakfast?"

"In bed?"

"Of course." She brought a tray to me from the cart. "Usually, you'd be eating breakfast downstairs, but Prince Edward insisted. He said you'd had a long day yesterday."

Yesterday. What happened again?

Oh, right. I busted Ed and was thrown in jail.

Productive day.

"That was nice of him," I commented.

"Yes, it was," she agreed. The other maid silently left.

I watched her bustle around the room, tidying up and moving things around. She seemed content, humming to herself as she worked. "What is your name, if you don't mind me asking?"

"You can call me Margaret," she answered with a smile. "What's your name, dear?"

"Elizabeth," I answered.

"Well, Miss Elizabeth, you'll be seeing a lot of me during your stay here. I'm your lady's maid."

My eyes widened. "I have my own lady's maid?"

She laughed. "Why wouldn't you have one? Now, eat up. I've been told you must be ready by eleven."

This I could get used to.

I complied, finally looking down at the plate she'd given me. The only things that were familiar to me were the eggs. Two of something that looked like hot rolls drizzled with butter caught my attention, and they smelled strongly of cinnamon and nutmeg. I broke one open with my hands, finding the center stuffed with warm cinnamon apples. With no hesitation, I took a large bite of the roll, groaning and falling back against my pillow as I savored the taste in my watering mouth. "This is amazing," I said through the bread as the cinnamon danced on my tongue.

"Don't talk with your mouth full," Margaret said. She busied herself by opening the wardrobe on the far end of the room and sifting through the clothing.

"We don't have much here," she said over her shoulder. "It's been a long time since we've had a young lady with us, but our seamstresses downstairs are working on more for you, and I think that Prince Edward has sent off for a few things as well."

"I could wear the same couple of dresses," I offered. "I don't need much."

"It's no fuss," she waved me off. "You need more than a few dresses if you're staying in Devereux a while."

Staying?

I hadn't thought about that. *How long will I be here? How will I get home?*

When I finished eating, I crossed my legs on the bed while she held up different garments.

"How about this one?" she asked, holding up another linen dress like what I had worn before. This one was a pale yellow. I wrinkled my nose.

"No, I didn't think so either." She held up two more, one green and one cream with thin brown stripes. "These?"

"I like that one." I pointed to the cream one in her right hand. She hung up the other one and took the cream dress off the hanger.

"Come here, let's get you dressed." She beckoned for me to come closer.

Dressed? She's here to help me get dressed?

I felt slightly embarrassed as she slipped the dress over my head, feeling a wave of heat rush to my cheeks. I cleared my throat awkwardly. She didn't seem to notice, or if she did, she didn't care.

"Joseph requested that you be brought to the dining

room this morning," she told me, stringing up the back.

"Joey asked that?" I straightened up as the dress grew tighter, breathing in so that she could easily tie it. "How do I even get to the dining room from here?"

"I'll show you." She tied the last knot. "You turn right from here and go down the big staircase, then left and into the Great Hall. Joseph and Prince Edward are waiting for you there."

"Thank you so much for everything. You've been so kind to me."

"Of course," she said with a smile. "We're going to be great friends, Miss Elizabeth."

Before we left, I remembered the leather bag that Ed had given me—the one that contained the Book of Aon. I made sure to grab it on my way out the door.

Margaret showed me the way to the Great Hall, down the stairs and through the large foyer. When we reached it, the door already sat open. She bowed before leaving me, and I hesitantly peered inside, spotting Ed and Joey sitting at the large dining table eating breakfast. Portraits hung on the walls around them, and a fireplace decorated the wall at the far end of the room.

"Good morning!" I called cheerfully, glad to see some familiar faces. Joey stood up as soon as he saw me, giving me a short bow and murmuring, "Good morning."

Ed smiled brightly as Joey pulled a chair back for me to sit in. "Morning, Liz!"

"How'd you sleep?" Joey asked. He circled around the table to sit down across from me. "I'll bet that bed felt ten times better than the dungeon. You were there until two o'clock this morning."

"That long?" I asked, watching as Ed placed his napkin over his empty plate. "I was glad to get an actual bed. I slept like there was no tomorrow."

"That's good to hear," Ed said enthusiastically.

I nodded. "How's the ankle, Ed?"

He stood up, jumping up and down. "Much better, thanks. Alec patched me up well last night, and it feels just fine."

Alec? A new name to learn, a new person to meet.

"Glad to hear it," I praised. "So, what's on the agenda for today? What do you guys do in a castle like this all the time? Will you answer some of my questions?"

"Well," Ed stood and pushed in his chair, "today, you're coming with Joey and me into the village."

"Great. What're we doing there?"

"Ed is visiting the orphanage, and I'm taking you to see Yula," Joey said, standing up next to him. "Yula knows more about the Book than any of us."

I glanced warily at Ed. *Joey and me alone? That didn't go so well the last time we were in that situation.*

"Be nice," Ed mouthed at me behind Joey's back. I sighed, changing my focus back to the Book.

"Who is Yula, again?"

"She's the original Keeper. She knows everything about the Book of Aon. She'll be able to answer your questions better than Joey or I could."

Nodding, I rose from my seat, and Joey walked around to pull out my chair once more. I walked with Ed as Joey led us out of the Great Hall and into the corridor, slipping the leather strap on the Book around my wrist as we went.

The doors opened into the courtyard when we approached them, revealing a horse-drawn carriage under a bright blue morning sky. I noticed things that I didn't see on my way here—no wonder; I was incapacitated on the back of a horse—like the carefully cut shrubs, the rows of black, white, and red roses, and the cobble that paved the yard.

Footmen flanked either side then pulled the carriage doors open, and one held my hand as he helped me into the carriage. Joey and Ed filed in after me.

The ride down to the village was considerably quiet. Joey and Ed made small talk opposite me, and I stared out the window at the greenery and the cottages that grew more and more dense as we rode on. Villagers pointed as we drove past, waving at Prince Edward with fascination and awe. He grinned, pressed his face to the window and waved back.

Ed seemed so much more comfortable here than he did when I first met him, only two days ago. I was happy to see that he actually had a family; even though his parents weren't here, Joey was enough for him. I was happy to see him happy.

Even though I hadn't known him for long, I felt like I was responsible for Ed and his happiness. I don't know why, but he felt like a little brother to me, and I promised myself that I would protect him; he was the closest thing to a family I would get during my stay in Aon.

Rather, he was the closest thing to a family I'd *ever* get.

I don't remember much about my family. I never had siblings, but there were many times growing up that I wished I had a brother to watch out for me or a sister to teach me how to use makeup or talk to boys. I lived in a girls' home all during school. The housemother never yelled or mistreated us, but she didn't have time to sit and bond with each and every girl. She made sure we had what we needed and then she moved to the next task.

I kept to myself. I never excelled in the art of making friends like everyone else, and the older girls intimidated me. When I left for college, I walked out that door with a laundry basket of my belongings and I didn't look back.

When at last we came to a stop, Ed opened the doors before any footman could do it for him. He leaped from the carriage, hugging the young boys that came to see him and waving to women and children.

"You'll take good care of him?" I heard Joey ask someone. I turned around to see Cyneward once again.

"Of course," he said with a bow. He smiled at me before following Ed towards the wooden building across the road, surrounded by a large group of boys of all different ages. A sign posted outside the house read *Alexander's Home for Boys*.

"Bye, Elizabeth!" Ed raced the boys, all of them trying to be the quickest to the door.

I waved back to him, smiling to myself.

When they all disappeared into the house, I turned around. Joey held his arm out for me with an amused expression. "Shall we?"

Things keep getting weirder and weirder. We're supposed to hold hands?

I reached out for his arm, but when I laid my hand on top of his, he laughed, shaking his head.

"Like this." He pulled me closer and adjusted the position of my arm.

That's close.

When our arms were linked, we made our way down the path. The cobble on the streets shined as the sun grew higher in the sky.

"Aon is a beautiful place to live," he said as we

ambled on a downhill street. "The winters are especially pretty."

"I'm sure they are," I responded awkwardly. I waited for a sarcastic remark from him, but it didn't come.

Weird. Joey hasn't made one snarky remark all morning.

I cleared my throat. "I was just wondering... Why is Ed the crowned prince? Isn't the first born usually the heir?"

"I'm illegitimate. I was born before him, but it was to a woman my father didn't marry."

My mouth fell open, but I closed it quickly, hoping that he didn't notice. "Do you wish you were the heir?"

He looked at me, and I thought for a moment that I had offended him, but he just shook his head. "No, I don't. I'm happy with my life. I take care of the politics for Ed and teach him what I know so he'll be prepared, and I'm fine with that."

"You don't wish your father and mother stayed together?" I asked.

He shrugged. "If they had, Ed would have never been born. I'm okay with it. Really, Elizabeth, I am; I've learned to accept things for how they are. Everything happens for a reason, does it not?"

Like me being pulled into a fantasy world?

I hope so.

"You know," he said, glancing at me, "I never knew people from your world could take to this so quickly."

"Take to what?"

"All of this." He gestured around us. "It's like you know what everything is around here, and none of it seems odd to you. Most Outsiders have taken weeks or even months to get used to all of this. A few almost had breakdowns."

"Believe me, it's odd. I just don't really know how to

react."

"All the same, you don't seem to mind. It's quite impressive, actually."

"Joseph," I gasped, "was that a *compliment?*"

"Hey, don't push it, or I'll take it back," he warned.

I shook my head, laughing. "Honestly, I just don't know whether to believe it all. For all I know, I could be dreaming, and I've had dreams weirder than this."

He frowned at me. "Do you honestly think you're dreaming?"

I shrugged. "There's always that possibility in the back of my mind. I really hope this isn't a dream, or I'll be very disappointed when I wake up."

He laughed. "This place is real, I promise. I can prove it."

I raised an eyebrow. "Ed said the same thing, and he twisted his ankle."

"If you were dreaming, you'd be able to make anything happen, right?" he asked, ignoring me. "You could control the dream?"

I laughed to myself. Ed and Joey may have only been half-brothers, but they thought the same way.

"I guess so, but I've never done it before."

"Okay, then, try." He stepped away from me. "Make it rain."

Skeptically, I agreed to try. "Fine. But don't laugh at me when I look like an idiot."

"You already look like an idiot," I heard him mumble. I hit him in the shoulder.

"What was that?"

"Nothing." He rubbed his arm.

I thought the word really hard over and over again, closing my eyes in concentration.

I hope this works.

Actually, scratch that—I hope this doesn't *work.*

Rain, rain, rain, rain, rain, rai—

My eyes snapped open when I felt drops of water hit my face. "Did I do it?"

Joey grinned as he continued flicking water in my face from his hands. I noticed a trough of water against one of the cottages behind him, so I ran over to it to submerge my hands.

The sun beamed high from its peak in the sky, beating heat down on our shoulders. The cold water broke the thick warmth, cooling down my skin. I turned around, throwing drops of water at him with my hands. He shielded his face as I laughed, taking off down the hill.

I heard his laughter as his footsteps came after me, catching me at the bottom of the hill. His hands grabbed my arm, and I lost my balance, falling backwards.

Instead of cobblestone, my back hit his arms.

He had caught me low to the ground, almost like you would dip someone in a dance. A smirk made its way to his lips before he spoke.

"I told you. You're not dreaming, understand?"

I gulped. He was closer than I had anticipated. "Got it."

He smiled. "Good."

He stood me upright before pointing down the street, a colorful lane with lots of cottages, villas, and shrubbery.

"This is it," said Joseph. "Yula's home is the one with the red door."

"Thank you." I tried to be as kind as possible. It was easier to be nice to Joey after he had been nice all morning. "Is there anything I can do? We could go wherever you need after—"

"I'm actually leaving now," he interjected. "There've been fires set out in the countryside, and there are casualties. I have to tend to my sister; she lives close to where the fires started. She's bound to know something about them. I strongly suspect that the Night Rider did this, but she'll know more than I do at this point. The journey is a day's time, but I'm a fast rider; I should be back late this afternoon."

"You have a sister?"

"Delia. Another bastard child, like me. She's my full sibling."

I shrugged. "It makes sense. Is she much older than you?"

"She's approaching her twenty-third birthday. I'm only twenty-one, so two years is the lot of it."

"Wow. It must've been fun growing up close in age."

He shook his head. "She was never there. When I was two, my mother shipped her off to a boarding school, and I didn't see her again until I was twelve. By then, Mother had died years earlier and Father had fallen ill. Young Ed was next in line and was about to inherit the throne of Aon at four."

Joseph nodded towards Yula's door once more.

"I best be off. I have to make it to Berkeley."

I did my best to give him a sincere smile, despite the pity I felt for his broken family. It must have been convincing because he returned the favor with a radiant smile and paced back up the street towards the carriage up the hill.

I took my time strolling the short distance to Yula's doorstep, swinging the leather sack by the strap. I admired the many flowers surrounding every window and filling any empty space around the cottage. An empty watering can sat outside the door.

Hesitantly, I rapped my knuckles against the wooden door. A faint humming could be heard through the barred wooden piece on the front.

The wooden piece swung open.

"Can I help you?" asked a woman's voice.

A pair of impossibly bright blue eyes stared out at me under dark chocolate hair.

"Yes," I said nervously, "I'm looking for Yula?"

The eyes darted back and forth behind me before the wooden slit slammed shut and the bright red door swung open.

"Come in," welcomed the dark skinned, slender woman standing in the doorframe. Her sincere smile filled me with a warm feeling—almost like home.

"Um, thanks," I murmured, sliding past her. She closed the door and bustled around me into the small eating area.

The room was open, well lit, with a few windows and a short table. The chairs had roughly sewn cushions placed on the tops, and a lace tablecloth covered the dark wood.

"What do I call you?"

"Elizabeth is fine," I responded. "And you?"

"I'm Yula. But you already knew that. Can I get you a cup of tea?"

"That'd be lovely," I replied in the politest voice I could manage.

As she poured the boiling water into two cups and tossed a teabag into each one, she glanced up at me.

"I have so many things to ask you," I started off.

She chuckled softly as she placed milk, honey, sugar, and lemons on a tray.

"I already know why you're here." She pointed to the leather sack that Ed had given me. "I'm assuming the

Book is in that?"

I gaped at her. I hadn't mentioned anything about a book.

"Don't act so surprised. You aren't the first to come asking questions."

I was still speechless.

She sat down at the table and handed me a napkin. Her eyes flicked up to the necklace around my neck.

"Where did you get that?" she asked, nodding towards it. My fingers came up to trace the stone.

"I wrote in the Book," I said. "I used to have one like this back home."

"You did well. It looks well made."

"Um, thanks." I awkwardly cleared my throat. "So, will you explain to me what this place is?"

"Let me start at the beginning. Here, I am known as Yula. In your world, where I'm from, I was Alice Dayton."

"Alice Dayton? That's the name written on the first page. So, you wrote in this book first?"

I clearly remembered the sophisticated handwriting on the first page of the Book and the curly letters spelling out the name.

"Correct," she remarked, crossing her arms and leaning back in her chair. "I found the journal, wrote in it, and the world where Aon exists was born. Everything around you is here because of my design." She gestured for emphasis.

"You *found* the journal?"

"I found it in an old bookstore. The owner, an elderly gentleman, told me that it had some sort of 'special qualities.' I had an idea for a story in my mind, though, so I forgot what he said and started to build the world in the Book. I woke up the next morning in a very simple, basic version of what you see now. I haven't been back since then."

"This place is real, then?" I asked.

"Yes," she said. "It's all real."

Was I supposed to believe it? Was magic somehow a reality?

I held my head in my hands. I felt a headache coming on.

"Does that mean you did everything that's happened here?" I asked. "Like Joey and Ed's parents? Are you... responsible?"

"You have to understand that when I wrote in the Book the first time, I had no clue that it was real," she said. "Joseph and Edward's stories are the first things I wrote. I had to watch them come true when I woke up here. Believe me, it wasn't easy watching them live the horrors I'd written, but once it was all past, I moved on and wrote things that affected Aon positively. I grew the kingdom, made it resourceful, and gave them allies."

"Did you intend for them to be close brothers?"

She shook her head and smiled. "Some things happen on their own. If I hadn't written the death of their parents then they never would have found comfort in each other. It's a butterfly effect—I don't write everything, but I've found that the things I do write set off a chain reaction."

It made sense to me. I couldn't blame her for what she wrote before she knew Aon was real—and I doubted Ed would either, if he knew.

"So when you got here and found that it was real, you just built your idea of a perfect world?"

"Oh, it's far from perfect." She waved me off. "But it's home. I made something that I wanted to live in. The neighboring kingdoms, like Baile and the ones across the sea are still a work in progress. Aon is the only one that I'm totally done with; I started writing Aon before the others. It always keeps me occupied, that's for sure. Devereux—that's the city we're in—was the first city that I finished.

"In your world, I wasn't happy. I was just a struggling writer with no friends and no family. Here, I could create everything I never had. I'm part of the village; I have friends. We have afternoon tea and talk about our favorite books. My only job is to take care of the Book, and I do it well. I love it here."

"You really did make a life here," I noted. "Do you ever want to go back?"

"Never," she said. "If I get bored, I write something new. I have everything I ever wanted."

"How does it all work? It seems complicated."

"The Book is always in Aon," she stated. "When someone new tumbles in, it disappears from my grasp, and I know we have a visitor. It moves itself to meet the new Outsider, like it has a mind of its own, so when he wakes up here, the Book is with him. When the visitor leaves, it's usually left unscathed wherever he left it. After all, more than one copy of that book in this world could get dangerous in the wrong hands. I usually take it back from the new visitor when one comes back around, but judging by the way it's still locked up tight in your pouch, I'd say you can keep it for now."

"Ed told me that you might let me keep it. What does he mean?"

Her amused smile didn't falter. She sipped on her tea. "He's bright, that one. I assume he mentioned something about the Keeper, too?"

Bewildered, I nodded. How did she keep guessing my questions? "Yeah, he did."

"Here's how you should look at it." Yula leaned onto her elbows. "I am the Keeper because I keep the Book, and I've always been the Keeper because I don't trust anyone else with it for a long period of time. Simple enough. When new people come in, I send the guards to search for them and I get the Book back; like I said, in the wrong hands, this could get dangerous very, very fast.

"Ed thinks you'll be the new Keeper, however, and you'll be the one holding the Book during your time here. You literally hold the key to the future of everything—the kingdom, the people, yourself—you can control it all."

I swallowed uncomfortably.

She continued. "He's right, too; I think you'll make a great Keeper. I can tell you have a pure heart, not because I think so, but because Ed thinks so. Ed is an excellent judge of character, and I trust him, therefore I trust you. Understand, though, that just because you have the power doesn't mean you should use it. The others before you have used its power, and they weren't always happy with the outcome.

"Here's the thing, though," she said, catching my eye. "People will try to change your mind. People will try to convince you to write things that could change Aon's fate in their favor, and people will try to convince you to tell them the future. You can't give in, Elizabeth. If you tell people what will happen in the future, things can go wrong. Do not tell anyone anything that's written or anything that you write yourself under any circumstances, understand? Even if it means you don't read anymore yourself, so you aren't tempted. *Do not tell anyone.*"

And just like that, I became the Keeper of the Book

of Aon. I wondered if I could handle the challenge, if the kingdom and I would be better off with me gone instead of holding onto their future.

I don't want to go home. There's nothing for me there.

*But one person—*me*—controlling the future of everyone?*

I don't think half of a history degree in college qualifies me for that.

I swallowed hard. *I'll hold onto the Book for now, until it becomes too much to handle.*

"Now, where were we?"

"You told everyone that Ed had come back," I said. "That's how the search party knew to go and find him."

She nodded. "When he left, he took the Book with him. I don't know how he managed to filch it without me noticing, but when his brother reported him missing and I couldn't find it, I realized that he'd run away with it. When he left Aon and slipped into your world, the Book came back to me, and that's how I knew he'd left the story. It just showed up on my doorstep. I don't know how he did it—my guess is that it's different for characters that were born into the story. Maybe he found some sort of loophole in the rules—no doubt there has to be one somewhere. As you can tell, I still don't know everything about it. I've never had a character leave the Book before. So, naturally, when it vanished a second time after his disappearance, I knew he'd returned."

"No characters have ever left?"

Yula shook her head. "Not one."

"Interesting," I mumbled. "How long has Ed known he lives in a story?"

"He's only thirteen, so it hasn't been long. He figured it out the first time he met an Outsider. It didn't surprise him, quite honestly; he came to ask me questions and told me that he always suspected something a little off about this place, even though he'd been born here. Some of the villagers know and some don't; some think it's a fable passed down from family to family or even that I started it as a children's story."

Yula didn't say anything for a moment, fiddling with her mug between her fingers. "It was a rough time for the people who believed it, when it got out. Several left the kingdom to find a purpose, something other than simply being written as a placeholder."

"That's horrible."

"They were bound to find out at some point, though, with all the writers that come and go. The Book fumbles from person to person and hand to hand in your world and new stories grow, and Aon changes every time something is written. A new Outsider reads the Book and shows up, stays a while, writes a piece of fate's script, and then decides he's had enough and leaves. I, however, made my choice. I didn't have the best life before, you see. This place was—is—my safe haven."

"Did you discover a way to leave?" I asked.

She raised an eyebrow in my direction. "Do you want to leave already?"

I thought of the piles of bills I had back in the real world, the essays I hadn't written, and the emptiness of the apartment I lived in that I couldn't even bring myself to call a home. Did I miss any of it?

Not at all.

"No, of course not, I was just wondering...What if you had changed your mind?"

"There's only one way out of here, and that's death," she answered bluntly. "For me, for you, and for any writer that comes through here. You probably could've figured that one out, though. There's no clicking our heels and wishing to go home here. I don't know anything about the death of the characters, though. I don't know what happens to them or where they go, and I still haven't figured out how Edward could have written himself out of the story. I've never had a character write in it before. Obviously, if he's alive and the same rules apply to him, then he didn't write in it."

Another question to ask Ed. I hoped I would remember later.

"Do you know how much time spaces out between coming here and leaving?" I asked. "I'm sorry. I have so many questions for you."

"Don't worry about it." She waved me off. "But to answer your question, I have no idea. I've never left, I have no desire to leave, and anyone who has left has never come back to tell the tale."

"What about the other authors after you? Darren and Maximilian and Josephine and the others I read about?"

"Didn't you read all the way through?" she asked, as if the answer was obvious. "All of them decided to go back home, wherever that is for them. In the experience I've had with them, they think that you write your story, live it, and then head back to the real world and get back to life. Almost like a vacation. " She grinned. "I, on the other hand, happen to find new things to keep my story going every day."

"So… What happened to Darren?"

"Died in a dragon attack. He valiantly defended the village until the end. Horrible, it was—he always was a man of violence. That's the first and last dragon we'll ever see around here. That thing was far too hard to get rid of, and no doubt it was terribly, terribly painful. He screamed the entire time. I don't know much about the death of Outsiders, but I know they physically feel the death here before they can wake up in their homes."

"Maximilian?"

She laughed. "He wished he thought of something as clever as a dragon. He decided that he would go by catching the illness the king and queen died from, being the *brilliant* doctor he was and all. After all, if you could choose your death, would you not make it memorable? He thought that trying to save the king was the best thing he could be remembered for, even though William was bound to die either way."

I frowned. "You mean that he never had a chance to save King William?"

Yula shook her head. "What's written is written, Elizabeth. There is no way to change what's been put down as fate. William would've died either way, no matter what Maximilian wrote to counteract it. Whatever is written first is what determines fate's course."

"How did Josephine go?"

"She wanted to stay, but the loneliness got to her. She missed her family, so she came to me and asked to tweak her entries. I couldn't stop her, so I let her write in her death. She died in a flood that made the waters in the lake between Aon and Baile rise. It flooded half the village."

"It's all rather morbid to think about," I murmured, feeling slightly uneasy.

"Yes, it is. But there are happier things here than stories of death. One of the things I rather enjoyed about coming here is being able to change my appearance." She grinned. "My eyes used to be green, the same shade as Edward's, but I've always wanted blue eyes, so I took the opportunity. Aging isn't much fun either, so I put an end to that for me. Not that it matters—Outsiders can't die of old age here—but I do like having forever twenty-one skin."

"I have another question," I said.

"Let me hear it."

"What's the situation on the royals?" I asked. "Joey has been out on business twice in three days, and he tells me that he handles politics for Edward. How did it end up like that?"

"Now, that's a long story," she said. "Long, complicated, and dramatic."

I leaned up onto my elbows, raising an eyebrow as a gesture for her to continue. "I've got time."

five

We drank our tea in silence for a moment before I urged her on.

"What about Joey's sister, the other bastard child? What's the story on her?"

She cleared her throat awkwardly. "It's a long story, and I really hate it for Edward and Joseph. I felt bad about it after I met them both; they really are lovely boys, but it was necessary to the story. Life isn't perfect, and this taught them that. I think they're both better people because of it. I wrote it all down in the Book," she said, nodding towards the pouch.

I looked down at the bag, untying it and pulling the Book out. The pages fanned out as I found where I left off. Yula put the water kettle back on the fire as I read.

When King William Valois was a boy, no older than eighteen, his best friend was a village girl name Melanie. She was very beautiful, and by the time he was twenty, William was totally in love. They ran, planning to elope, knowing that the king and queen, William's parents, would never approve a marriage.

"Wow," I said. "William and Melanie were going to elope?"

She grinned. "I wrote a little romance in my day."

Melanie conceived a child not long after they ran away, before they could marry, and William struggled. He worried about being a father, and his parents were both old in age. He knew his time to be king was approaching fast. Melanie forced him to return to the palace to take his place as king and take care of his mother when his father died.

Though it was true that William loved Melanie and cared for the child, he had not yet married her. He'd begun to think about what a marriage would mean for him and decided against making her his queen for the sake of his people.

The child was born many months later and was given the name Delia Rose. William loved the child, and for a short time, he considered legitimizing his family. Melanie conceived another child two years later, and that child was named Joseph Peter.

Melanie grew sick after Joseph was born. She knew that Delia would have no life as a bastard child, being a girl, so she sent her child to a boarding school in a neighboring kingdom. She decided that William loved Joseph enough to make a life for him, so she left him her quaint cottage in the village below the castle grounds. She died when Joseph was six.

"Did Delia come back for her mother's funeral?" I asked, looking up from the script. She shook her head.

"Her father forced her to stay in school. The king sent her letters and started paying for her education when her mother died, realizing that his children needed him. He also realized that if he didn't marry soon, then an illegitimate child would rule the kingdom. Aon would be the laughing stock of the world."

I frowned. I felt horrible about Joey and Ed's past,

but Yula was right. If none of this had happened, the brothers would be very different people.

William grieved, but not for long. He was introduced to a beautiful young princess named Isabel from a kingdom across the sea, and it was love at first sight. He didn't think twice when a marriage between the kingdoms was arranged. He was surprised he was able to fall in love after Melanie's death had taken such a toll on him, but he went into the marriage eagerly.

Isabel conceived a child when Joey was seven, and Edward was born shortly after Joseph turned eight.

"Why didn't Delia come back after Edward's birth?"

She grimaced. "For one, Delia had pent up anger at her father for remarrying and keeping her in school when her mother died. Second, she didn't care for little Edward—he was, after all, her father's son, not her brother. Lastly, she began to develop… certain talents."

"Talents?"

"Delia has an uncanny ability to move things with her mind," she explained. "When she realized she had the talent, she didn't dare come back. The few adults that knew were terrified of her and her powers. She moved to a chateau in the country when she turned eighteen. People are burned for heresy, you know. She'd be burned, accused of being a witch. She didn't take the chance of her father's protection faltering. Now she lives in the countryside close to a village called Berkeley."

"That makes sense."

She eyed me curiously. "You aren't surprised?"

"Not at all. It's a story, remember? Anything can happen."

She smiled at me.

"Isabel died about six months before William did. Edward has been without his parents for a while now. Joseph looks out for the both of them and handles the politics. Once Edward has finished his schooling and the coronation takes place, he'll have control over everything. Until then, Joey teaches him what he knows and hopes that he can leave everything in good standing when his younger brother takes over."

"That's a lot for one person to handle. Just the death in the family alone is enough to drive someone crazy. How *did* Isabel die?"

"The same illness that took Melanie took Isabel, and there were no doctors that could help them. The sickness was far beyond their expertise. Since then, I've made some entries in the Book of Aon relating to the young medical trainees. Actually, Lord Alexander is the top of his class. No doubt he'll do great things when he's finished his schooling."

I nodded. "It's all trial and error, isn't it? You write something and wait for the reaction, then fix it and repeat. Does it end?"

Her lips curled to one side as she shook her head. "I don't mind it. This is what I want. It does end, though— or at least it has for me. I stopped writing about Aon's future permanently. I don't interfere with what goes on here. I did my part and now it's time for me to sit back and watch. What other writers write is their business. They can come to me and write whatever they want, but my job is done. Now, I just live here. I'm a resident."

"You don't write at all anymore?"

"I write for the bordering kingdoms. They have interesting stories... so far. But that's a story for another time." She pushed her chair back and stood up. "Did that cover all of your questions?"

"For the most part, I think. If I come up with more, I'll be back." I closed the Book and slid it into the leather pouch.

"Good idea. I'd fancy another cup of tea with you some time soon, all right? And be careful with the Book."

I grinned before standing up and pushing in my chair. "Thanks for everything, Yula. I was almost positive this place wasn't real."

Yula laughed. "It's as real as you and me, I can assure you. Come back anytime, Elizabeth."

I left Yula's house in a great mood. I was glad to have some answers but even more thrilled to be sure that Aon wasn't a dream or a figment of my imagination. I'd always wished I could be one of the characters in my favorite novels, like Elizabeth Bennet, with a big family and a rich suitor, or Dorothy in Oz, with an aunt and uncle and a yellow brick road, but this took dreaming to a whole new level.

"Elizabeth!" Ed called as the orphanage came into view. He jogged towards me, three boys his age running along behind him.

"Hey, Ed."

"These are my friends." He gestured to the boys behind him. "Zac, David, and Zeke."

I gave them a wave. "Hello, boys."

They all waved back at me.

"Are you ready to leave?" I asked Ed.

"Yeah," he responded. I noticed his friends' shoulders begin to sag.

He turned around to console them. "Don't worry, guys. I'll be back before you know it."

The boys did some sort of handshake, and his young friends took off back towards the orphanage.

"How old are your friends?" I asked on our walk back to the carriage. "Are you the same age?"

"Pretty close. Zac is twelve, Zeke is fourteen, and

David is thirteen, like me."

"Do you visit them often?"

"As often as I can. It's hard being the only child in a big castle, you know. All I have is Joey, tutors, and an endless supply of books."

"That sounds amazing," I commented. "You know, maybe minus Joey."

Ed laughed. "It's great sometimes, and I love my brother to death, but he's always busy dealing with the nobles or out on business or handling treaty and trade negotiations. I'm glad you're here; you can keep me company."

"I'd be happy to."

We got in the carriage together and sat in a comfortable silence on the way back to the palace. I peered out the window, taking in everything I hadn't seen on the way to the village. As the courtyard of the palace came into view, Ed swung open the door and jumped out before we were even stopped.

"Come on, Elizabeth!" he called, waving me on behind him. I pulled my dress above my ankles and jumped down after him, not waiting for the footman to offer his hand.

Ed obviously had energy to burn as he barreled towards the huge, wooden front doors detailed with intricate carvings of vines and scroll patterns. A large, pearl-like stone was encrusted into the center of each door, and it glistened as the doors opened for the little prince.

"I want to show you around," he said once I had caught up. "The most you've seen of the castle is the dungeons, and that's sad."

I didn't bother trying to agree out loud. I tried to savor the air I still had left in my lungs.

Following him through the foyer, I noticed the portraits on the walls. Kings, queens, and other royal figures were painted in beautiful colors. I almost tripped over Ed's feet, not watching where I stepped. The strikingly realistic eyes memorized me; they almost seemed to follow us through the foyer.

"You were in this room this morning," Ed commented, opening a set of dark, polished double doors on our left and a set on our right. "This is the Great Hall, and through the small door in the corner is the kitchen. And over here is the throne room, the courtroom, and the chapel; those are all in their own section of the palace."

Before I could get a good look of the room, he started down the hallway again. The foyer opened up into a large room with big windows, sparkling marble tile floors, hallways branching off from each side, and a large staircase on the right. A white scroll-carved trim positioned in arcs adorned the ceiling and walls. Straight ahead, a set of doors were next to the windows. I could see an elaborate garden through the glass.

Ed pointed to the staircase. "That's where all of our rooms are. Yours, mine, and Joey's are all up there. There's another staircase that leads to the third floor, but we'll get to that later."

He pointed to two more hallways, one on either side of the staircase covered in a lush red carpet. "The one on the left side leads to the ballroom, the parlor, and my father's old office. This one over here leads to our training rooms and the passage to the dungeons. Obviously, I'm not mentioning every room in the entire castle, but you get the idea."

"You have training rooms?"

"Of course we have training rooms," he said, as if I

should've known. "How else would we protect ourselves?"

I frowned. "Don't you have guards and escorts for that?"

"Self defense is a priority here with the Night Rider out and about, Liz. Joey and I have to know at least a little to be able to take care of ourselves if something goes wrong... though I'd say Joey knows more than a little."

He went on to tell me that the two hallways on the left wall, opposite the staircase, led to servants' quarters and a large library and music room. After he pointed up, I noticed that there was a balcony on the inside of the room.

"The barracks and armory are connected through a passage in the training room at the end of the hall," he said, walking to the door straight ahead. "And this door goes out to the gardens. Joey and I used to play out there as kids."

I laughed. "You are a kid, Edward."

He shot me a playful glare. "I meant when I was a toddler. There's a maze out there, you know; we had the most fun playing hide and seek and tag."

"That sounds great. You'll have to let me play sometime."

Ed grinned from ear to ear. "Yeah, I will. Now, are you ready to go upstairs?"

Nodding, I held my dress above my ankles once more so that I could keep up with him on the staircase; he mounted them two at a time and beat me to the top.

A large hallway lined with windows on the right and doors on the left stretched and intersected another hallway at the end.

"Ed, how many of these rooms are actually

occupied?" I asked curiously.

"You'd be surprised. We have nobles from Baile that love to take advantage of the resources here. They come to visit and negotiate and stay for a few days extra. Right now, there are only a few of them being used, but when my birthday rolls around, they'll be full to the brim with people trying to catch Joey in a good mood."

"Do you make any of the kingdom's decisions?"

He shrugged, casting a side-glance at me. "I'm not of age, remember? It'll be another five years before I have total control. For now, Joey takes care of everything that heavily affects the kingdom and takes my input into consideration."

"At least you get a little bit of a say in what goes on around here," I commented, trying to cheer him up. "Joey's taking what you're saying and thinking about it."

"Yeah." Ed had slowed to a walk, and I was thankful for the break. We reached the end of the hallway, turning left into an identical hallway. Lush, deep red carpet covered the floor, white, flowing drapes hung open on the windows, and tall doors lined the left-side wall.

"The main upstairs hallways make a square and then branch off into other hallways," Ed explained. "There's a door to the inside balcony on the last hallway. The entire second floor is just guest suites and the occasional guest office and parlor. There are also several wardrobe rooms."

The tour continued all the way around the main square of the second floor until we reached the hallway where the first and the last edges of the square connected.

Ed ushered me through the third floor rather quickly where we found another library, another music room, and the gatehouse; he told me we'd have other times to explore because even he didn't know what some of the rooms were. Joey ran into us as we were leaving the music room.

"Ed," he said, swinging the door open, "you're late for your lessons. What've you been up to?"

"Sorry, I had to give Elizabeth the tour." He gestured towards me as he spoke, and Joey's eyes flicked from Ed to me several times.

"Get downstairs, please," Joey said. "I'm sure she's seen enough for now. Run along."

Ed smiled at me before jogging out of the room, past Joey and down the stairs.

His brother watched him leave. An emotion I didn't recognize flashed on his face, and then disappeared as soon as it came.

"What do I need to do?" I asked curiously. "Any lessons I need to go to?"

I had meant it as a joke, but he took it seriously.

"Well, you'll be taking riding lessons rather soon," he said, "but not today. You're free to do whatever you want."

Glancing around the music room, my eyes rested on the caramel colored faces of lions carved into the legs of the pianoforte. "Can I stay in here?"

"Sure. Do you play?" He nodded towards the instrument.

I shook my head. "Nothing but simple melodies."

"That's something. I play a little, but it's been so long."

Giving him a sideways glance, I approached the pianoforte and slid onto the bench. "Will you play something?"

He seemed hesitant, almost leaning towards the door, but he gave in and came to sit next to me. His fingers caressed the ivory keys, sliding over the smooth surface before they found their place on the board.

The rich sounds sent a chill down my spine as Joey played a melody, then added in a faint harmony with his left hand. Goose bumps covered my arms.

"That's beautiful," I said quietly in awe, watching him play the keys. "Where did you learn it?"

He gave me a crooked smile, his eyes still trained on the ivory. "My father taught me when I was very young. He heard my mother playing this song through an open window in the Forum, and he said that when he finally saw her sitting at the piano it was love at first sight."

I raised one of my hands to the keys at the far end of the piano before playing the baseline of the song. The notes were easy to pick up on, and the low notes with the high, soft melody sounded amazing.

"You loved your father very much, didn't you?" I asked him.

He nodded. "He was a great man and an even better father."

"You're very accepting of his past," I noted quietly, casting a sideways glance at him. "Were you ever mad at Yula when you found out that she wrote it?"

"No one is perfect," he answered simply. The song changed to something simple and soft, but ambient. "If she had never written my parents meeting and having me, then she never would have written Ed's mother meeting my father, and he never would have been born. I love my brother. I wouldn't wish for change if it affected him. She didn't know what she was doing. Besides, Father acted beyond what she wrote. She just set the dominos in motion."

He cleared his throat, his eyes trained on the keys. "Even the people we think are the best of their kind have problems. She never wrote it, but my father became an alcoholic for a short time after my mother's death. I loved him anyway. We aren't flat pieces of paper, Elizabeth; we're people. Yula doesn't bend us to her will; she influences our actions. What we decide to do or how we decide to react after that is entirely our own. My father decided to drink; he didn't have to, he wasn't made to, he just did. I don't blame him, despite what you might think. It's best not to focus on the mistakes, but rather to focus on who we know the person as."

"And who did you know your father as?"

A ghost of a smile appeared on his lips as he prepared to answer.

"I was very close to my father, despite the fact he pushed my sister away. I loved him very much. I accepted the mistakes he made. He was kind and caring to me, even though he spent more time with his new wife than with his son. When I did see him, I was very happy." His face fell slightly. "My sister wasn't as fortunate."

"You're very strong, you know. Not many people have the strength to think about these situations in a different light. I know that it was hard, but it's best to just keep your head up and focus on other people."

Comparing my childhood to Joey's, I could see some similarities. He grew up most of his life without his parents, and I could relate. I guess I could feel what he felt: the loneliness, the confusion, the pain.

Perhaps we did have something in common.

The corner of his lip turned up as he responded. "I'm not nearly as strong as I'd like to be, El. All the same, though, thank you."

six

"What do you mean?" I asked as I followed Ed through the inner courtyard. He weaved around stone benches and skirted around the fountain. He cut straight across the grass, headed towards the door.

"Exactly what it sounds like." He nodded hello to people who passed us by. "You need to learn some self defense if you're going to stay here."

"*Self defense?*"

"Yep."

"*Me?*"

"That's what I just said, did I not?"

"Ed, I've never needed self defense before. I don't know the first thing about it!" I protested. I peered up at the sky. Gray clouds streaked the sky, and it looked like it would rain.

"That's what the term *learn* is used for, Liz. Breathe for a second, okay? It's going to be fine. Even I know basic self defense."

"You're a prince. It's necessary for you. Why do *I* need to learn it?"

"Liz," he said, stopping to meet my eye, "listen to me. Self-defense is necessary for anyone within a mile of the castle. Do you want to leave?"

I shook my head. "No, of course not."

"Then quit arguing with me. Do you remember how close we were to the Night Rider? That's why we need self defense. There's always someone after the royal family and anyone close to them. I know you like it here, and you may not want to leave, but if you get caught alone with the Night Rider then you may not have a choice in the matter. Now, will you please cooperate and just take the class?"

I sighed in defeat. "When you put it like that, I guess I will."

He smiled and continued walking. Small water droplets started to fall as we headed inside the castle.

"So," I started, looking at him out of the corner of my eye, "does Joey know much self defense?"

He snorted. "You're asking me about Joey?"

"Yeah," I answered, hoping that I wasn't blushing. "I'm just curious."

"He knows more than any of us. Joey is one of my appointed protectors, on my protection detail. He's strong and fast and picked up fighting really quick, so he just stuck with it."

"Impressive."

"You could say that." He shrugged. "But I'd just call him a show off."

I laughed.

"This way." He led me down a hallway that branched off of the foyer. I had no memory of this corridor, but I'm sure he told me what was on it during his tour.

"Where are we going?"

"To see Rose. She's the only woman on the royal guard, you know. They wanted her for the militia, but she's too skillful not to have around here for protection."

"Why is she the only woman?" I asked.

"So far, she's the only one brave enough to show us her skills and adept enough to take on a man and win. She's top of her rank."

"Wow," I said in awe.

Something slammed against the wall just to the right of the door as we entered. I ducked out of instinct, covering my head with my hands.

"Sorry about that," a woman's voice apologized. Hesitantly, my eyes moved up, watching for any more flying objects before straightening my back.

Ed didn't seem fazed by the object that almost decapitated us, surprisingly. A thin, tan skinned woman with pixie cut, silver-blonde hair dusted her hands off in front of him.

"Who might this be, Edward?" she asked, placing her hands on her hips.

Awkwardly, I cleared my throat.

Why did Ed drag me here? There's no way I can do this. She's going to think I'm a freak.

"Rose, meet Elizabeth. Elizabeth, Rose."

Her eyes traveled up and down my body as she slowly circled my figure. "The new Keeper, eh?"

Wow. That news must have spread fast.

"Yeah," Ed said, walking with her. "Perfect, isn't she?"

The heat that rose to my cheeks embarrassed me, but I couldn't hide it.

"She is," Rose agreed. "She looks rather fit. Are you an athlete, dear?"

I tried to find words, but I was still in shock from the object that came near my head and how self-conscious she made me when she circled me, so I gave up. I shook my head instead.

"I could've sworn you were," she said. "Well, we'll make one of you yet. You did bring her to train, didn't you, Ed?"

"Yes. If she's going to be here for a while, she's going to need some self defense, and if it's for as long as I'm hoping, then I know Joey will eventually put her on my protection detail."

"Understood. We'll get to work straight away, then. Elizabeth?"

"Yeah?" I asked. It came out more like an embarrassing whimper than a question.

She laughed. "What're you afraid of? I'm not sentencing you to death. Come on. Let's get you changed and then we'll start on some basics."

Ed waved at me as he turned to leave. "Have fun, Liz."

"Where are you going?"

"Elizabeth, I'm a prince. What do you think I'm going to do?"

"Lessons?" I guessed.

"Bingo," he said lamely.

I grimaced. "Have fun."

He rolled his eyes. "I'll try."

As the door closed behind Ed, Rose snatched my hand and pulled me along behind her into a door on the far end of the training room between racks of weapons and armor. Inside, rows of boots, jackets, pants, shirts, and other assorted articles of clothing were set out neatly in stacks.

"This is the wardrobe room specifically for training," she explained, pulling me to a wall where jackets hung. "You obviously can't train in that dress, so we'll have to get you something you can move in."

I felt relieved. Dresses were fine, but they weren't my favorite thing to wear.

"Let's see… Ah hah." She pulled out a jacket, thrust it into my arms and set off to find something else.

Minutes later, I struggled as my arms almost buckled under the weight of all the gear. She waved me off.

"Try everything on. I'll be back in the training room, so come out whenever you're ready."

She left for me to get dressed on my own, and I breathed a sigh of relief.

After sliding out of my dress and folding it up, I inspected the clothes she gave me. To me, the pants appeared to be something like leggings, but they were a little baggier than what I had seen. There was also a plain shirt, a jacket, and a pair of boots.

I stepped out into the training room, unclasping my necklace from around my neck and putting it in my pocket.

"Perfect." Rose surveyed my appearance. "I know these may seem a little odd to you, but the only people that are seen wearing anything like this are on protection detail. They'll feel weird for a while, but people will know you're training with me if you wear them in public."

Rose beckoned from a mat in the center of the room. Hesitantly, I shuffled over.

"To get started," she said, "we're going to learn basic defense."

I gulped.

"Don't worry, you'll do fine. You look tough."

Without warning, Rose's hand came to my wrist, gripping it tight.

"Now, if someone grabs your wrist, what do you do?"

"Um... Pull away?" I guessed nervously.

"Wrong." She shook her head. "Turn your wrist so that your palm is up in my hand."

I followed her instruction, rotating my arm.

"I want you to jerk back at the elbow as hard as you can," she guided. "On three, ready? One, two, three."

Jerking back my wrist at my elbow, I broke free from her grip, almost losing my balance and falling backwards.

"Great job. Let's try it again, and then move on. There's a lot I want to cover with you today."

We completed the same drill several times, moving on to learning how to break someone's nose, the best places to elbow someone for a quick getaway, and how to block attacks. It shocked me how much we'd done by the end of the day. My exhausted body didn't want to move anymore, and I had learned about twenty different ways to incapacitate an attacker.

"You did really, really well today, Elizabeth," Rose praised. "You've picked everything up very quickly. It won't be long before you'll be able to fight me without a problem."

I coughed, almost choking and inhaling water. "But I don't want to fight you!"

She laughed. "For practice purposes, you will. Don't worry; you'll become more comfortable with it. I promise."

For my sake, I hoped she was right.

———

"Where are you going?" I asked, jogging to keep up

with Joey's fast pace as he covered the long stretch of the upstairs corridor. I almost tripped following him down the staircase.

"Scouting," he answered. "Every week I take a team of guards out to the surrounding forest area to search for evidence of the Night Rider's whereabouts. It helps us get a good idea of what area to prepare the most with reinforcements."

"Does it actually help?" I asked.

That must've been a bad thing to say, because Joey didn't respond well.

He stopped walking and shot me a glare. "Well, aren't you brutally honest this morning. And what do you mean by 'does it actually help?'"

Rude. What's gotten into his cup of tea this morning?

"Precisely that. Do you actually get any benefit from it? Or does it just make everyone feel better?"

Joey turned away from me and kept walking without answering my question. I continued following him anyway.

"Can I come?"

He looked at me.

"I don't know, El. You aren't that great of a rider or a fighter."

"Wow," I said, rolling my eyes, "you don't have to sugar coat it."

"I'm just telling you how it is." He shrugged. "We run into rouges more often than not, and most of them like to pick fights. I don't like the thought of you getting beat to a pulp if there happens to be one twice your size."

I crossed my arms. "So, you think I'm weak?"

"I didn't say that. Don't twist my words."

"You didn't have to say it. You're thinking it, aren't

you?"

He turned away from me to face forward.

"You aren't going with us, Elizabeth. Not this time." He cast a side-glance at me as he rounded the corner. "By the way, I have something to ask you."

"What is it?" I answered, still peeved.

"I thought, since you're the first Keeper that isn't the author of the Book of Aon, would you read ahead for me?"

I froze. Read ahead? *Yula warned me this would happen.*

"Well, I…" I had no words. *What am I supposed to say to him?*

"Thinking about it yesterday, I kind of realized that we have a valuable tool in front of us. This could save lives. If you read ahead and report to us what will happen, then we can prepare ourselves and maybe even prevent unnecessary deaths."

"I don't know, Joey."

"Come on, Elizabeth. It's not a hard request. Just do some reading tonight. You know what," he said, snapping his fingers, "you don't even have to tell me what happens. You can keep it to yourself until you find something bad, and then you can tell me. Okay?"

He smiled at me expectantly. "You will read some, won't you Elizabeth?"

Lie to him.

"Yeah, of course I will," I said with a forced smile.

"Great. See you later."

I stopped walking with him and let him go on. As soon as he was out of sight, I sprinted back to my room to get the Book.

Should I read it? I asked, battling against my conscience. *Yula said not to.*

But I could save someone's life.

No, I decided. Who knows what could happen?

___

I woke up early the next day for training with Rose. My eagerness surprised her, but she didn't question it.

"All right," she said, "today we need to cover hand-to-hand combat. Grab a dagger and a sword over there." She pointed to a rack against the wall. I did as she instructed, bringing the items back over to the pad in the center of the room.

"We're going to need those a bit later, so put those to the side. We're going to start with fencing so you can get used to the motions, then we'll move on to using the actual weapons." She removed her boots, throwing them to the side and telling me to do the same. A fencing sword was tossed my way, and I caught it by the handle.

"Good," she praised, nodding in satisfaction. "Your hand-eye coordination is improving. Now, onto the mat. We've got a long day of training ahead of us."

I released a deep breath and prepared myself as we dove in at full force.

The majority of the day I spent with Rose in the training room. Margaret came in with food at mealtimes, and Ed came in to observe for an hour or two after lunch. As he left, and the door closed slowly behind him, I caught a glimpse of Joey walking the halls. He peered into the room, catching my eye before shaking his head and continuing down the corridor.

Rose rested on the floor against the wall, sipping her water. I was on the floor on my back, a towel around my neck as I tried to catch my breath.

"Good job today. You caught on faster than most people do."

"Thanks," I huffed.

"You're pretty decent. Rather good, even. Careful,

you might be competing with me real soon if you keep this up."

"What about Joey?" I asked. All my energy from today came from that snarky remark he made the day before, and my blood boiled in my veins.

You aren't that great of a fighter.

"You're already competing with him."

"Really?" I asked, excited.

She laughed, shaking her head. "No way. Even I'm below Joey. He's probably got the most skill of anyone here."

I frowned. "He knows it, too."

"Yes, he does. Maybe it's time someone took him down a notch, hmm?"

I looked up at her. "Think I can do it?"

"I know you can do it. You just need more practice is all. Real practice, no fencing or sword fighting me when I'll stop before it gets too serious."

"Real practice... Got it."

"Good. Let me know when you're ready to go again; I have all the time in the world to be spending here."

I jumped to my feet, wiping my face and hands with the towel before reaching out to shake Rose's hand. "Thanks for everything."

"Don't mention it," she said. "Go get some rest; you'll need it."

The door squeaked as I swung it open, jogging down the corridor and towards the grand staircase. I took the steps two at a time, making it to the top exhilarated. I didn't slow down all the way to my room.

It was late, and most of the maids and other servants had gone to bed. I found a note on my dresser from Margaret telling me that I would have to prepare for bed myself that night. I didn't mind, glad to be alone for a while. A pot of water sat by the fire, so I put it on the hook and waited for it to heat before pouring it into the tub in the bathroom.

The hot water relaxed my muscles after the physical strain of the day. I brought water to my face with my hands, washing away the sweat. As soon as I finished, I got dressed and went straight to bed, falling asleep as soon as I hit the pillow.

I woke up early yet again but for different reasons than that of the morning before. I slipped on a simple dress from the closet as well as my boots and a navy cloak that Margaret had made for me. I scribbled a note and left it on my dresser so she wouldn't worry.

I snuck down to the training room, taking the sword and knife I had practiced with the day before and a satchel of supplies (including the Book of Aon—it never left my side when I left the castle) before heading towards the stables silently. Galloping out of the palace grounds and towards the city, I rode towards the woods, intending to do a little scouting on my own. The sky was clear, having rained out every ounce of water in the past two days that I spent inside with Rose.

The woods were quiet, as expected. No one seemed to be around. I rode silently, observing my surroundings and searching for any evidence.

Around lunchtime, I still hadn't found anything. I stopped to eat, building a small fire with some matches I had smuggled from the training room. It wasn't big; just enough to warm some bread and cheese.

I remembered the greasy, sugary food from the real world: the pizza, the hamburgers, the cupcakes, the brownies, and the soft drinks. While I did enjoy a good hamburger, none of it compared to the food in Aon. Even the cheese tasted rich and elaborate, made with salty spices and specked with flecks of a different kind of cheese. The smooth texture and warmth tickled my taste buds.

I ate in silence, staring up into the trees. I got up to walk around and explore on foot for a while after that; I'd tied my horse to a tree, so I had freedom to go off without it. I didn't find much, just the same thing I'd been seeing for the past couple hours. Tall grass, lots of trees, and puddles of water and mud were nothing new.

As I gathered my supplies and stuffed them carelessly back into my satchel, I noticed the bottom of my dress caked in a thick layer of mud.

That'll have to go, I thought, sitting down and gripping my knife in hand. Carefully, I cut away the ruined fabric up to my knees. *Much better. Margaret won't be happy, but now I'll be able to run faster if I get caught without my horse.*

Tossing the scraps onto the dying coals of the fire, I took up my satchel and mounted my horse. Not long after I journeyed back into the tree line, however, I heard a branch snap behind me.

"Can we help you, miss?" a voice asked me. A short man stepped around a tree into my line of view.

We?

Almost as if he had read my thoughts, another man stepped out where I could see him.

"No, thank you," I said coldly, trying to convey that I had no time for them. As I urged the horse forward, however, the first just blocked my path.

"I could use a cloak like this, you know," he said thoughtfully, pulling at the navy fabric tied around my neck. "It'd sell for good money."

I stepped back. If they wanted a fight, that's what they were going to get. No doubt it was late enough in the morning that Joey and Ed would realize I'd left if anything went wrong.

I prayed that what I had learned from Rose so far would be enough.

Real practice, eh? This seems good enough.

Jumping from my horse, I pulled out the sword I'd taken from the training room and prepared myself for a blow.

"There's no need for that, sweetheart. Just give us what we want and we'll be on our way."

"No, I'd rather not."

He laughed, as if it were amusing. "I don't want to hurt you."

"Pity," I remarked, a confident, snarky tone in my voice. "I was hoping to get some swings in."

The confidence I had surprised me. I'd never been confident in anything, but for some reason, the sword made me feel powerful, and I was comfortable with it.

He gritted his teeth, and after motioning to his partner, the two closed in. I held up my sword in front of me, nervously waiting for someone to make a move.

The shorter of the two barreled at me, dodging my sword and tackling me to the ground. I struggled to get him off as he landed one punch after another on my face. My hand fumbled for the sword. When it found the handle, I brought it up behind him and slashed it at his back, breaking open a long but shallow gash in his skin.

He cried out, rolling off of me and onto the grass, the blood staining his shirt red. When I looked up, the other man had advanced, and he cracked his knuckles. I scrambled to my feet, gripping the sword.

"There's more where that came from," I warned.

The second man had at least triple the height of the first. He didn't hesitate to seize my arm and try to twist it behind my back. Before he could, however, I turned my wrist over and jerked my hand back, causing him to stumble. His head dipped towards the ground, and I hit it as hard as I could with the butt of my sword. I heard him groan and he stumbled towards the ground, doing his best to steady himself on the grass.

While both of them were incapacitated, I used the opportunity to sprint to the saddle and pull out the dagger I'd stashed in the bag. They regained their balance, their eyes widened at the sight of another weapon threatening them.

"Now," I said, tossing the dagger up and catching it in my palm, "who'd like another turn?"

———

"How you could you be so *utterly* reckless?" Joey paced back and forth across the floor of the kitchen while I held an ice pack to my eye. *"You could've been killed."*

"Oh, come on, Joey, lighten up," I said. "It wasn't that bad. They only got a few hits before I pulled another sword and they ran off."

Ed kicked his chair back in the corner, laughing his head off. Quite frankly, I thought the situation was hilarious, and I tried to fight a smile.

"You think this is funny?"

Ed shook his head, covering his mouth so he wouldn't laugh anymore. That plan failed when I turned around and flashed a grin at him and he started laughing all over again.

"Why are you so worried about me anyway, Joseph?" I asked teasingly. "It's almost as if you actually *care*."

He stiffened. "Don't call me Joseph."

"Why not?"

"He hates his full name," Ed said.

"Shut up, kid," Joey retorted.

"Why? It's true." Edward shrugged his shoulders. "He says it sounds condescending."

"To answer your question, Elizabeth," he sneered, "I don't care. I just don't want to have your blood on my hands when you get killed for not telling anyone where you're going. They placed your safety on my shoulders, so you better stay out of trouble."

I laughed at his cover up.

"It sounds more like you care," I taunted. "I thought you didn't like me."

"I don't hate you."

"But you don't like me?"

He smirked. "It takes a lot more than fighting off a pack of rogues to make *me* like you."

Ed leaned over my shoulder to whisper in my ear. "He likes you; he's just too proud to admit it."

We both giggled.

Joey threw his hands up in frustration. "I'm done here."

"Go sulk in a corner somewhere, Joseph," I said again. "We can have plenty of fun without you."

Joey shot me a deadly glare before taking long strides out of the room.

If looks could kill, I'd have died about a hundred times by now.

"Don't worry about him," Ed reasoned, standing up. "He's just grumpy. He's never found much interest in the girls around here, so this is the first time he's felt something."

"Felt something?"

He nodded. "He likes you, no matter how many times he denies it. I'm pretty sure he's convinced himself that he hates you."

He likes *me?*

No. No, that's impossible.

"Maybe." I raised an eyebrow. "But I think he's just really annoyed with me at the moment."

He grinned at me. "He'll get over it." He pulled more ice out of the icebox. "In the meantime, keep ice on that eye. I'd like you to be able to see out of it by tomorrow. What good is sightseeing if you can't *see?*"

Bringing the ice pack up to my eye, I relaxed in the chair. This wasn't so bad. I *did* get the practice in, and I was confident that those rogues wouldn't bother anyone else again. Joey would get over it eventually.

Ed took the seat across from me. "So, are you going to come to the ball?"

My face dropped. "Ball?"

"Yeah." He ignored my expression. "It's a ball for my birthday. It's not for another two months, but I wanted to know ahead of time."

"Oh," was my only reply.

"What? Have you never been to a ball before?"

"It's not exactly something that happens every day where I come from," I reasoned. "But I guess I can make an exception for you, if I'm still here."

"Thanks," he replied with a grin. "Hopefully you will be. I'll have Margaret help find something for you to wear, yeah?"

I sighed. "Couldn't I just find a t-shirt somewhere?"

He wore a confused expression as he shook his head. "No, Liz, it's a ball. You'd think I wouldn't have to explain what to wear to a ball to a twenty-year-old."

I stuck my tongue out at him playfully.

"Fine. I'll wear your fancy clothes to the ball. But," I said, giving him a glare, "I'm *not* dancing."

"Fine by me. We can hang out in the corner

together, so I don't have to dance with—" he stopped short.

"Dance with who?" I raised an eyebrow suggestively.

"No one." He glared, ending that conversation. "I'll see you tomorrow?"

"Yeah, I'll see you tomorrow."

"Goodnight, Elizabeth."

"Goodnight."

Edward smiled at me once more before pulling open the heavy door and disappearing into the dark hallway.

Too lazy to find somewhere to put the ice pack, I took it with me. It would most likely melt during the night, but I didn't care.

I pulled open the door just as Edward had, watching the light from the kitchen spill onto the red carpet of the corridor. The moon streamed in through the big windows and illuminated the paintings on the ceiling. Curiously, I tilted my head up to admire them. The paintings were of angels and cupids and roman goddesses and gods. Golden auras were painted around them, as if they were some source of light.

Suddenly, I ran into something hard, falling backwards onto the floor. Someone laughed hysterically, and I balled my fists up, ready to punch whoever knocked me over.

"You should've seen the look on your face!"

I glared up at Joey, who shook with laughter.

"I'm so glad that you thought mowing me over was a good idea," I snarled.

"In my defense, you were walking around with your head in the clouds. You weren't even watching where you were going."

I cursed under my breath, earning an amused expression from Joey.

"Now if you'll excuse me, Joseph," I said, smiling at his expression when I used his full name, "I'm headed back to my room so I can... What was it you said again? Stay out of trouble?"

"Fine. You're better in there than out here."

"Fine," I said, amused. "See you tomorrow, Joey."

Joey eased up when I called him by his nickname, unclenching his fists. "See you tomorrow, El."

He's the only one who calls me El... I realized, *and I can't say I don't like it.*

He offered a small smile before calmly taking me by the hand and pulling me to my feet. He bowed politely, then stepped around me and continued on his way down the hallway. His footsteps were silent.

seven

The next morning, bright and early, I woke to a sharp knock at the door. Before I could answer, Margaret bustled in and collected things from my wardrobe.

"What're you doing?" I asked, rubbing my eyes. "What time is it?"

"It's six in the morning." She closed the doors and laid a dress on the chair next to my bed. She threw the covers off my legs, and I curled into a ball to protect myself from the cold morning air. "Get up; you're going into Baile with Joseph today."

I perked up. "I'm going on a trip with Joey?"

"Yes, now get up and get dressed. He's already waiting for you."

I complied, slipping into the plain linen dress and throwing a cloak over it. I pulled on my boots and perched on the edge of the bed while she braided my hair.

"You're going to see his sister," she explained, her fingers nimbly braiding the strands. "He thinks you need to meet her."

His sister?

As in the one with sci-fi powers? The one who can move things with her mind?

I gulped. *Is she still bitter towards Aon? Will she hate me because I'm associated with Edward?*

I shook my head, scattering my thoughts. *What a stupid idea.*

When she was done, I clasped the clear teardrop stone around my neck and tucked it into my dress.

Margaret pushed me out of my room with the Book in my arms. Joey leaned against the wall with a book in his hands.

"You had enough time to read?" I asked, closing my bedroom door behind me. His eyes flickered to me and then back down to the page before he closed his book.

"Well, you did take forever to get dressed. I even had time for a cup of tea this morning."

"Hey," I said defensively, "you didn't tell me I was leaving with you today."

He led me down the stairs in silence, not bothering to answer me. The hallways were dim; I realized that the sun hadn't even broken the horizon yet.

"Why are we leaving so early?" I asked.

"Berkeley is in Baile, which is the next kingdom over. Even though it's on the outskirts, it's still a long ride. I want to be back by tomorrow."

"Tomorrow?" I raised an eyebrow. "It's that long?"

"We can't ride there and back in one day; you'd die of exhaustion," he said, as if it were obvious. "We'll stay with my sister overnight and leave early tomorrow morning."

Instead of leading me out through the front doors of the castle like I expected, he led me down the hallway to the training room. He muttered a quiet, "Wait here," before disappearing into the dark room. He reappeared a few moments later with a dagger, a sword, and a belt.

"Hold these." He thrust the weapons into my hand. Before I could respond, the belt came around my waist under my cloak, and he was tightening it in front of me. The sword was taken from me and put into place on the belt.

"What are these for?" I asked, wary of the close proximity as he slid the dagger into the sheath on my belt.

"It's just a precaution," he said, avoiding my eye. "There's no reason we should run into the Night Rider in Baile, but just in case, I don't want to be found unarmed and vulnerable."

He turned on his heel and started towards the front of the castle. I matched his fast pace.

The horses were saddled and ready by the time we got to the stables. Even though I could mount on my own, Joey clasped his hands together to boost me into the saddle. I managed to mutter a "thanks" before he mounted his horse. I stuffed the Book into my saddlebag. The cold morning air crept around my body, and I pulled my cloak tighter around my torso.

"I'm sorry if you wanted to take the carriage," he apologized, "but we can take short cuts if we're on horseback."

"It hadn't crossed my mind," I admitted.

He didn't respond. He only spurred his horse with his heel, and I followed close behind.

For a while, the only sounds we could hear were the

hooves hitting the cobble and the birds singing. The morning grew brighter and the village buzzed with life. The sun breached the horizon, spilling bright yellow light into the sky. We passed cottage after cottage and a few people as we trotted through the city. Shopkeepers opened their shops, women carried baskets of goods, and children started on morning chores. A few people waved to Joey, and he nodded back politely.

When the road changed from cobble to gravel and then to dirt, I knew that we'd left the city limits. At a fork in the road, Joey chose the path that wound into fields instead of the forest.

Probably a good thing. We'd get lost in the woods.

About three hours later, I wasn't so sure it was a good idea after all.

The sun had come up and it warmed the air around us. Since we had no trees overhead to block the light, we had to take off our cloaks and roll up our sleeves.

"Can we take a break?" I asked, turning to him.

He snorted. "It's only nine in the morning, Elizabeth. We won't stop until at least noon."

I huffed, wiping my sweaty forehead with my sleeve. He glanced at me before rummaging through the saddlebag at his side and pulling out an apple. He tossed it to me.

Catching it with both hands, I scanned over it with my eyes. "What's this?"

"Breakfast."

I blinked. "Thanks." I ate it quickly, suddenly aware of how hungry I'd been. I tossed the core into the grass as we continued our journey.

True to his word, we stopped riding at noon, pulling off into the trees for shade. I was extremely happy to stretch my legs. Joey held a hand out to help me off of my horse, and I jumped to the ground, stretching my arms up and brushing my skirt out straight.

"Next time we go riding," I commented, "remind me to wear pants instead of a dress."

"That'll be a sight." He chuckled, tying his horse's reins around a tree. "A woman wearing pants isn't something you see everyday here."

"I'll make it something you see everyday. Dresses are exhausting."

Joey laughed, pulling another apple out of his saddlebag and tossing it to me.

"What's with all the apples?" I asked, taking a bite out of it once I had caught it.

"Aon is known for its apples." He fished another out of the bag for himself. "We grow the best."

I took another bite. It was tart and sweet at the same time and extremely juicy. The juice dribbled down my chin, and I wiped it away with my sleeve.

I weaved between trees and observed our surroundings while I ate. The leaves were turning orange, yellow, and brown. Fall was coming.

Wow. Seasons change fast here.

"We can't stay for long." Joey tossed the apple up and down in his hand. "We're only about half an hour from Berkeley."

"Only half an hour?" I snorted. "So, every time you go to see your sister, you have to ride six hours?"

"No, I can usually make it in three or four."

"*Three or four?*" My mouth dropped open in shock. "Why in the world is it taking us six, then?"

"Because you aren't exactly the best at riding, Elizabeth. You'd fall off if we had to ride that fast for that long."

"That's rude," I muttered through gritted teeth.

"It's the truth." He shrugged his shoulders.

All of a sudden, his face dropped, and he perked up. He scanned the area before untying his horse.

"What's the matter?" I asked, approaching him.

"Nothing," he said over his shoulder. "We need to keep moving."

I turned around and listened, trying to see or hear whatever made him perk up.

"Elizabeth," he called impatiently.

"I'm coming," I answered. Throwing my apple core into the forest, I untied and remounted my horse. Joey tapped the side of his horse, sending it into a gallop as we darted from the cover of the trees.

When the first cottage of Berkeley came into view, relief washed over me. The fields we had been trudging through were running together and giving me a headache.

"Does she know we're coming?" The hoof beats changed from a soft thud to a low clop; the terrain faded from soft earth to smooth cobblestone.

"She knows *I'm* coming."

"And you didn't mention you were bringing me with you?"

"No. The thought didn't occur to me at the time."

I gulped. "And she won't be angry, will she?"

She won't make something fly at my head, right?

"Well, she hasn't pulled a sword on anyone in a long time, so I guess you're safe."

My head whipped towards him, eyes wide. He laughed.

"I'm kidding," he said. "Sort of."

He led me through the cobble roads. I noticed that Berkeley had more of a rural population than Aon's capital city. The cottages were spread out, and each had a small expanse of land around it.

Only a few minutes later, Joey stopped in front of a large, beautiful, stone and brick home. Roses were planted under the windows, and land stretched from the house all the way to the forest. A smaller building was attached to the main house from the side.

Joey jumped off his horse, offering a hand to help me down. Together, we led our horses by the reins to the smaller part of the house where we found a stable. After leading each of the horses into a stall, I pulled the Book from my saddlebag. No way would I leave it outside.

Joey had a bright grin on his face. His mood improved significantly as we approached the front door. Nervously, I smoothed my skirt and rolled my sleeves down, tucking the Book protectively into my chest.

He watched me fiddle nervously with my clothes. "You look fine. She's not going to bite." He raised his hand and rapped his knuckles against the wood.

"You don't know that," I muttered more to myself than to him.

Just then, the door opened.

A beautiful young woman in a long, pastel dress appeared in the doorway, an apron wrapped around her waist. She had long, flowing dirty blonde hair and Joey's blue eyes.

"Joseph!" She opened her arms wide. He hugged her around the neck, kissing the top of her head.

"Hello, Delia," he said, pulling away.

"You're late." She pushed his shoulder.

"I'm sorry, but I got held up."

At that moment, Delia noticed that I was standing there. Her eyes raked my body, scrutinizing me as if searching for an imperfection.

"Delia, this is Elizabeth. She's the newest Outsider."

"An Outsider, is she?"

I squirmed under her harsh gaze. Something was off—why was she observing me so closely?

"She is," Joey said. "I wanted her to meet you. She's the only Outsider that Yula named the Keeper."

Delia extended a hand towards me. I accepted it only to be welcomed with an iron grip.

"Welcome to Wellington Place, Elizabeth." She offered a kind smile. I managed to smile back, but something behind her gaze made me feel like it was forced.

"Let's go inside, shall we?" Joey asked. "I'm starving."

Delia let go of my hand to put both on her hips. "Don't eat all of my food, Joseph, or you're buying me more groceries."

"I guess I'll be buying you more groceries, then." He grinned, walking into the house. I followed silently behind him into the small foyer, all too aware of Delia behind me.

Relax, Liz, I scolded myself mentally. *You have no reason to be afraid of her.*

"Joseph, go wash your face." Delia closed the door behind us. "I'll show Elizabeth her room."

He nodded before leaving us.

"I'm sure you had a long journey," his sister said once he was gone. "Joseph can be quite difficult to put up with sometimes."

"Sometimes," I agreed. "Maybe a little more than sometimes."

She laughed, and something in her eyes twinkled. Immediately, I relaxed.

"You're the first girl he's ever brought here." She

took my cloak from around my shoulders and hanging it on a knob by the door.

"I find that hard to believe," I answered. She snorted, wiping her hands on her apron and motioning for me to follow her.

"Believe it. He claims he's too busy to court anyone, and I don't doubt it."

"Oh, no!" I waved my hands out in front of me. "No, you don't understand. We're just friends—acquaintances, at that. We can't even get along well for more than a little while."

She raised an eyebrow, seemingly amused. "I see."

Leading me through the foyer into the hallway, we walked to the door at the end. She pulled a key from her apron pocket, and after waving it at me, she inserted it into the lock and pushed the door open.

"I like to keep this room clean all the time," she explained, motioning for me to walk in first. "I'll let you wash up. I'll be in the kitchen when you're ready for something to eat; it's not hard to find."

I thanked her before she curtseyed and pulled the bedroom door closed behind her.

Once the door clicked closed, I observed the room. It was simple, clean, and small. The bed was on the wall facing the door, a short night table next to it. A desk and a stool rested on the wooden floor under a window, and a washbasin leaned against a pale blue wallpapered wall.

After rolling my sleeves up and taking off my belt, I stepped up to the basin and washed my face and arms. The cool water felt amazing on my skin after the long day riding in the sun with no shade. The weather may have been cooling off, but the sun sure wasn't. With eyes closed, I reached for something to dry my face off. My fingers grasped what felt like a small cloth.

When my face was dry, I opened my eyes to see a small, white towel. Tiny stars were embroidered in gray. It made me think of Edward and his talk of stars from the first night in Aon, only a week ago.

"I think some stars shine brighter than others on purpose. The brightest ones are the people who were secretly great," he explained, resting his arms behind his head on the ground.

"Not all of them are secret, though," I said, lying down next to him on the ground and sharing the view of the night sky. "Some of them are so obviously great that you can't help but stare."

"Like that one." He pointed up into the sky. My eyes focused on the biggest, brightest star.

"Yes, like that one. Who do you think that one is?"

He was silent for a moment before he answered. "I think it's my mother."

A nostalgic feeling rushed over me and instantly put me in a better mood. I really felt so much happier in Aon than I had been in the real world. I didn't miss a thing about my old life—not the stress, the loneliness, or the work. I didn't even miss the food or anybody I knew; I didn't have friends apart from the occasional class project partner, and I had no desire to visit anyone from the girl's home. Here, I had a life. I had Ed, and I had Joey.

I have Joey.

A sharp knock on the door interrupted my thoughts.

"Come in," I said, putting the handkerchief down next to the washbasin. As I rolled down my sleeves, Joey pushed the door open.

"Are you hungry?" he asked, stepping inside. I scrutinized my reflection in the mirror and then shifted my eyes to watch him sit down on the edge of the bed through the glass.

"I could eat," I admitted, tucking in loose strands

from my braid. Pacing to the bed, I slid the Book under my pillow and hung my belt on the bedpost. He seemed amused as he watched me hide the journal.

"Delia's preparing an early supper. I wanted to discuss the Night Rider with her, and I want you to be there."

Raising an eyebrow, I turned to face him. "Why me?"

"Because you have the Book," he explained. "You can tell us if anything big is going to happen, right?"

Before I could protest, he held a hand up. "I know you don't want to mess with the destiny of Aon, so you don't have to tell me any of the little details. I just want to know if we're in danger, and that's all. Okay?"

Lie to him. You can't tell him the truth, or he'll press further.

I nodded. "Okay."

"Great." He grinned, hopping off of the bed and standing by the door. His arm moved in a gesture towards the hallway. "After you."

A soft light filled the window-lined hallway. The feeling I got while walking through it comforted me; it felt like a home. I noticed portraits on the walls. One in particular reminded me of Delia. I stopped and let my eyes scan the portrait.

"That was my mother," Joey informed me, standing next to me.

"You both look just like her. I see where you get your eyes."

"Yes, I do hear that a lot. Delia is a spitting image of my mother, though. I'm not quite as much like her as she is."

"Joey?" Delia's muffled voice called.

"We're coming."

Joey stepped in front of me and led the way to the

kitchen. I followed him, tossing a glance at the portrait once more before turning the corner.

The kitchen was bright and open. Delia sat at a wooden table pouring tea. We took the seats opposite her.

"Joseph," she asked, sliding a cup of tea his way, "has anything happened since the last time you were here?"

Joey glanced at me out of the corner of his eye before answering.

"Not particularly, but Elizabeth did fight a pack of rogues on her own."

"Did you really?" Delia asked, shocked. "How extraordinary."

"Not really." I shrugged. "Rose taught me everything I know."

She frowned. "Who is Rose?"

"She's the only woman on Edward's protection detail, besides me, now, I suppose," I said.

Joey nudged my foot under the table, clearing his throat awkwardly. Delia shot him a glare.

"Just because I don't like the child doesn't mean you can't talk about him, Joseph," she scolded.

"I'm sorry," I apologized, feeling guilty.

"Don't feel sorry, Elizabeth. You've done nothing wrong. Now, please continue. Rose taught you how to defend yourself?"

"She did. Joey and Edward told me it was necessary."

"Because of the Night Rider, correct?"

"She hasn't encountered him yet, though," Joey said. "She hasn't used anything she's learned against him."

Frowning, I shook my head. "Yes, I have."

"You have?" Joey seemed bewildered. Did Edward

not tell him?

I looked over at Delia, who had her gaze trained on me. I shifted uncomfortably in my seat.

"The day Edward and I got here," I explained. "We had to climb a tree to hide. He rode right under us. I didn't have to fight him, but I was close enough to know I didn't want to."

"I see." He clenched his jaw. "I'll have to ask Edward about that."

Whoops. Sorry, Edward.

"You're the new Keeper, correct?" Delia asked me.

"I am."

"So, you're the one that all of our lives depend on, correct?"

"I wouldn't say that." I started to get a little nervous. Did she think I needed to read it, too?

"Whether you say it or not, you do." She leaned back in her seat. "Have you read anything about Baile or Aon?"

I raised an eyebrow. "This thing can control Baile, too?"

"The Book of Aon is only named after Aon because that's where it originated," Joey explained. "It was the first kingdom created. The Book itself can control anything in this world; it's not limited to Aon."

"Have you read anything?" Delia asked again, getting impatient.

Thankfully, Joey answered for me.

One less lie I have to tell myself.

"She's reading ahead to ensure the safety of the people," he said. "She's worried about disrupting what's written, so she's not going to tell us anything unless it's life threatening."

"Are you now?"

Delia's gaze made me extremely uncomfortable. It seemed like she knew I'd lied as soon as Joey started talking. The smile that twisted across her lips unnerved me, but Joey didn't seem to notice a thing.

She thinks I'm the bad guy. She thinks that it's wrong of me not to try to save them, just like Joey does.

"And have you read anything bad about either of our fine countries?" she asked sweetly.

"No, I haven't." I forced a smile.

At least that part isn't a lie.

Joey's sister seemed to linger on my words for a moment before clearing her throat and breaking her concentration. Her smile disappeared.

"The Night Rider has been here, Joseph." Delia shifted her gaze from me to her brother. "He's burned the village just north of here."

"He burned another village?" Joey asked, snapping out of his oblivious daze. "Was anyone hurt?"

"Most of the village evacuated and are being taken to the capital to stay," she explained. "There were several casualties."

"What was the death toll?"

She grimaced. "Fifteen."

Joey rubbed his forehead with his fingers, obviously stressed out. "I swear, I'm going to find this man, and I'm going to kill him myself."

"Joseph, there's no reason to give yourself the label of a murderer."

"Murdering to defend my kingdom sounds pretty damn good right now."

Delia scoffed. "Use better language at my table, Joseph."

"I won't tolerate this *terrorist* taking the lives of innocents."

"What are you going to do about it?" she asked.

"I'm going to take a patrol out, and soon," he said. "We're all going to train up, then we're going to go find the bastard."

"*Language*," she hissed again. He ignored her.

"The townspeople here have mentioned seeing him ride past the forest border," she offered. "You could start there."

"Have any forest dwellers seen him?"

"You know there aren't many left, and the ones who still live there don't come to town very often. I'd go and ask them yourself; no one here would know."

"Have you seen him?" I asked Delia.

Nodding, she sipped from her cup of tea. "I have. He's come rather close by before. He's run through the village at night several times; you can't see him unless you stay up long enough to watch. We've all learned to blow out all of our lamps so that he doesn't target us."

"Isn't it tiring?" I questioned, frowning.

"Isn't what tiring, dear?"

"Living in fear and bending to his will. Doesn't it get tiring?"

She seemed to ponder for a moment. "I suppose it does. No one is brave enough to stand up to him, though, so we'll be in the same routine for a while. The King of Baile himself can't even speak to him because he can never find him."

"I'm going to find him," declared Joey, "and when I do, he'd better be prepared for the worst."

"I think you're tired," Delia corrected. She realized that Joey wasn't listening to a word. "Enough talk of death for now. I have soup over the fire. Would you like to eat?"

The rest of the evening was spent at the modest

dinner table. We ate soup and I listened to Delia and Joey tell stories of their childhood. Delia talked about the friends she made while in boarding school. Surprisingly, she didn't mention her powers or use them at all. Joey didn't say anything about them either. By the time we cleaned up dinner, I had almost forgotten she even had them.

Delia lent me a nightgown to use for the night. After thanking her for the meal and saying goodnight to everyone, I found my way back to the room she had designated as mine, closing the door behind me before slipping into the nightgown and crawling into bed.

The room was pitch black when I opened my eyes. I stared at the ceiling, trying to will myself back to sleep for lack of a better thing to do, but it didn't seem to work.

I was about to sit up to go get a glass of water but quickly changed my mind when I heard the floorboards creak.

Who was up at this hour?

Either way, I didn't move. I didn't want either of them to know I was awake. It was too late to be butting heads with a cranky Joey, and I didn't want to risk an awkward situation with Delia.

There was something strange about the footsteps that echoed through the house. They didn't sound like Delia's—they were way too heavy—and Joey's footsteps sounded more... formal, for lack of a better word. Joey never trudged when he walked, even when he was tired.

As I wondered who it could be, I realized that the footsteps were right outside of my door.

My breath hitched in my throat as the creak of the door on its hinges sent a chill down my spine. One by one, the footsteps drew closer until they stopped at the end of my bed.

In a temporary moment of bravery, I flicked my eyes down to try to make out who the intruder was. A shadow was all that I could see.

One second, I laid in my bed, and the next, I was thrown to the floor, nearly meeting the wood with my face. Pain shot through my arm as I landed right on my elbow, and I cried out.

Before I could turn around to see my attacker, he latched onto my ankle and trudged down the hallway with me in tow. Unable to turn my body, I lunged for anything I could to slow him down.

Remember something, I thought, forcing myself to focus. *My thoughts were scrambled and chaotic in my mind. Anything from combat training. Anything Joey has said. Come on, remember something!*

That's it!

Joey!

"Joey!" I screamed, clawing at the door frame. I heard the front door being slammed against the frame of the house when it swung open, and I knew that the intruder hadn't planned to just scare me or hurt me.

He was going to abduct me, and if he succeeded, I knew that I had no chance of making it to morning.

"Elizabeth?" I heard Joey say. "Elizabeth, where are you?"

"Joey!" I screamed again, my voice cracking. I managed to grasp the frame of the door, digging into the wood with my fingernails. The pain made me cringe, but I held on for my life. He tried to pull me from the house, outside into the darkness of the night.

"Elizabeth!"

Suddenly, Rose's voice popped into my mind.

"Turn your wrist so that your palm faces up," she had said.

"Pull back as far as you can. Your elbow will have more leverage."
Would the same tactic work with my ankle and my knee?

It was worth a shot, and at this point, my only option. My fingers were losing their grip, and Joey hadn't found me yet.

Mustering every ounce of strength I had, I turned my ankle over in the mystery man's grip. When I had the leverage, I used my arms to pull myself back into the house and jerk my knee up with it. My body slid across the wood, scraping my skin and knocking my head against the wall.

Once again, I heard the footsteps draw close. Instinctively, I tried to kick at the attacker through the darkness that crept into my vision.

"*What the hell* is going on in here?"

Joey's familiar voice put me at ease, and a sense of calmness washed over me. I blinked, trying to clear up the blurry images. The door hung wide open, but the dark figure had disappeared.

"Are you two okay?" Delia's voice called. She burst into the room, taking in the sight of me sprawled on the wood and the door hanging open. She crouched next to me, pulling me up by the shoulders. The fast motion sent my head spinning, and I gripped her arm to hold myself steady.

I got an odd feeling having Delia next to me, and it wasn't a good one. I pushed it aside, trying to focus on staying conscious.

"Joseph, go get a wet cloth from the kitchen." Delia kept her voice level.

"Oh, *crap*," Joey breathed. "Delia, she's *bleeding*."

"Joey, go get a cloth, please," she urged again. "Quickly." She helped me slide back down until I sat propped against the wall.

Reluctantly, Joey ran down the hallway and reappeared moments later. He crouched down next to me, holding the cloth to the back of my head. I winced at the pressure.

"What happened, Elizabeth?" he asked.

"I don't know," I slurred, trying to regain focus. My head ached. "Someone came into my room."

"*Your room?*" Joey's voice was deadly.

"It was dark... I couldn't see."

Delia scanned the area and her expression dropped. A burning lantern rested in a windowsill down the hallway.

Joey followed her gaze.

"Delia, you left the lantern burning?"

The lantern.

"We've learned to blow out all of our lanterns at night so that he doesn't target us."

He.

The Night Rider.

Oh, no.

"I don't remember blowing it out," she admitted.

"Elizabeth could've been killed!" he yelled. I flinched at the sharpness of his words. "How careless can you be?"

"I'm sorry!" she said. "I'm so sorry, Elizabeth."

"S'okay," I managed to say. "I'm not dead yet."

"Where did he go?" Joey asked, springing up from the floor. "Where'd the coward go? I swear, I'm going to rip the life out of him—"

"Joseph, if you think one more murderous thought in my house, I'm making you sleep in the stable. Now isn't the time."

Reluctantly, Joey sat back down with his back pressed against the wall next to me.

"Here, El," he said, his voice quieter, "rest your head. Does it hurt?"

I nodded, wincing at the fast motion. I rested my head in his lap, watching Delia's feet move beside me to go to the open door and close it. I heard a muted click as she locked the door into the frame.

"Like that will help now," Joey murmured. "I don't think doors are much of a match for the Night Rider."

"It gives me peace of mind," his sister said simply.

I closed my eyes, listening to the sound of Joey's breathing as I lay on the cold wood floor. My head felt better when I didn't move, but when I was totally still, I could feel the ache of my other injuries settling in.

A few minutes later, in a hushed whisper, Delia spoke.

"Will she be okay?"

Sleep began to creep in, but I fought it so that I could listen.

Joey's response was just as quiet. "She'll be fine. She's tough. I think it just scared her more than anything."

Silence, and then: "I'm sorry, Joey."

"Don't worry about it," he answered. "What's done is done. Let's just move on."

"Do you care about her?"

I found myself anxious to hear his reply, though I couldn't figure out why. A pit formed in my stomach, but I had to energy to do anything about it.

Joey didn't speak for a moment before he answered. "I don't know."

"Judging by the way you're holding her right now, I'd say you know more than you're letting on."

The pit in my stomach was carved deeper by butterflies that seemed to erupt. What does she mean?

How is he holding me?

I wanted to open my eyes, but my eyelids were so heavy that it was impossible.

"*Geez*, Delia. She was almost abducted only *half an hour ago* and you're asking about my *love life?*"

"I'm just pointing it out, Joey, because you can be pretty oblivious sometimes."

"I don't want her dead. Can we leave it at that?"

Delia let out a breathy chuckle before answering. "For now."

The butterflies faded and allowed me to drift before I could hear anymore. Their words rang in the back of my mind as I fell into a deeper sleep.

———

An unfamiliar silence settled in my ears as I came to. I didn't open my eyes; I was afraid of seeing that awful figure again if I opened them.

Instead, I settled for calling out. The Night Rider would answer if he were standing there, right?

Idiot.

"Joey?"

I heard light footsteps echo off of the floor, and then Joey's quiet voice.

"Are you okay, Elizabeth?"

I opened my eyes, figuring that I was safe if Joey was here. It was morning, and I had to squint before my eyes could adjust.

Joey's familiar blue eyes met mine. He loomed at the foot of my bed, leaning against the frame. His dark hair was tousled and messy, but it didn't seem to bother him. His clean, white undershirt was unbuttoned, loose across his chest, but he didn't seem to care about that either. The morning light streaming through the window made him seem refreshed.

I wonder what I look like right now.

"Did you hear me?" he asked. "Are you in pain?"

"No." I sat up, wincing as the pain erupted from my head. My hand flew to my temple. "Yes."

He wasted no time in retrieving a cloth from the washbasin in the corner. The edge of the bed creaked as he sat down next to me, pressing the cold cloth to my forehead.

"Do you remember what happened?" he asked, speaking slowly.

With wide eyes, I swallowed hard. "Too well," I whispered in a hoarse voice. "All too well."

A sad smile graced his lips as his eyes flicked from my forehead to my eyes, then back again. "If you're feeling okay, then we'll head back to the castle today. If you need another day to rest, though, I underst—"

"I'm ready to leave," I said, cutting him off.

"I'm not rushing you, El. You can stay if you—"

"I want to go," I urged. "Please. It makes me uncomfortable that the Night Rider just rides through here on a daily basis. I don't want to risk seeing him again. I have a feeling he won't give up."

Joey nodded. "All right. We'll leave soon, then. We aren't riding on horseback, though; there's no way I'm letting you on the back of a horse with a concussion."

"I don't have a concussion."

The glare that Joey gave me made me back off. "I mean... yeah, you're right. Horseback riding is a bad idea right now."

"Besides." A slow smile formed on his face. "You aren't that great of a rider anyway. You riding with a concussion would be an absolute disaster."

"Hey!"

"Keep your voice down, Elizabeth. You'll give

yourself a headache."

"*You* give me a headache."

"You need to lay down," he said, ignoring me. "Get another hour's rest while I call for the carriage. Delia will pack your things while you sleep."

"She doesn't have to do that," I argued.

"Let her help you," pleaded Joey, giving me a look. "She feels bad about last night."

I sighed. He pulled the cloth away from my head and leaned closer to examine my forehead. I felt butterflies erupt in my stomach—something unexpected.

Calm down, Liz.

"You're not bleeding where you hit your head anymore, so that's good."

Oh, right. I bled last night.

Great.

He stood from the bed to put the cloth back at the washbasin. When he reached the door, he pointed at me.

"Sleep, please. Get some rest."

In a blink, he was gone. Taking his advice, I settled into the sheets to go back to sleep.

When I woke up, Delia was in the room. She packed a cloth with what appeared to be a couple of apples.

"Are apples a big deal here, too?" I asked curiously, sitting up against the headboard. She turned and smiled.

"No, that's just Aon. Joey brings me a basket every once in awhile, though, and I had a few left from the last time he visited." Her dress brushed the floor as she came closer and held a hand against my head. "How do you feel?"

"Better than last night," I admitted, "but I'm sore. I'll bet I look horrid."

She tried to smile, but it came out more like a grimace. "You don't look *that* bad."

"Your expression says otherwise."

Hesitantly, she reached into the drawer in the side table and pulled out a hand held mirror. Her hands rested it into mine.

I glanced warily at her, holding the mirror to my face. Was it worse than I thought?

Ouch.

Yes, yes it was.

My left eye was tinged with a sickly yellow color where a bruise formed under the skin. The same color stretched across my jaw and the side of my face where I hit my face against the wood. Dark spots dotted my skin, and I truly looked sick.

There was a faint streak on my forehead where blood had dried and stained my skin. My hand reached up to touch the spot on the top of my head where the flow started. I flinched when the pressure started to hurt.

"You'll heal," Delia said, trying to give me some solace.

"I know," I said, "but *wow*."

"I'll go get some ice for your elbow." She ignored my comment. She nodded towards my arm before pacing from the room. When I straightened out my elbow to look at it, another ache started on my arm.

"Did I bruise every part of my body?" I asked in exasperation, observing the ugly purple color that my elbow had taken on. Throwing back the sheets, I scanned my legs for bruises, finding them littering my legs and hips. I had one particularly nasty one on my right hip that hurt whenever I moved it.

Delia's footsteps echoed down the hallway, and I flinched at the sound. It seemed louder in my head than it probably really was. She came back with ice wrapped in a cloth and immediately pressed it to the bruise, making me shiver. As she held the ice to my swollen arm, Joey came sauntering down the corridor and into my room, my cloak in his hand. He was fully dressed now, jacket and all.

"Are you feeling up to leaving?" he asked, sitting on the edge of the bed. "The carriage is ready if you are."

"You really should stay here and recover another day," Delia reminded. "You took a beating. You need rest."

"Thank you, Delia, but I really should be getting home."

Home. Did I just call Aon home?

Huh. I guess I did.

"Thank you for coming to visit," she said. "I'm so sorry this happened. You'll probably never come visit again!"

"I'll come back," I promised.

I wasn't sure whether that was true or not. I appreciated Delia's kindness, but I got a horrible vibe from her. She watched me too closely, like I planned to do something horrible and she knew it.

"I'm ready to leave," I told Joey.

He stood up and rounded the bed. Delia moved out of his way as he held an arm out to help me up.

Shaking my head, I held my hand up. "I don't need it."

He seemed like he wanted to protest but changed his mind, moving back to let me up. Hesitantly, I put one foot on the wood floor and then the other.

Once I stood on both feet, I smiled triumphantly, happy that I had the strength to walk. That is, until I stumbled.

I hit Joey's arms before I could hit the floor, and he pulled me into him. I looked up at him and raised my eyebrows.

"Don't need it, huh?"

"Thanks," I mumbled, aggravated.

If I'm going to have to be carried around and fussed over for weeks, I'm going to scream.

"I folded your dress and put it in the carriage with your belt," Delia said, watching me lean on Joey's arm. "Don't worry about the night gown. You can keep it."

"Thank you." I forced a smile. Joey threw my cloak around my shoulders and fastened it for me before helping me limp to the door.

"Oh!" I exclaimed, whipping around. "I forgot!"

"Crap, El, you scared me," Joey said. "What'd you forget?"

"The Book." I pointed at the pillow. "It's under my pillow."

Delia raised an eyebrow before lifting the pillow. Her hands wrapped around the worn leather of the Book's cover, and she rubbed her hands across it. Then, she stepped forward to hand it to me.

My eyes traveled carefully from Delia to the Book.

"Thanks," I said, taking it cautiously from her hands. She offered a smile, but there was no warmth in it.

Joey let me use him as a support until we passed through the front door. There, he let go of me, hopped down the steps, and then picked me up and carried me to the carriage.

"That was unnecessary." I scowled at him.

"You were walking too slowly," he said.

"Were *you* just brutally attacked?" I asked. "No, I don't think so."

"I'm brutally attacked by your words every day." Joey opened the carriage door and helped me inside. "I literally take a beating."

I rolled my eyes. "Hardly."

He laughed, shaking his head at me. Delia stepped outside and strode towards the carriage.

"I really am sorry about all of this." She smiled apologetically. "I hope you come back to visit."

"Don't worry about it. You'll see me again."

"We must be off," Joey stated. "I don't know when I'll be back. Things will be pretty busy for a while."

"Just come by whenever you can," she said. "Joseph, I think I left your food back in Elizabeth's room. Will you go get it, please?"

"Sure thing," he answered. As he walked away, Delia turned to me.

"I want you to understand something," she said, drawing closer. "I don't pity you because you got a little beat up."

I blinked. "Excuse me?"

"It's happened to me before. I don't pity you," she repeated. "I know you haven't been reading that," she nodded to the Book, "and if you're not careful, things will start to hurt a lot worse than a little beating. Joseph may be oblivious to it, but I certainly am not."

"How did you—"

She pulled me down into a hug just as Joey reappeared in the doorway.

"If you hurt my brother, I will make sure you pay," she hissed in my ear. "Understood?"

Before I could answer, she pulled away, flashing me the brightest smile I'd ever seen.

She's nothing but a fake, I realized. *She's a liar.*

You're no better than her, my conscience reminded me. *You've been lying to Joey.*

I forced a smile, trying not to let my grimace show through as Joey approached his sister and gave her a hug.

"Goodbye, Joey." She kissed his cheek. "Be careful."

"I will," he answered.

Joey waved goodbye through the window as we rode away.

"Joey?"

"Yes?"

"Why doesn't Delia use her powers?"

He looked at me, alarmed. "You knew?"

"I visited Yula," I reminded him.

It took him a moment to find his words. "Well... I guess she didn't want to scare you. Neither of us knew that you knew about her... talents." He turned back to the window. "She doesn't like to use them much, anyway. She doesn't like feeling different from everyone else. She likes doing things the hard way." He bit his lip and paused for a moment before continuing. "It tires her out if she does it too long. She doesn't think it's worth it."

I looked down at my hands and clasped them together in my lap.

Does he know what she's really like? Is it just me?

Is Delia right? Are things going to go wrong if I don't read it?

No. I have to trust Yula before anyone else. She told me not to read it, so I'm not going to read it.

"Are you okay, Elizabeth?" Joey wore a worried expression when I met his gaze.

"I'm a little achy, but I'm okay," I said.

"Not that." He shook his head. "I mean, you seemed a little worried for a few minutes. You were kind of out of it."

Should I mention Delia to him?

No. It isn't important.

"I'm fine," I reassured him.

He raised an eyebrow. "Are you?"

Lie.

"Don't worry about me, Joey. I'll be okay."

eight

Four weeks of training, horseback riding, and reading every book in the library passed in the blink of an eye. Everything became routine and normal, and more often than not I totally forgot about the world I lived in before. I no longer stayed in a guest room, I stayed in my room; every member of the staff knew my name and I was in the kitchen helping and chatting often. Surprisingly, we didn't see much from the Night Rider. It was as if he went MIA for a month and was laying low.

I moved on from my uncomfortable confrontation with Delia. I wouldn't see her for months, anyway; there was no reason for me to drag down everyone's happy moods by being bitter. All the while, though, theories brewed in the back of my mind—ridiculous things, like she was out to get me or that she had an agreement with the Night Rider. I never told Joey of my suspicions.

Training with Rose became easier and easier to handle. We moved on to more advanced things. I even took her down in more than one of our skirmishes.

"You've learned so fast," Rose said. "You're probably as good as Joseph by now, if not better."

"Really?" I asked, my back turned to her as I drank my water. I didn't feel as tired as I did when I first started.

I heard a slight sound, like something cutting air. Instinctively, I turned sideways, and a knife whizzed into view. I brought my boot up and kicked it just before it passed me, and it hit the wall with a thud and stuck.

"Yeah," she answered with a chuckle, "I'd say so."

She went over to the wall, and I followed her.

"There's really not much more for me to teach you, Elizabeth." She released the knife from the wall. "You can come back to stay in practice, but I'd say you're done for now."

"So, what I'm hearing is that I can come back tomorrow to train?"

She chuckled. "Sure, if you want. See you tomorrow, then."

I smiled at her, waving before stepping out into the hallway. When I did, I ran right into the man himself. Overwhelmed with the happiness of my accomplishments in the training room, I decided to share them with him.

"Don't you have somewhere to be, Elizabeth?" Joey asked, annoyed as I followed him through the winding hallways.

"No," I said, satisfied. "I finished my training. Isn't that great?"

"Superb," he said through gritted teeth. "Is there something I can do for you?"

"Yeah, actually," I admitted. "When is the next scouting trip?"

"Why do you want to know, especially when you could just go on one by yourself again?"

I stopped in my tracks. "Hey now, no need to get snappy just because I proved to you that I could do it. Can you get over it?"

"You didn't prove anything," he said, turning around to face me, "except that you're stupid enough to take on reckless tasks."

Someone woke up on the wrong side of the bed this morning.

"Did someone slip something into your morning tea?" I asked sarcastically. "And I'm not stupid. I just want to know when the next one is. Would you please quit acting like a child, Joseph?"

He turned his back and kept walking. I jogged to catch up to him.

"We leave in an hour." He turned into the training room. I hadn't even realized that we were here; he must've taken an alternate route. He walked inside and gathered weapons.

"An hour? With who?"

"Cyneward, Rose, Alec, and me. Why?"

Alec. I've heard that name before.

"I'm coming with you," I stated simply.

"No, you're not," he growled. "The last thing I need is to be dragging you around trying to keep you upright on a horse when you get hurt."

"Who rode all the way back to the castle on a horse and wounded by herself?" I asked. "Oh, that's right. I did. And by the way, I don't remember asking your permission to go scouting."

"You're not coming."

"Yes, I am."

"No, you're not."

"I am."

"I could stand here all day, Elizabeth. How much time you got?"

"More than you. You leave in an hour."

He shot me a deadly glare. "Just do yourself a favor and stay here. We don't need you to tag along on this one."

"Fine." I crossed my arms. "I'll stay here."

He raised an eyebrow. "Really?"

"No. Now, which dagger is mine?"

An hour later, I stood next to Joey in the stables in a very bubbly mood. I rocked back and forth on my heels, impatiently waiting for us to get on the road.

Joey, on the other hand, was brooding. It was like his whole aura radiated anger, and I could feel him shooting daggers at my back; I ignored him and I jogged ahead to ready my horse.

"Elizabeth!" Rose called with a smile. "I'm so glad you're coming. It's time you put the rest of those skills to use."

"Thanks!" I exclaimed. "Joey isn't particularly happy, though."

We both turned around to glance at him before continuing. He shot a glare back at me.

"He'll get over it. My husband was extremely nervous and annoyed when I told him I'd joined the royal guard, but he got over it, too."

I blinked. "You're married?"

She nodded. "My husband lives in the village."

Huh. You think you know someone after two months and you still don't know her.

"Wow. It must be tough."

She shook her head. "It's not great, but it's not nearly as bad as it could be. Thank you for your sympathy, but it really isn't needed."

I gave her a crooked smile.

"Everyone ready?" someone called from the other end of the table. I perked up at the unfamiliar voice.

A tall boy with pitch-black hair and green eyes was coming our way. He looked about my age, and he appeared to be just as fit as Joey. Cyneward followed behind him, silently readying his horse.

"Who is this?" he asked, raising an eyebrow at me. His eyes assessed me before he turned to Joey, a puzzled expression on his face.

"This is Elizabeth," he mumbled, clearly still aggravated.

"Ah, so *this is her.*" He turned to me with a wicked smile. I couldn't help but laugh at his mischievous expression.

"You've heard of me?" I asked.

"Heard of you?" he snorted. "You're all Joey has talked about for weeks."

"Very funny, Alec," he spat. "That's enough."

"Oh, contraire." He smiled at me before he shot a grin in Joey's direction, "I'm just getting started. What should I tell her about first? The angry rant or the heartfelt conversation you spilled?"

Joey launched himself at Alec, but Alec merely stepped to the side and let him fall to the ground, chuckling to himself.

Alec held his hand out to me, ignoring Joey's body sprawled on the floor. "Alexander Fell, medic in training."

He's a medic. He's the one who patched up Ed when we got here.

"Elizabeth." I took his hand.

He raised an eyebrow. "Just Elizabeth?"

"Just Elizabeth." We shook hands.

"So, you're going to be coming with us today?"

"She's not," Joey said as he took to his feet and dusted himself off.

I ignored him. "Yes, I am."

He laughed. "I like you already. You're a breath of fresh air."

"Thanks. You're not so bad yourself."

He smirked at me before walking towards a stall and unlocking it, guiding his horse out. "Let's get going, shall we?"

We did well that day. There was no evidence of any more killings close to the village and no run ins with thieves. We returned later that night unscathed.

I joined in on more scouting trips after that. Alec commented it was strange that we hadn't found anything after a couple of trips, but we tried to take it as a good sign and keep our eyes open.

We took another scouting trip per Joey's request. He said that the probability of an assassination attempt was a higher risk; the ball wasn't for another month, but no one questioned him. The trip started out normal. We entered the woods straight ahead of the city, working our way farther in as we searched for any evidence of the Night Rider.

"If I were terrorizing an entire kingdom, why would I be a coward and hide in the woods?" Alec asked after a moment.

"He's trying to intimidate us," Joey answered. "He knows most people don't venture here because they're afraid of getting lost. He has the advantage here."

"About that," I cut in, "how do we know the Night

Rider is a guy?"

"We don't," Rose answered. "It's just easier to call it a male."

"Maybe you could expand your search to women too," I offered. "You'd have a better chance of finding whoever it is that's doing this."

"We've already done that," Cyneward said. "Thanks for trying to help, though."

We rode in silence for a while before I spotted a knife stuck in a tree.

"Guys, look at this."

Everyone rode towards me, surrounding the tree.

"Finally, we found something," Rose said. "At least we know how far he is from the village now."

"Over there." Cyneward pointed towards another tree. I rode towards it, finding cuts in the bark.

"We should follow them," I suggested. "Maybe we can figure out more about the Night Rider's place of operation."

"Good idea, Liz," Alec said. "Maybe we should split up. I'll go with Elizabeth, and Joey can go with Cyneward and Rose. Sound good?"

"No, it doesn't sound good," Joey argued, suddenly irritated. "Why are you going with Elizabeth alone?"

"Why not?"

"Enough, boys," Cyneward interrupted. "Splitting up is a bad idea. We don't know who could be in these parts; it's best that we stick together."

"He's right," agreed Rose, "but we do need to follow these markings before it gets too dark to do so. Let's get a move on."

We followed those markings for two hours, but we still were nowhere. When we stopped for a break, I noticed what appeared to be another knife stuck in a tree.

I dismounted, jogging to the tree to examine it. All of the cuts were in the same place, and the handle pointed upwards just like what we had seen before.

"Uh... guys?" I called.

"What is it?" Joey asked.

"I don't want to make you panic or anything, but I think we've been riding in circles."

Everyone perked up at that, dismounting and joining me at the knife-marked tree.

"It's exactly the same as the last one," Rose marveled.

"Because it *is* the same one." Alec scanned the area around us. "That can't be good."

"This is too strange," said Joey. "There's no way."

"He's toying with us," Alec realized.

He was right. The sound of hoofbeats reached my ears, almost too soft to make out. I sprinted to my horse, jumping into the saddle and grabbing the reins. Everyone else followed my gesture, not bothering to ask questions.

"Move, now!" I urged, tapping my horse's side. I took off, loping into the woods with everyone else at my heels.

"What's happening, El?" Joey asked, catching up to my side.

"Hoofbeats. He's hunting us." I glance warily behind us, on my guard.

I reached down to my saddlebag to grab my extra dagger just as an arrow soared above my head and into the woods.

"The Night Rider's men!" Rose exclaimed. She let out several curse words when more arrows soared our way, narrowly missing her ear.

He has followers?

"Let's go!" I called, weaving through trees to lose the mysterious riders.

"Let me take over," Joey advised. I shifted over so his horse could take the lead.

More arrows shot at our heads, and we tried our best to dodge them. We came to a small clearing, and Joey was the first to race across the bare area.

Just before he made it to the cover of the other side, an arrow pierced his left leg.

He let out a cry, trying to hold onto his horse to continue riding. I caught up to him.

"Hold on, Joey." I tried to keep the worry and hysteria down until later.

Now's not the time to come apart, Liz.

"Doing my best," he retorted through gritted teeth.

"We've got to get them farther behind." I peered over my shoulder. They had gained a lot of ground behind us, but they were barely close enough for long-range weapons.

Like that hindered their accuracy.

As if on cue, another arrow shot through the trees, meeting its mark on Joey's left side.

He cried out again, this time letting go of the reins and nearly falling off the horse. I reached out and supported his shoulder, keeping him upright so he wouldn't fall off. Our horses continued to ride at full speed.

"Hold on, Joey!" I yelled.

His face in a twisted expression, he struggled to stay on the horse while the pain took over his body. His hand found mine, and his limp grip was outweighed by the overwhelming grip I had on his hand. The image of his bloody torso put a pit in my stomach.

"This way! Over here!" I heard a voice call. I turned my head to see Cyneward behind all of us, standing still on his horse. He was waving towards the Riders.

"What is he doing?" I asked. "Cyneward!"

He ignored me, taking off on his horse in a different direction. The Riders changed their direction to follow him.

"He's leading them away." Rose caught up to the other side of Joey. She seized the reins that had fallen from his hands and used them to steer his horse to follow her. Alec followed suit, and the four of us left Cyneward behind.

Focus on Joey, Liz. Cyneward will be fine; just focus on Joey.

Rose led our pack further into the woods, stopping by a small stream.

"We don't have long." She halted Joey's horse as well as her own. "We do have a few minutes, so do what you can with him before they realize we've gone a different route. I'm going to go keep watch."

I immediately jumped from my horse, not letting go of Joey's hand. I helped him lower himself to the ground, but as soon as his feet touched the grass, he fell to his back.

"Joey!" I called, my hands on either side of his face. He struggled to keep his eyes open as the blood poured from his wound.

"El, please, help me up," he asked, gripping my hand.

"No way." I shook my head.

Alec moved the horses away from us. He knelt next to Joey.

"Can you sit up against this tree?" he asked. Joey nodded.

Together, Alec and I moved Joey as gently as we

could.

"Just bandage it or something," Joseph forced out. "I can still ride."

"Are you joking?"

"Alec, you can bandage it, right?" he asked hopefully.

"Do you honestly think you'll be able to do anything with an arrow in your side and in your leg?" he asked. "I'll do my best, but no promises. I don't have many materials with me."

I watched Alec examine Joey's wounds. It was amazing how fast he could go from carefree to concerned and focused.

"Take them out, please," Joey pleaded.

"Are you crazy? If I take these out, there won't be anything keeping your blood from the ground. You have nothing to clot the wound with."

Joey's grip on my hand tightened. "Please. Anything's better than this."

Alec glanced at me. "I'm sorry, Joey. If I take them out, you'll lose too much blood. You wouldn't survive it. You're going to have to hold on until we get to the castle."

His face turned a horrible shade of white, and the sweat on his forehead formed into drops.

"I'm sorry, Joey," I said, holding his hand to my face and squeezing his hand back. The pit in my stomach grew deeper; the pain in his expression and my fear together made it almost unbearable.

His hand dropped from mine as he fought to stay upright. "They're coming. We need to... move..."

"Can you help me get him on a horse?" Alec asked me. I nodded.

"You need to hurry," Rose called from the woods.

"You only have another minute or two."

"He'll have to last until I can get him to the palace. I don't have the necessary items to take care of him properly here. I'm sorry, Joey, there's nothing I can do."

"Get me on my horse and let's get out of here," he muttered, gritting his teeth. His back arched from the intense pain.

I got up, running to Alec's horse. My nimble fingers quickly untied the horse from the tree and led it over to the pair.

"Joey," Alec said, using his dagger to cut off the bottom of Joey's shirt, "I understand you're obsessed with Liz, but I don't think she'd enjoy your funeral. Give me a second."

Obsessed? No way.

...Really?

I clenched my fist, trying to focus. *Not the time, Liz.*

"Shut up," he managed to mumble.

"Joey," I said, "do me a favor and chill out, okay? You're not going to do much good to us dead."

"I want t-to— I want to help." He grimaced, gripping the ground as Alec tried to tie the strip of fabric around his waist. The fabric nudged the arrow in his side, and Joey writhed against the tree.

"Elizabeth," Alec called, wiping the sweat from his forehead and tying a knot, "cut the leather belt off of my horse's saddle. I need to use it as a tourniquet."

"Elizabeth," Joey pleaded. I narrowed my eyes at him.

"Stay," I replied firmly. Pulling out my dagger, I loosened the leather under the belly of the horse and cut it off at the base.

Alec focused on tying the rest of the shirt around Joey's leg, and didn't say a word, but took the leather strip from me and tied it firmly above Joey's wound, on his left upper thigh. Joey groaned when he pulled it tight.

"I'm sorry. That's all I can do until I can get you back to the castle."

"Thank you," Joey managed to force out. "Elizabeth, get your horse."

"No, Joey. I'm staying here to make sure they don't follow you."

"I'm not leaving you here defenseless," he argued weakly.

"Joey, I understand it's your job to protect me and everything, but I think that I'm in the better position to protect you this time. Just do yourself a favor and get back to the castle—you can't protect me if you're dead."

"Ride back with me. Your life is just as precious as mine is, if not more."

"If I die here, I have another life, remember?"

I didn't want to have to pull that card on Joey, but it was the only way I could get him to shut up. I totally didn't want to go back to my old life, no matter what I said to him.

He was silent.

"Elizabeth," Alec cut in, "as much as I hate to say it, you may *have* to stay here. I don't know which of us is the faster rider, but if anything happens on the way to the palace, I have more medical training. I'm afraid to let him go right now."

"Don't worry about it," I reassured him. "I'll handle it. Ride as fast as you can, please; I wouldn't like coming back to the castle to the death bell."

"I don't want to hear a death bell either, so make sure one doesn't ring for you," Joey warned.

"Shut up, Joseph."

"But I—"

"Joey, focus on being alive right now. I'll see you later, okay?"

I helped Alec get Joey onto the horse.

"The last thing I need is to be dragging you around trying to keep you upright on a horse when you get hurt," I mocked him, mumbling under my breath.

He groaned in pain. "Shut up, Elizabeth."

When we had successfully secured him on the horse, Alec mounted next to him. He waved to me before taking off into the woods with Joey.

I unleashed a deep breath, relieved that Joey was finally on his way to safety. I couldn't live with myself if he died when I could've stopped it.

The sound of horses and yells of men grew closer.

"Elizabeth, are you ready?"

I turned around to see Rose, mounted on her horse with sword in hand.

"Ready." I climbed onto my horse and cut Joey's steed free—I hoped it could find the capital city.

With dagger in hand, I followed Rose. Our horses covered the forest floor at an alarming speed. She reached up to break branches on our way, trying to create a false path for the horsemen to follow.

The sound of rushing water filled our ears, and I guessed the river was close. We both dismounted when the brook came into view.

"We could lose them here," said Rose, placing a hand in the water. "The current is really strong.

"Could their horses make it through?" I asked.

"It's possible, but unlikely. Our horses are trained for this, though; I think we could cross here then run south towards the rapids and try to get them to cross there."

"It's worth a try. Let's go."

We were off again, except this time, our horses moved slowly across the water. Rose was right—our horses could tolerate the current, but not without difficulty. We finally reached the other side and started riding again, this time slower so that the horsemen could see us. The riders caught up just as we reached the rapids, parallel to our position across the water. One man seemed to be feeling overly confident, and he led his horse straight into the water.

That was his first mistake.

His horse reared up at the cold water, trying to gain balance on the slippery rocks. It threw him off, and he disappeared into the water, only to resurface a few feet from the horse. He threw the reins back onto the land, shoving the horse out of his way.

That was his second mistake.

Unfortunately for him, the horse kicked backwards when it felt his hands forcing it ahead. It kicked him right in the chest, causing him to fall back into the water and be propelled downstream with the rapids.

Rose grinned, happy her plan had worked. However, we still had three horsemen behind us, and we couldn't just depend on the water to survive.

We slowed our horses, watching the man get pushed downstream in the unforgiving waters. The others looked at each other before one by one they filed into the water. Rose didn't expect them to make it all the way across, and even though one more washed downstream without his horse, the other two were making good progress and were almost all the way across the water.

"Come on!" Rose yelled, urging her horse to gallop again. I followed close behind.

We led the two remaining men into the woods once more. We were well ahead, but they had just been released from the water and were catching up rather quickly.

"I have an idea!" I said, taking the lead. I led Rose on a twisted path through the trees, trying to confuse the horsemen. Soon, I gestured up to the branches above us. She nodded.

We adjusted our stance on the horses.

"On three," I called. "One, two, three!"

We sprung from our saddles and each wrapped our hands around a thick tree branch. The horses kept on running, and we struggled to pull our weight up as fast as we could.

Rose was up first, taking me by the hand and pulling me straight up so we were both crouched on the branch. We climbed fast, now, seeking the cover of the foliage before the men could ride under our tree.

Rose perched on a branch high up, and I was almost there. I took another step, stretching to reach the limb before my foot slipped, and I ended up hanging by my fingers.

I struggled, trying to hold my grip and trying my best not to let out any sound. I knew a yell would only echo from our position. Two hands grabbed mine and once again pulled me up higher into the foliage just as the men trotted under our tree. Rose pushed me back against the trunk, leaning forward slightly to see the riders that had stopped under us. She raised a finger to her lips before beginning to climb around the tree to the other side.

Her footsteps were silent. She gripped each limb with an iron fist. I tried my best to copy her silent maneuvers.

The men seemed to look around for a moment. One of them made a gesture for them to keep riding. Suddenly, the branch Rose was sitting on cracked, and it started to buckle under her weight. She scrambled for another branch to support her but decided too late, and the branch fell.

Rose hung from a branch by her hands, gripping for dear life.

The sound startled the horses below, and the men dismounted to inspect the branch.

Don't look up, don't look up, don't look up, my mind silently pleaded.

Unfortunately for us, the one on the right tilted his chin upward. He nudged the man next to him, pointing at Rose. Neither of them said anything as the other pulled out his bow and loaded an arrow into it.

Rose! I wanted to scream. My eyes went wide. What was I supposed to do?

"Stay," she mouthed back, trying to keep me calm.

I was far from calm.

In a fraction of a second, two silent arrows shot through the branches.

nine

J oey grimaced, holding his leg and side in pain. He tried not to think about Elizabeth, for he knew it would only make things worse.

"If Elizabeth gets herself killed, I'm going to kill her," he said, his mouth betraying his thoughts. The horse jumped over a log, and he groaned in pain, cursing under his breath.

"Try to hold on, Joey," Alec consoled him. "It's not much farther from here."

"It's not me I'm worried about," he spat through gritted teeth.

"She'll be fine. She'll have my head if I don't get you back alive, so please, just cooperate and focus on staying conscious."

"A lot of murderous thoughts going around, aren't there?"

"You could say that."

The horse jumped again, and this time, the pain was almost unbearable. Joey's vision became wobbly as he struggled to gain his breath.

"Joey?" he heard Alec ask. "Joey? Can you hear me?"

"I can hear," he answered, forcing the words out of his mouth. His vision faded and went blurry.

"Keep talking to me, Joseph," Alec prompted. "Try to stay aware, please. Joey?"

Joey tried to open his mouth to respond, but it was as if his body has shut down on him. He couldn't stop himself as he slumped forward, pitch black clouding his vision.

———

The feeling of stiff linen slipped through Joey's fingers. It was the only thing he could move; it felt like his entire body was paralyzed with cold.

He felt a dull ache set in as he remembered what happened.

Forcing his eyelids open, he squinted, taking in the bright room around him. It was relatively quiet, but there were nurses bustling all around the infirmary.

He tried his best to sit up, hoping his limbs weren't really paralyzed. They seemed to warm up, though, and ever so slowly, he lifted his head from the pillow. No longer were there arrows protruding from his side and leg, and he sighed in relief.

"You're awake. Finally."

Joey finally noticed Ed, who had been sitting at the foot of the bed, but who now moved to his brother's bedside.

"How did I get here?" His voice came out raspy; it surprised him.

"Cyneward got back before you," he explained. "He told us what happened and sent a group of guards out after you guys. Alec rode into the village almost immediately after they left, pretty much holding you up on the horse."

"He brought me all the way to the palace by himself?"

Ed nodded. "You looked horrible when you got here. You were soaked in blood and unconscious. Alec didn't leave until he made sure the nurses gave you pain medication and cleaned your wounds correctly. He scared everyone half to death when he came in—he was drenched in your blood. You'd be dead if it weren't for him."

"Huh," was all he said.

Joey held a hand up to his head and winced at the fast motion when it sent a sharp, piercing pain into his side. Hesitantly, he lifted the edge of his shirt to reveal the bandage that wrapped around his torso. He could feel the padding under his left pant leg, and realized that the wound there was bound, too.

"How long have I been out?" he asked his little brother, inspecting the bandages on his arms.

"About two hours—plus the half hour you were unconscious on the back of a horse and the hour it took for them to pull the arrows out."

Joey cringed at the thought. He was glad he wasn't awake for it.

"What about Elizabeth?"

Ed shook his head. "She hasn't come back yet."

He sat up. "Hasn't come back?"

"Rose hasn't, either."

Joey let out an agitated huff, running a hand through his hair in frustration.

"Don't worry, they have to have found them by now. They should be on their way back, but if they aren't back in half an hour, I'll send another group out. Okay?"

"She has the Book, Ed. If the Night Rider or any of his goons catch up to her, horrible things could start to happen."

"Joey, we'll find her."

"I want to go help in the search."

"Sorry," Ed said, putting a hand on his shoulder, "but Alec made us all take an oath to keep you under strict bed rest. He threatened to behead several people, including me."

"He can't hurt you."

He shrugged. "If there's one person I will not cross, it's Alexander Fell."

"This is ridiculous. What am I supposed to do until they're found?"

Just then, a piercing sound broke through the quiet of the infirmary. The nurses bustling around all perked up, exchanging glances as if someone in the room knew what had happened.

Unfortunately, both Joey and Edward knew that sound well.

It was the bronze bell, the one that hung in the castle tower. It was the bell that was only rung when a close friend of the monarchy was lost. It was the bell that released that familiar somber tone, the very same that tolled once at the death of Edward's mother and tolled again at the death of their father.

It was the same bronze bell that tolled at that moment.

Joey's breath caught in his throat, and his hands trembled as the bell rang a second time.

"Two tolls," Ed breathed. "Joey, you don't think…"

He didn't answer. He pushed past Ed, staggering when the pain of his wounds crept back in. He reached the window and caught glimpse of the guards, galloping through on horses with two wagons in tow.

No, no, no! Joey silently repeated. *Elizabeth, Rose... It can't be them.*

"Joey!" Ed's wavering voice cried from behind him. He hardly noticed; his mind was trained on Elizabeth.

He pushed through the swarm of nurses, footmen, and maids that filled the room, aiming for the door. The sound of Ed calling his name seemed to fade into an unbearable silence. He rushed into the hallway, the adrenaline drowning out the pain his leg caused him only for a moment.

A moment was all he needed. He just had to get to the courtyard.

Limp by limp and corridor by corridor, he made it to the stairs. The room swam before his eyes as the pain became intense and black crept into his vision. Skipping steps along the way, he bounded down the large staircase, falling against the wall halfway down. His hands found the railing, and he gripped it, willing himself to push forward. A pair of hands held his arm, helping him off of the ground. It was then that he realized that Ed stood beside him. He forced air in and out of his lungs, trying his best to stay conscious until he could find her.

He had to find her.

Their bare feet carried them all the way down the corridor and to the large front doors. They opened just in time for them to sprint through without hitting the edge. Ed stopped on the stone porch, but Joey kept going.

Joey's feet carried him down the steps and into the stone courtyard. He fell to his knees on the grass, then further down onto his side as pain shot through the left side of his body. He forced himself to his feet, his breathing seized in his chest and his mouth hanging open.

In dead silence, a dozen guards dismounted, all of them moving to either side of the first wagon draped with black material. The two standing closest to him picked up the edge of the fabric before lifting it off the motionless figure.

Rose.

Rose's figure laid on the wagon with her arms crossed, the blood that stained her shirt peeking out from under them.

Joey let out a short breath, his eyes wide. How could Rose be dead? She was one of the best fighters he knew; there was no way she could've lost a fight.

Unless there wasn't a fight.

Joey was sure his heart wasn't beating as the second wagon rolled into view. Just like the first, the men surrounded the wagon and rolled back the cover.

This time, the figure that lay motionless was a man wearing a guard's uniform.

As was tradition, the entire courtyard fell into silence. While most people had their heads bowed in mourning, Joey's was up and his eyes searched frantically for Elizabeth.

Where is she?

His muscles tensed. He'd spotted her across the courtyard.

She stared at the ground, her brow furrowed in frustration. Her hair had fallen and hung on her shoulders, and the scratches on her face still bled. She looked up, casting her gaze at Rose before her eyes caught his.

The moment the silence was over, she was off the

horse and Joey was already halfway across the courtyard.

"Joey—"

She stopped. Joey reached her and engulfed her in a hug, burying his face in her neck. He ignored the discomfort in his side, just taking her in. Breathing her in. Feeling her warmth.

She's here. She's alive. She's okay.

"I thought you were dead," he told her, finally able to breathe properly. "I thought you were gone."

"I'm not dead." She brought her arms around his waist and held on tight.

He closed his eyes, breathing heavily and calming down his frantically beating heart. *She's okay. She's safe.*

"Joey?"

He pulled back, looking her in the eye. A few tears streamed down her face as she stared back at him. She closed her eyes, taking a deep breath.

"We were hiding in the trees and a branch broke," she recalled solemnly, looking over his shoulder. Her eyes weren't focused on anything. She seemed in a daze. "Rose was hanging from one, trying to pull herself back up, but they shot two arrows at her and she fell. They took her dagger and left to hunt me in the other direction."

Joey stayed silent, watching the way her lip quivered when she held back tears and the way she'd look away from him before she spoke.

"The guard died taking another arrow for me," she explained. "The palace guards came looking for us, and they found Rose and me. By then, the Riders had come full circle and were on our tail. One of them shot an arrow at me, and a guard threw himself in front of me before it hit."

She opened her eyes, biting down on her lips to keep

from losing it.

"It's okay," he said. "You can cry. No one here is going to blame you."

"Tears do nothing," she replied. "They don't help anyone or do anything."

"They don't help when you hold them back, either."

Her eyes met his. She hesitantly let go of his waist and stepped back.

"I'm okay." She wiped the tears from her cheeks with a shaking hand.

"Are you really?" he asked.

She nodded, but slowly, she changed her mind, and she shook her head. The tears flowed more freely this time, and she buried her head into the crook of Joey's neck. His arms came around her waist once more, and he held her tight.

"You're alive," he breathed again, more to himself than to her. "Thank the Lord, you're alive."

ten

I observed the sea of people wearing black, watching the captain of the guards present a man and young boy with a pale gray-blue flag—the two who I assumed were Rose's family. The funeral was almost over, and the villagers had already placed black roses on the casket.

Thankfully, Joey explained to me what they were for. The black rose was used as a sign of respect in Aon, he had told me. When someone died, roses were placed on doorsteps, strewn in the streets, hung in windows, and last but not least, placed on the casket by the villagers attending the funeral.

The young boy looked up at his father, tugging on his sleeve. His father crouched next to his son and hugged him.

Suddenly, I remembered the last thing Rose told me.

She let out a cry, losing her grip on the branch and falling down to the ground. I reached for her, covering my mouth with my other hand so I wouldn't make a sound.

The men stood over her body. One retrieved his arrows, and the other searched her for weapons. They took her dagger and gold before they rode off on their horses, most likely searching for me.

As soon as I couldn't see them anymore, I got as low as I could before I sprang from the trees. I crouched next to Rose, who barely opened her eyes. Her shirt was soaked in blood.

"Elizabeth," she rasped, "t-tell them about m-me."

"I will," I promised, taking her hand. I did my best to remain calm. "They'll all know about what you did here today. You'll be a hero."

"N-not the village," she struggled to say, "my f-family. Tell t-them it wasn't p-painful. T-that it was v-valiant. Tell them I-I love them and I'll see them again."

I was surprised. She rarely talked about her family.

"I will. They'll be the first to know."

"Thank you," she whispered. "St-stay safe, L-Liz."

I nodded, the tears rolling down my cheeks. She closed her eyes as her breathing slowed then finally stopped.

When the ceremony concluded, I left Joey and Ed to find her family. I found them sitting on a bench together, the boy's hands rubbing back and forth over the flag.

"Hello," I greeted when I reached them. The man, her husband, gave me a sad smile.

"Hello," he said, standing up to bow. "You must be Elizabeth."

"Yes." I shifted my eyes from him to the boy. "I was with Rose the day she died."

The boy looked up at me as I crouched down to his level.

"Do you want to know what she told me to tell you?"

He looked from me to his father, then back to me

before he nodded slowly.

"She told me to tell you not to worry about her," I said. "She said that she's in a better place now, but she loves you both very, very much."

"Did it hurt?" the little boy asked quietly. "When she died?"

Her husband looked from the boy to me with wide eyes, mouthing an apology for his son's boldness. I took the boy's little hands in mine.

"She died a valiant death. It hurt her a little bit, but it can't hurt her anymore."

He stared down at the flag in his hands.

"She wants you to know she'll see you again."

All of a sudden, the little boy's arms came up around my neck and squeezed me into a hug. I hugged him back.

His father wiped tears from his eyes, hugging me after his son. "Thank you so much."

"Don't worry about it," I said, drying my own tears before they had the chance to fall. "I'm just the messenger."

Rose's husband pulled away, bowing politely before taking his young son's hand and walking towards the casket that held his wife.

I stood up straight and exhaled. I was doing better today than I had been, but it was still hard.

"Edward," I said, turning around, "you don't have to be apprehensive about approaching me, you know."

Edward wasn't trying to make his footsteps light while I talked with Rose's husband.

"I know," he said. "I just didn't want to interrupt."

A half smile somehow managed to form on my lips as I ruffled his hair. "What's bothering you?"

He shrugged. "Nothing, really. I'm fine."

I raised an eyebrow. "Are you sure?"

"Honest, I am. I was just going to ask if I could hang around you today."

"Of course you can. I don't want to be alone on a day like today," I said, shifting my gaze from his face to the view of the hills and the distant village.

"Me neither," he admitted.

"Let's get going, then." I held my hand out for him. He looped my arm through his and led me back towards the carriages.

That day, my mind wandered to places I wouldn't dare speak out loud. *How did the Night Rider know we were there? Did he have people watching us? Could he see or hear us the entire time?*

There's only one person besides us who knew we were out there. Delia knew we were eventually going on patrol.

I shook my head as an absurd idea aroused. Was Delia working with the Night Rider?

Was she the Night Rider herself?

Impossible. There are so many reasons why that's wrong. Not to mention, if you mentioned that to Joey, you'd probably lose your head.

I put those thoughts to rest, and the days grew easier, one at a time. It was at least a month before I could smile without effort. Ed and I did our best to keep each other happy, and Joey used every ounce of his effort in trying to make us both smile. I think it hurt Joey more seeing us unhappy than it hurt us.

Joey healed after slow therapy and long days of pain. When he recovered, however, he walked with more confidence. He still had a faint limp, but he did his best not to let it show. Soon enough, things went back to normal.

One afternoon, the rain drummed against the

windows harder than I'd ever heard. It wasn't thundering or lightning—there was only rain. The sound of it pelting the glass echoed in the large, hollow hallways of the castle. Ed and I reclined next to the fireplace in the parlor.

"Does it pour down like this often?" I asked, closing my book louder than I meant to. The repetitive sound had hit a nerve. "I'm sorry, I just can't focus. It's so incredibly loud against the windows."

"You learn to get used to it," he said, peering over the top of his book. "It's not unusual for us to get rain like this all year round. I find it rather soothing."

"That's insane. I'd go crazy."

He grinned. "It's impossibly loud, yes, but it makes a great opportunity for some fun."

I raised an eyebrow. "What kind of fun?"

He shut his book, laying it on the table in front of us. "Come with me. We have to be quiet."

Ed rose from his position on the couch and led me to the door. Carefully, he cracked the door open just wide enough to see the corridor.

"The maids hate when I do this," he explained in a whisper, "but Joey and I used to do it all the time."

"Do what?" I whispered back.

He flashed me a crooked grin before turning back to the door. "We ran through the gardens in the rain. Most of the time we played hide and seek, but we've done all sorts of things."

He wants to play in the rain? But I don't like the rain.

Shut up, Liz. Who knows how much longer you'll be here.

"Joey played hide and seek?" I asked, ignoring my pessimistic thoughts.

"Yeah, why?"

"It's just… Well, it's a child's game."

"It's more fun than you'd think."

Ed opened the door slowly, making sure it wouldn't make a sound before motioning to me. Quietly, we tiptoed down the corridor. When we reached the corner, we thought we were home free.

…Until we ran straight into a footman.

Ed looked up at the elderly man, giving him a guilty smile.

"Good evening, Daniel," he said. "We were just out for a walk around the castle."

"You mean outside of the castle," he corrected.

"Precisely," Ed agreed, before realizing what he'd said. "Wait! I mean…"

Daniel shook his head, chuckling softly to himself. The wrinkles around his eyes grew deeper with each laugh.

"Don't worry, Your Highness," he said. "I won't tell. Run along, and don't let anyone catch you."

Ed grabbed my hand, sprinting down the corridor with me in tow. When we reached the door, he threw it open and pulled me outside.

The warm air helped make up for the cold rain, but I shivered nonetheless. Ed grinned, holding his face up to the sky. The rain drenched us in seconds.

"Come on," he yelled, pulling me by the hand down the path into the gardens.

As soon as we stepped into the gardens, Ed let go of my hands, sprinting around the cherub crowned fountain and off into the maze of shrubbery. "Count to thirty!" he yelled over his shoulder as he disappeared into the greenery.

I laughed, running to a wall of shrubbery just inside the garden and turning to face it. Out loud, I started counting to thirty.

The rain made the material of my dress heavier and heavier, and my stockings and my boots soaked up water. Although I was slightly cold, I couldn't help but grin at the feeling. I threw off my boots and my stockings, tossing them off towards the door and letting my feet feel the softness of the wet grass. My hair stuck to my cheeks and my neck, but still I stood counting in the rain.

When at last I hit thirty, I bolted into the gardens at full speed to find Edward.

I ran hard, holding my dress above my ankles so I wouldn't trip. I veered left, then right, then left, choosing random pathways through the garden maze to find Ed. When at last I came to a dead end, I looked around, trying to find some other pathway.

"Boo!" someone yelled, and I fell to the ground in fright.

Edward laughed hysterically behind me, falling next to me while holding his stomach. Water and mud splashed up from the ground, and I held my arms up to keep it from reaching my face.

"You should've seen your face!" he yelled through his laughter, closing his eyes. I pushed him over into the wet dirt playfully.

"You're it!" I grinned, jumping to my feet and sprinting off the way I came. "Thirty seconds!"

I heard his laugh echo through the rain as I ran once more, a smile plastered on my face. I took more random paths, jumping through mud puddles and skipping along the hedges. The olive colored fabric of my dress started to turn brown at the bottom, and I spun, sending droplets of water off into the grass.

When I was out of breath, I stopped running, ducking around a hedge on my left and turning back towards the way I came. I estimated that it had been at least three minutes since I left him, so I hoped he hadn't taken the same path as me.

I backed away slowly, checking to be sure Ed wasn't following me. I stayed on my toes so that I could make a quick getaway if he popped up out of the blue.

The rain made it impossible to see in front of me anymore, so I stopped, holding still to listen for sounds. My heart thundered in my chest when I heard breathing rather close to me. I backed up faster.

Soon, I hit something strong, causing me to let out a scream. Someone's arms came up around my waist and lifted my feet off the ground.

"You're it," a laughing voice said in my ear as I tried to catch my breath.

"Joey!" I exclaimed, recognizing the voice. I jumped to the ground as soon as his arms loosened their grip and spun around, only to find Joey with a smug grin on his face. His hair was sticking to his face and the back of his neck, like mine.

"You nearly gave me a heart attack!" I hit his arm with as much force as I could. He feigned being hurt as he laughed.

"I know," he said, shaking out his hair that was plastered to his forehead, " I heard your scream loud and clear, love."

Butterflies erupted in my stomach, something that was becoming more common around Joey. *Love. I can't say I hate that.*

I crossed my arms. "What're you even doing out here, anyway?"

"Alec and I saw you and Ed at the door," he explained, yelling over the rain. "We followed you out here and jumped into the game when Ed found me before you. Did you know you have mud all over the back of your skirt?"

"That's comforting," I breathed. "So what I'm hearing is that you've followed me since we got out here? And Alec's out here?"

"Bingo." He grinned, poking at my shoulder. "You're not very hard to follow, either. You never check behind you."

"I did before I ran into you!"

"But I wasn't behind you, was I?" he asked. "I've lived here my whole life, El. I know this maze like the back of my hand."

"You're insane." I shook my head, splashing water off the ends of my hair. He wiped rainwater from his face before taking off again to hide.

Ed, Joey, Alec, and I stayed out in the rain playing hide and seek for what felt like hours. I'd find Ed, then Ed would find Alec, then Alec would find Joey, then Joey would find me, and the cycle would go on and on. It wasn't on purpose, but it was rather hilarious. We'd run into each other a time or two, laughing as we chased each other down the green halls of the maze. Surprisingly, I only ran into Alec once.

"We should go inside," Joey yelled over the rain, after he had found me again. "Ed and Alec already went in."

"How does he know we ended the game?"

He smile mischievously at me. "Ed found him, and they went in together. They're drying off."

"So, you came out here just to find me? Alone?" I pretended to be disgusted by holding my hand over my mouth and rolling my eyes. "How scandalous."

He rolled his eyes at me. "Come on, let's go." He reached down and took my hand.

"Do you know the way out?"

"Who do you think you're talking to?" he asked, pulling me along behind him. I tried to ignore the butterflies that holding his hand sent through me.

This place isn't real, remember? my conscience brutally reminded me. *It will never last. Save yourself the pain, please. Besides, you don't like Joey, remember?*

I waved away the thoughts, focusing on keeping up with him and his weaving patterns in the maze. When we reached the entrance and the small fountain, Joey stopped me before I could start up the path to the door.

"Wait," he said, pulling me to him. My cold cheeks warmed up as his hand took mine and the other rested on my waist.

"I can't dance," I warned.

"Sure you can." He grinned, taking one step at a time. As one of his feet moved backwards, one of mine moved forwards. "Besides, how often can you say you actually danced in the rain?"

I rolled my eyes as he continued to lead me in the dance. This was cheesy, like something straight out of a movie. Secretly, being out there was the most fun I'd ever had, but I wouldn't tell him that.

"See, you're dancing."

"Barely." My bare feet moved in synchronization with his, and I was surprised at how fast I picked it up. Soon, we were dancing and jumping and skipping in circles around the fountain. An exhilarating feeling welled up in my chest, and I couldn't wipe the grin from my face..

"What'd I tell you?" he asked smugly, spinning me with one hand.

I fell back against his chest, trying to hide a smile. "Just be happy I'm dancing in the first place."

"I am. Believe me, I am."

All too soon, Joey stopped and dropped one of my hands.

"Ed is waiting for you. I think he's worried you got lost."

"I doubt it," I said, turning my head towards the door. As my eyes found the handle, I found the door cracked open. I felt a pang of disappointment that I didn't understand when I realized we weren't alone anymore, but I shoved it to the back of my mind.

"Hi, Ed," I yelled, grinning widely and waving.

The door slammed shut. Joey pulled me down the path and out of the gardens.

The heavy door swung open again as soon as we reached it.

"Enjoy your time, sir?" Daniel asked, holding the door open for us. I blushed, hiding behind Joey's shoulder, but he wasn't affected. I noticed that Ed was nowhere to be seen.

Daniel's eyes wandered down, and I realized that we held each other's hands. I coughed awkwardly, pulling my hand away from Joey's and taking a small step away from him.

"Very much, thank you," he answered, nodding at him. He didn't seem to notice or care that I let go of his hand. Margaret and another footman appeared, each holding a fluffy white towel.

"You look a fright," Margaret commented, throwing the towel over my shoulders and rubbing it through my hair.

"I know," I smiled at her, playfully swatting at her hands and wrapping myself in the towel. Water dripped onto the floor, creating puddles around my feet.

"Where are your boots?" she asked, glancing at my

feet. "And no stockings?"

"Sorry." I shrugged. "They would've gotten ruined."

"They're already ruined," said the footman tending to Joey. "Daniel picked them up out of the gardens earlier. Violet has already sent off for another pair of each."

"But I like my boots!" I said.

"Should've thought of that earlier," she scolded.

"They can dry by the fire," I offered. "I like my boots worn in, honest. Send the new pair to the village shelter. Give them to someone who needs them."

Margaret gave me a wary glance before nodding. "Fine. I'll have them sent there instead."

"Thank you," I said. I didn't need another pair of boots. I was spoiled enough by being at the castle.

"You're soaked! Up the stairs to your room, now. You'll catch a cold if you don't hurry."

"Fine, *Mom*." She tried to smack my behind and I dodged her, skipping to the stairs with a huge grin on my face.

I flashed Joey a smile before running through the corridor. The sound of his laugh echoed behind me.

————

Alec dried his hair with a towel, watching the gardens from the window. Beside him, Ed leaned against the windowsill on his elbows.

"You're purposefully leaving them alone together?" Alec asked, looking down at the little prince.

"Yeah," Ed said, his eyes scanning the maze. The rain still poured, but they both could catch glimpses of Joey and Elizabeth running every few seconds.

"Are you going to tell me why?" Alec mused. "You know, they could end up actually liking each other."

"I know." A ghost of a smile made its way to Ed's

lips. "That's the point. In case you haven't noticed, Joey's kind of a dummy."

Alec chuckled. "Believe me, I've noticed. He's lucky, though, because this castle happens to be full of dummies. Do you think she'll admit it at the same time he does?"

"Admit that they like each other? No, I think he'll admit it before her. She's hard headed and stubborn."

"But so is he," reminded Alec. "Maybe even more than she is."

"Fine." Ed turned to face Alec. "Wanna bet on it?"

A grin broke out onto Alexander's face. This was a bet he could handle.

"All right. What're the wages?"

Ed thought for a moment. "The winner gets to dump the loser in the pond fully clothed," he said, "and then lead the winner's horse through town."

"Get ready to be made a fool of, Edward," Alec said with confidence. "You're on."

The boys turned their heads back towards the garden where they caught a glimpse of Joey and Elizabeth dancing around the fountain.

Ed grinned. "I think this bet will pay off real soon."

———

"I *told* you so," Margaret scolded. "I told you that you'd get sick."

"I said I'm sorry. How many times do I have to say it?" I sniffled and sneezed then fell back onto the pillow.

"Until you're better," she responded, lifting the corner of the sheets and placing a hot pan in the folds. "Stay here, understand?"

I nodded hesitantly. I crossed my fingers underneath the sheets.

"Good. I'll be back in an hour with soup and a glass

of water. You had better be here when I return."

I watched Margaret slip out the door and close it softly behind her.

As soon as the door latched, I was out of bed. I tiptoed to the door, silently opening it and peering out after her. I watched her walk to the end of the hallway and down the stairs.

My nightgown trailing behind me, I sprinted the opposite way down the hallway.

Stay in bed all day?

No way am I doing that.

I rounded the corner, taking the right hallway instead of the left hallway. At the end of the corridor was a large window and a bookcase.

Perfect. Something better than doing nothing.

I jogged all the way to the bookcase, searching for something to read.

There was nothing there.

"Who keeps an empty bookcase here for show?" I asked aloud, throwing my fists down to my side.

Now I have to climb more stairs. Great.

I jogged back down the hallway and took the alternative extending corridor, going all the way down until I came to another staircase. Unlike the impossibly huge, grand staircase that ran from the ground floor to the second floor, this one was smaller and plain, a solid color with no etchings in the wood. I padded up the steps one at a time until I reached the top.

The third floor was more spacious than the second. There were fewer confusing corridors and more open space. I went in the first door on the right into the large library. A wave of cold air hit me as I walked in, the smell of parchment wafting to my nose. The smell had comforting warmth to it.

I meandered between the rows of shelves, inspecting the covers of random books as I went. My bare feet carried me to the bookshelf at the very end of the room where I spotted a brown book with gold trim. I reached on my tiptoes to grab it, groaning when I realized I was way too short for the extremely tall bookcases.

Suddenly, someone grabbed my legs, and I was lifted to the perfect height to be able to grab it.

"Hey, thanks!" I pulled the book out of place with both hands. I looked down to find Joey holding me up on his shoulder.

My fingers wiggled back and forth at him. "Hello."

"Hello," he greeted, flashing a grin at me before dropping me down lower into his arms. I grinned, holding up the book in front of my face. He switched his position to holding me bridal style. "Shouldn't you be in bed?"

"Maybe," I said, sticking my tongue out at him from behind the book.

"You're sick, El. You should be sleeping."

"I'm not sick." Just then, I felt a tickle in my nose, and I sneezed into my arm.

"Right." He rolled his eyes, turning and walking towards the door with me in his arms.

"The book is dusty."

He ignored me, keeping on his path towards the hallway.

I realized he wasn't going to stop. "No! You can't take me back there!" I struggled against his grip. "I can't sit still in that bed any longer!"

"Sorry," he apologized sarcastically.

"How are you not sick?"

"Unlike you, I didn't want to spend an hour looking for Ed before I changed out of my wet clothes," he said, a smirk growing on his lips. "I'm actually smart."

"You know, you're putting a serious dent in my ego," I commented. He laughed as he descended the stairs and headed back down the corridor towards my room.

He nudged the door open with his foot, stepping inside and dropping me on the bed. I laughed, continuing to bounce with the book in my hand.

"Elizabeth, if you don't settle down, I'm sending Margaret in here to—"

"Sending Margaret in here to what?" Margaret called, walking in with a tray of food in hand. She eyed Joey and me suspiciously before setting the tray on my bedside table. Pointing to the soup, she narrowed her eyes at me and said, "Eat."

I wasn't about to argue with her, so I complied.

"Joey, you should stay," Margaret said, fluffing the pillows and straightening the comforter. "Isolation has been driving her crazy."

"I'm not isolated," I argued with a mouth full of noodles. "You're in here."

"Don't talk with your mouth full," she said, patting my leg lightly.

"I doubt we'd be able to get along long enough for me to stay in here," Joey said, tossing a skeptical glance at me.

"It's worth a shot," I said after swallowing. "Yesterday was fun."

He eyed the door before sitting down on the edge of the bed next to me.

A weird feeling filled my stomach. I decided it was just hunger.

"I'm off to do chores." Margaret pointed her finger at me. "Behave."

"Yes, *Mom*."

She rolled her eyes, closing the door behind her as me and Joey laughed.

As soon as the door shut, I was up again, running to the window. "Do you think it'll rain again today?"

"Does it matter?" he asked, coming to stand next to me. The weird feeling in my stomach grew stronger, and I realized it was because Joey was so close to me.

"Yes," I scoffed. "I want to go play in the gardens again. Maybe not hide and seek this time. Maybe we could play capture the flag, or tag, or we could race, or—"

"Elizabeth," Joey said, cutting off my new found love of rain and steering me by the shoulders back to the bed, "go to sleep. You aren't going outside to play in the rain again today."

"But this is so boring!"

"Not my fault," he said.

"You're no help."

"I don't try to be." He pulled the covers back, and I crawled under them. He walked around the bed and hopped on top of the covers, his arms behind his head.

"You're really frustrating, you know that?"

"I've been told."

"Aren't you going to argue back? Come on; say something infuriating."

"But then you'd be satisfied. Plus, I think I've done a good job so far; you seem pretty annoyed at the moment."

I groaned. "At least hand me that book before I beat my head through a wall."

He handed me the book before leaning back again and closing his eyes.

I opened the book, trying my best to read the words

on the first page but failing miserably. I peered over at Joey who still had his eyes closed.

"You know, staring at me isn't reading."

I felt the heat rise to my cheeks as I turned a page and stuck my nose back into my book. "I wasn't even looking at you, big head."

"Big head?" He opened his eyes, covering his heart and pretending he was in pain. "I'm hurt."

I rolled my eyes. "Whatever."

He laughed before closing his eyes again, resting his hands across his chest.

"I thought you were supposed to be keeping me company," I said, annoyed.

"I am."

"You're sleeping!"

"I'm enjoying the silence." He opened his eyes. "Oh wait, there isn't any. You keep talking. Do me a favor and shut your mouth, Liz."

I huffed as his eyes drifted closed again.

"He likes you, no matter how many times he denies it. I'm pretty sure he's convinced himself that he hates you," Ed's words came rushing back. I stole a quick glance at Joey before putting my nose back in my book and trying to focus.

Keep things the way they are, Liz, I thought. *Don't ruin anything. Friendship is enough for now. Baby steps.*

I heard a knock at the door.

"Come in," I called, closing the book. I'd been staring at the same page anyway. It wasn't going anywhere.

Joey opened one eye just in time to see Ed peer in through the doorway.

"You guys seem like you're having a party in here," he said with a grin. "Mind if I join?"

"Come on in." I eagerly beckoned to him, grateful

for the distraction. "You're way better company than Joey will ever be."

"Hey!"

"Shut up, Joseph." I could see him clenching his jaw out of the corner of my eye at his full name, and I took satisfaction in it. "What's up, Ed?"

"Nothing much," he answered. "Margaret has been asking me questions about what I want at the ball on Friday, and I really need a break."

Although the ball was at least a week away, the maids were frantic in trying to plan the party. Food was constantly being brought in from the village only to take up space on the kitchen shelves. Just yesterday, the footmen carried in four tables and new sets of chairs for the ballroom. Carriages were being polished, horses were being groomed, and everyone on staff was sent off to get fitted for new uniforms.

"This is the first event we've held in a while," Ed said. "The last one we had was before Mom and Dad died."

"Really?"

"Yes. Margaret keeps asking me questions about placemats and silverware and napkins, but I don't know what's right. I'm a thirteen-year-old boy! I shouldn't be expected to know this stuff."

Laughing at his moody expression, I patted his shoulder. "Come now, Edward. It's absolutely necessary to know what color napkins to use at a ball when you're king."

"I don't want to be king, either."

"Ed," Joey warned, suddenly sitting up against the headboard. His tone was sharp.

"I know," Ed snapped back. "Give me a break."

The look in Ed's eyes was different. It was hurt and

slightly menacing, like he was fed up. I hadn't seen Ed get angry with Joey before, and it made me wonder what had happened behind closed doors.

Glaring over at Joey, I shoved his shoulder. "Back off, Joseph. He's just a kid. What did he do wrong?"

His hands flew up in anger. "Why are you so defensive of him? He's not your brother, Elizabeth. You don't decide what's best for him. I do."

"And what's *best for me* is forcing me to take on a kingdom in four years?" Ed cut in. His hands clenched into fists at his side.

"Edward, stop," Joey said in a warning tone. To me, it sounded almost condescending.

"No, *you* stop," his little brother retorted.

I froze. Edward was definitely losing it.

"I love you, Joey, because you're my brother," he said as his voice grew louder, "but stop trying to choose my path for me. I don't want to be king; I don't even like being a prince. You can tell me it's the best path for me, and maybe it is, but it doesn't change my mind. Stop trying to convince me this is the only way my life will go. For all you know, I could die before I reach eighteen. What will you do then, Joey? Who will you have to force onto the throne? Yourself?"

All of us were quiet.

Joey didn't say anything. He looked away from his brother, got off the bed, and left the room without another word.

Ed was obviously uncomfortable. He looked at me, his shoulders sagging as the guilt set in.

"I crossed a line," he said quietly. "Sorry, Elizabeth."

"Don't apologize to me," I responded. "Nothing happened to me."

The boy seemed to squirm, as if he didn't know what

to do. He started to get up but then sat back down.

It surprised him when I got out of bed and tied my robe around my waist.

"Where are you going?" he asked. "You should be in bed, Elizabeth. You're sick."

"Whatever." I waved him off. "I'll be back soon. You can stay in here if you like."

"What are you doing?" He grabbed my wrist.

"I'm going to talk to your brother," I snorted, as if it were obvious. "He's right about a lot of things, but thinking that I shouldn't care about you isn't one of them. I need to set the record straight with him."

Edward let go of me, shaking his head and laughing under his breath. "You really are something, Elizabeth Knight."

I rolled my eyes. "So I've heard."

I found Joey on the balcony on the front of the castle. If he heard me open the door, he didn't show it.

"That was brutal," I said, going to stand next to him.

He didn't answer.

"You know, you really should give Edward a break. He's only thirteen."

"He's also the heir to the throne," Joey cut in. "He has an entire country to think about."

"Let him have a childhood."

"Listen, Elizabeth," he said, looking at me, "he's not your concern. He's mine."

"I care about him too, Joseph," I snapped. "I don't care what you say about him or me or anything that has to do with it. I can and will care about your little brother because he's the closest thing to family I've got, just like he's the only family you've got."

"I don't like forcing him to do this, but I have no choice. The nobles are getting tired of having me do his work; they want to be able to manipulate Edward into doing what they want. I have to explain to him how it works. I have to teach him everything there is to know before the nobles decide to try to overthrow him."

"Why didn't you just explain that to him?" I asked, leaning over the balcony rail to look at him.

"I don't want to worry him."

"He's already worried about you. He's upset at what he said to you back in my room."

He laughed, but there was no trace of humor in his expression. "He's right. Everything he said was true."

"All the same," I encouraged, "you should go talk to him."

Joey looked at me, seeming to realize that I was right. He pushed himself off the railing and headed towards the door.

"I'm sorry, Elizabeth," he said over his shoulder before he left. "And thank you."

eleven

Margaret woke me up as soon as the clock hit seven, telling me we had work to do. I felt much better (even though I never really felt sick in the first place).

I moaned, falling over back into the pillow and pulling the covers over my head. "Five more minutes."

Cold air hit my skin and gave my arms and legs chill bumps as Margaret pulled the covers off of the bed and smacked my leg.

"Ouch!" I yelled, falling off of the bed and onto the floor. "What was that for?"

"Get up!" she said, bustling around my room with a ghost of a smile on her face. She had acted almost as if she was my mom, taking care of everything I needed since I'd arrived at the palace. It was nice to have a parenting figure in the picture since I'd never really felt that before.

Rubbing my stinging thigh, I found my balance and

stood. "What do you want me to do?"

She hummed in satisfaction. "You're going into the village with Edward and Joseph to buy the material for your dress and ribbons, as well as a few other things. When you get back, you better be ready because we have a lot to do to get things set up for the ball this week."

I tried my best to keep the groaning to a minimum. I offered a polite smile before she helped me get dressed.

"Pants?" I asked in astonishment.

"Don't say I never did anything for you," she said with a wink. "Now, how's this?"

When I'd finished getting dressed, I wore a pair of fitted pants with a riding jacket in a light gray color. The jacket was more like a fitted dress, and it reached down just below my hips. I was glad that Margaret had taken my taste into account and made the suit fit me tightly. She had pulled my hair back into an elegant but still casual braided ponytail. I made sure to grab the journal and clasp the teardrop necklace around my neck.

"Now, get a move on," she said, making the bed. "Joseph is waiting to escort you. Don't forget the ribbons, and do not come back any later than three o'clock! We have things to do!"

I smiled, hugging her before swinging the door open.

To my surprise, Joey was already standing there, adjusting his sleeves so they were rolled to his elbows. He raised an eyebrow, taking in my appearance from head to toe.

"You look very... interesting today, Elizabeth."

"Thank you," I replied easily. It seemed easier to be nice to him now than it had been. It was almost like our friendship was bipolar—great one day and horrible the next. I decided to try to keep up this good mood for as long as it would stretch.

All I had to do was ignore that feeling that kept piercing my stomach.

He took my arm and looped it through his. "Has Margaret told you the schedule for today?"

"Yes. We're to go to the village with Edward to buy several things for the ball."

"Right." We descended the stairs, in step with each other. "Except Ed isn't accompanying us today."

I raised an eyebrow. "Why not?"

"He's busy." He gave me a look. "He has to learn how to dance by Friday. Besides, I think you'll want to buy a gift for Ed?"

"Yeah, I do," I replied instantly. "Thank you. Are you and Ed on good terms now?

"We are, thank you for asking. I apologized, and thankfully, he accepted it."

"That's good. I'd hate to see you two angry at each other."

"Me too."

"So, why does Ed have to learn how to dance?" I asked curiously as we continued down the wide corridor and out the huge front doors.

"There's a young girl who lives in the palace just there," he said, pointing to the shadow of a tower across the lake. "It appears closer than it is. It's actually more than two days' ride, but it's a small kingdom called Baile. Baile stretches from that side of the lake to the east, and as you have probably figured out, our kingdom stretches in the opposite direction. The girl is the next heir to the Bailian throne, and her name is Aileen. She's only a year younger than Ed, but he refuses to answer the invitations she sends to him."

I frowned. "Why should he have to?"

A ghost of a smile appeared on his lips as he waved

off the footman who offered him the carriage. He quietly informed him that we planned to walk, and the man bowed and scurried away. I tried my best to ignore his skeptical glances at my attire.

"Because," he said amused, "Aileen is Edward's betrothed."

"*Betrothed?*" I asked incredulously. "At thirteen?"

"Fourteen on Friday," he corrected, "and it's not uncommon here. It isn't official. Edward still has to formally accept the decree. It's a wonder he has to give his consent; were Father still here, poor Ed wouldn't have a choice either way."

"But he really doesn't have a choice."

He shrugged. "It's true that we strongly advise him to accept the engagement because it's what's best for our kingdoms, but this is one thing I won't force him to do. He understands this, so more than likely he'll think about it and give his consent in the future. They won't get married until they're about our age, anyway. We just have to seal the agreement with a formal engagement."

I shook my head. "There's no way I could be told who to marry."

"You'd be surprised at how many accept it. Many learn to love their match."

"I'm leaning more towards eternal fury towards each other."

He grinned, chuckling softly to himself.

"That didn't answer my question," I reminded him. "Why does he have to learn how to dance?"

"Aileen is coming to the ball. His advisors have told him that he has to dance with her at least once."

"'His advisors' being you, right?" I asked, a grin spreading across my face. "I'll bet she's just as reluctant as he is. Maybe they can find something in common."

"Maybe," he agreed.

The sun shone brightly, and there wasn't a cloud in the sky. Plants decorated every inch of the pathways, and luscious trees provided shade as well as fruit. Joey reached up to one on our way down, picking an apple and handing it to me. He and I descended the cobble paths down the hill where the castle stood, and I tried to savor the scenery. "Beautiful, isn't it?"

"It is," he remarked. "A view like this never grows old."

"I wish I could stay here forever." I sighed, dodging a rose bush that had grown into the pathway. I bumped into Joey, apologizing and getting back into sync with his footsteps.

"Isn't your world much better?" he asked. "You have all sorts of things there that make life so much easier."

"I like it here. Life is so much simpler. You don't have to face all sorts of horrible things here like you do in my world."

"Except the Night Rider," he mumbled.

"Except the Night Rider," I agreed.

At last, we reached the bottom of the hill, and beyond that, the iron archway that led into the village. We followed the main street until we found what we were searching for.

Today, the Forum bustled with life. Children ran about, playing as knights and damsels in distress. Wooden swords hit as they dueled. Women carrying baskets bought food and fabrics from the booths lined up in rows, some gossiping amongst the jewels. Men talked and laughed in pubs lining the outskirts of the area. A few men and women cast me a wary glance before returning to their activities.

"People keep staring at me," I muttered.

"Don't worry about it," Joey mused. "It was your decision to wear something so... eye catching. Besides, you look pretty."

"Wow, Joseph," I said, turning my head to him in shock, "was that a compliment?"

The corner of his lips twitched. "Don't push it."

A group of children rushed past us, racing to the fountains and jumping in. They splashed each other with water, laughing and giggling.

A little girl, smaller than the rest, dawdled along, struggling to catch up. She stopped next to me to catch her breath, leaning on me before realizing that I was a person, not a wall.

She grinned apologetically, blushing with embarrassment. I laughed, crouching down next to her.

"Here you go," I said, handing her the shining green apple that Joey had picked for me earlier. She gasped, taking it in both her small hands before giving me a wobbly curtsey and running off towards her friends with a giggle.

"Do children just naturally like you?" Joey asked.

"I don't know." I shrugged. "I never had any younger siblings or anything, but I've always wanted children. The closest I got were the girls at the home I was placed in, but I was the youngest for a long time."

"I see," he muttered, more to himself than to me.

"What all do we need?" I asked. "Margaret mentioned fabric for my dress and ribbons?"

"Yes, and your present for Ed, as well as three dozen eggs, five pounds of flour, and four pounds of sugar."

"Wow, that's a lot of ingredients," I noted. "Do they not have someone assigned to shop for the kitchens?"

"They do," he explained, "but on nice days like this I

offer to go just to have some excuse to get out of the palace and stay outside."

I nodded in understanding. "Where to first?"

"I'll order the ingredients to be sent to the palace," he said, pointing to a booth where a man in an apron tossed and kneaded dough on a wood table. "I'll meet with you over there where the fabrics are, yeah?"

Glancing over to the left, I noticed a booth overflowing with colorful fabrics and threads. "Yeah, I guess I'll just… start looking."

"Good. I'll be there in a few minutes."

Reluctantly, I let go of Joey's arm. "All right."

He gave me a small bow before pacing off towards the ingredient booth.

Walking to the colorful fabrics, I was hit by a wave of sweet smelling perfume. I closed my eyes unknowingly, breathing in the scent.

"Can I help you?"

My eyes snapped open as I realized a woman wearing an expensive dress made of satin stood directly in front of me. Her dress was covered in gold ruffles and jewels. It was obvious she took pride in her job.

"Sorry," I said apologetically, "I'm just looking for some fabric."

"Well, you've obviously come to the right place," she said playfully. "What is the fabric for, might I ask?"

"A gown, for a ball."

"Prince Edward's ball, I assume. I may have just the thing. Come along."

The woman reached out and grabbed my wrist, pulling me along behind her. She led me to the other side of the booth where the more expensive and luxurious fabrics laid over the display.

"What color were you thinking? The ball is a black

and white ball, so I assume you'll want a different shade of black or white than others. You may even get away with gray, if you wear it right."

"I'm not sure," I said, thinking for a moment. "What about white?"

"Excellent choice with your hair color," she said, pulling several spools of fabric out to compare.

"Thank you."

"Tell me when you've decided. These spools," she pointed to a section of whites, creams, and pastels, "are most likely the best options for you."

She winked and stepped back to the front of her booth.

How much longer is Joey going to be? I glanced around the front of the booth, searching for him. He negotiated with the man covered in flour. I laughed as he pulled out a huge sack of flour and the dust flew up into his face.

"Mind if I join you?" A young man paced up to the booth next to me, seemingly admiring the colors. "I hope I don't interrupt your browsing."

"Not at all." I assessed him out of the corner of my eye. His hair was a golden shade, and his eyes were a tawny color. He towered over me by at least four inches.

"Devin," he said, holding his hand out. Ready for a handshake, I placed my hand in his, but he swiftly raised our hands to his lips and kissed the back of my hand. My cheeks felt hot.

"Elizabeth." I retracted my hand to my side.

"Pleasure to meet you." He flashed a bright grin at me. "I've never seen you here before. Are you new to these parts?"

"I am," I answered.

"Well, Elizabeth, you're very beautiful," he said, no shame in his voice. "Are you here alone?"

"No, actually—I'm here with a friend."

"How lovely."

"It is," I agreed. This boy was charismatic; I'd give him that.

"What do you need the fabric for?" he asked, eyeing the fabric I admired. "The prince's ball, perhaps?"

"Right. Are you attending?"

"Maybe," he mused.

"If you don't mind my asking," I pried, "what is your business in the Forum today?"

"I was going to run some errands, do some things, meet some people; I suppose I've gotten lucky. I've met you, haven't I?"

I couldn't help but smile.

He returned it with a grin. "How would you like to walk with me? Just around the Forum?"

Hesitantly, I glanced over at Joey who was still conversing with the baker. "Well, I don't know, I should really—"

"It'll only be a moment," he urged. "Come on. It's not every day you meet someone new here. I'd like to learn a little more about you."

His arm extended for me to take, and with one more glance at Joey, I slipped my arm through his.

"See? That wasn't so hard," Devin said.

"I suppose not."

"I must say, Miss Elizabeth, you look amazing. I've never seen anything like what you're wearing."

"Thank you," I said. "I haven't either, to be honest, but I'm not fond of wearing dresses all the time."

"How amusing," he chuckled, leading me through the crowds of people between stalls in a slow-paced walk. I looked around, trying to find Joey, but I couldn't see him anymore.

Quit looking for Joey, I scolded. *He's not your babysitter, and you aren't his.*

"Tell me about yourself, Miss Elizabeth. I'd love to know more about you."

I raised an eyebrow at him. "What would you like to know?"

"Where do you come from?" he asked me. "If you're not from Aon, you must be from Baile, or one of the kingdoms across the sea."

Should I tell him where I'm from? I wondered. *I suppose it isn't really a secret. Yula said most of the villagers knew about the Book anyway.*

"I'm from somewhere rather distant," I said. "You've never been there."

His eyes went wide. "You're the new Keeper, aren't you?"

Hesitantly, I nodded.

"My, how interesting," he said as we continued walking. "What are the odds that I'd meet a beautiful girl today who also happens to be the Keeper of our destiny?"

"You make it sound more extravagant than it really is."

"But it *is* extravagant. You have all the power in the world in your hands, you know; you can read our future before we know what's happening. You can control our future; you can make anything happen that you desire. This could be a useful tool to you and the kingdom."

"I'd rather not," I said. "I feel better not knowing any more than anyone here."

He shrugged. "I guess I can kind of understand."

"Enough about me." I felt uncomfortable talking about the Book in such an open area. I directed the conversation away from myself. "What about you?"

"There's not much to me," he said, taking a detour through more stalls. We were now on the outskirts of the Forum, walking in front of the less crowded shops that lined the perimeter. "I'm a rider for a living; I run errands for a nice lady that lives out towards Baile. I don't have any family, and my circle of friends is rather... limited."

"Limited?" I asked. "Well, consider your circle of friends to have grown. I'd love to be your friend, sir."

"Devin," he repeated. "And thank you; that's very kind. Who knows? I may call upon you in the future."

"Excuse me," said Joey from behind me. Once I turned around and my eyes met his, I could see he was livid.

"Pardon me, sir," Devin apologized before I could speak, "I was just leaving."

"Good," Joey bit back.

Devin looked from Joey to me with a forced smile, bowed, and then he stalked off in the opposite direction. "I'll write you, Elizabeth," he called over his shoulder.

"What was that all about?" I asked Joey once he was out of earshot. "What did he do?"

"It's complicated." He grimaced watching Devin leave. "Don't worry about it. What were you doing with him?"

"I *was* having a nice conversation with him," I retorted, "but not anymore. I suppose I won't have another one with him if you act like that."

"Good."

Later, I promised myself. *I'll ask him about it later. Remember: keep the peace.*

Joey sighed, frustrated, running his hand through his hair before looking at me again. "Are you ready to go?"

"I didn't get the fabric," I remembered. "I should

probably go pick it out."

Suddenly, Joey took my hand, pulling me along behind him with no intention of letting go. It was as if he was adamant about making escape impossible.

"Do you remember which one you liked?" he asked as we approached the same shop as before.

I showed him the fabric I'd picked.

"Great." He waved over the woman running the small street shop.

"Have you decided?" she asked me with a genuine smile.

"Yes ma'am," I responded, pointing to a thin, opaque white fabric. "This one is perfect." The woman reached over to begin cutting the fabric.

"We'll also need thread and a little more fabric in the same color, as well as the finest black for a set of tails," Joey added kindly.

"Of course."

His smile faded as the woman turned her back. His eyes were still trained towards the direction Devin went.

"He didn't actually buy anything over here, did he?" he questioned quietly. "When he came to speak to you?"

"Um, well... No, I don't think he did. I don't think he even looked at anything here. "

"Hmm," he said, unsatisfied. "Thought so."

I stepped back to frown at him. "Were you watching me?"

"Of course not. It is hard to ignore him when he's within a mile of me, though."

"What does that mean?"

"When I say don't worry about it right now, I mean it, Elizabeth," he said. "I'll tell you when it becomes... What's the word?"

"Relevant?" I asked lamely.

"That's right. When it becomes relevant."

I huffed like a child as Joey reached over to ruffle my hair. I swatted his hand away, though I was glad he seemed to be moving on from the subject.

"Why did you get more of the fabric?" I asked. He watched the woman measure out the fabric.

"Because I need some of it," he answered.

"Why are you wearing the same color as me?"

"Escort," he pointed to himself, "duh. And in case you haven't noticed, it's a black and white ball. Everyone's going to be wearing the same color as you."

"Hey, no need to get snappy." Honestly, I was just worried I would have to dance with him again. One dance was enough for me.

No doubt I'd trip over my feet or get nervous and say something stupid.

Lately, I started getting a feeling in the pit of my stomach whenever he was near me. I couldn't decipher it, and I couldn't tell whether or not I liked it. All I knew is that it put thoughts about him in my head that I didn't know what to do with.

Not that I'd ever tell him that.

Joey grinned.

"Do you have to get fitted for a suit, then, too?"

He smirked. "Nope. That's all you, love. I already have a suit that fits. I just have to have a bowtie and handkerchief in the same color. The black fabric is for Ed's new tails."

I groaned. "Lucky bastard."

He laughed. "The irony of that sentence."

The woman came back with the fabric and thread, naming her price. It sounded outrageous to me, but Joey smiled and paid more than she asked.

Joey grabbed my hand and pulled me over to a

wagon where the flour, sugar, and other ingredients he had bought were already loaded. Carefully, he placed the fabrics in the front before patting the horse on the back.

"Why are you still holding my hand?" I asked, pulling our intertwined hands up to eye level. The feeling in my stomach grew stronger, and my cheeks felt warm.

"To make sure you don't go running off," he said, as if it was the most obvious thing in the world. "I don't need you to have another encounter with rogues, or horsemen, or worse, Devin."

"What makes you think I'll go running off?"

He gave me a look.

"Never mind," I murmured. He adjusted his grip on my hand and pulled both our hands back down to his side. Smirking in victory, he pulled me along behind him towards a few trinket booths.

"What are you thinking of getting Edward?"

I thought for a moment. "I changed my mind; I'll just give him the necklace I made. I have a few ideas of tweaking it in the Book, so maybe he'll like it."

"He'll like it no matter what," Joseph said. "So, if you aren't getting him anything here, can we leave?"

"I think so," I said, pondering for a moment. "Wait! I promised Margaret I'd buy ribbons, but I have no idea what they're for."

"Oh, I nearly forgot! This way."

He pulled me by the hand through row after row until we reached the perimeter of the Forum. In a large square that ran all the way around the marketplace stood shops in small buildings. Above the door in front of us, a sign read, "Anne's Lace and Ribbons." As we walked in, an old woman stood in front of us.

"Filthy child," she muttered. Her shoulder purposely brushed his with a surprising amount of force. Joey grimaced but didn't speak a word.

"That was incredibly rude," I said once she had passed. "Do you let people treat you like that all the time?"

"I'm an illegitimate child, remember?" he asked, forcing a smile. "There are a few people in this kingdom who don't approve of me."

"You should say something back. That must be awful, listening to them all the time."

"I've learned to ignore them," he answered evenly. "It's okay, really."

"No, it's not okay. You don't deserve that."

"Let it go, Elizabeth. It's not worth the trouble."

Before I could say anything more, he pulled me through the door of the store.

"Anne!" he called.

"Joseph, is that you?" a voice answered.

Joseph? I thought he hated being called Joseph.

A young girl ran on her toes to meet us. She was beautiful, to say the least, with long blond hair and emerald eyes. She all but launched herself into Joey's arms, breaking his hold on my hand. A twinge of jealousy hit me before I shook my head to clear it away.

"How nice to see you, Anne!" he exclaimed, pulling away from their embrace. He made a quick bow.

"And you, Joseph, and you!" she responded with a curtsey. "What brings you to the Forum?"

"Her, actually." He placed a hand on my lower back to push me slightly forward. I managed an awkward curtsey and a small smile. "This is Elizabeth."

"She's absolutely gorgeous!" she exclaimed, taking my hands. "Is she yours?"

"His?"

"Relax, El."

I tried to ignore the heat that seemed to have a newly permanent residence in my cheeks.

Joey turned back to Anne, a radiant smile on his face. It was almost strange to see him so content and in such a good mood—he'd been so serious since I'd arrived. "Sorry to disappoint, Anne; we're just friends. She's visiting with us at the palace for a while, though."

"Ah, how exciting! I take it you're out and about to prepare for the ball, then?"

"We are. Mind showing us the best ribbons first?"

"Of course! Nothing less for someone as beautiful as she is," she said, pointing at me. "Come, this way!"

As we followed Anne through the shop, I whispered to Joey. "She's very... *exciting*, is she not?"

He chuckled, speaking back into my ear. "You don't even know."

We finally stopped at the wall where hundreds of colorful ribbons decorated the shelves and hung from the ceiling.

"These are the best we have so far," she said, gesturing to the tables and shelves. "Let me know when you're ready to pay!"

Joey thanked her with a smile; she curtseyed before happily skipping away.

"Now that we're here," I said, turning around to face him, "can you *please* explain to me what these are for?"

"*Wow*, did *you* say please?"

"Joseph!"

"You've never worn ribbons before?" he asked, dismissing my outburst.

"In my hair, as a kid," I answered, holding a thick blue ribbon that I'd randomly picked up against my head.

"You have so much to learn," he said, rolling his

eyes before taking the ribbon from my hands, grabbing my shoulders and turning me around. "You wear it around your waist." His hands raised the ribbon over my head and tied it behind my back tightly.

"Like a belt?"

"Women don't wear belts here, but I guess it's similar. We're here to find a ribbon for your dress for the ball, and ribbons for your day dresses as well."

He finished tying the ribbon, his fingers lingering for a second before he guided me by the shoulders to a full-length mirror.

My reflection took me by surprise. The outfit that Margaret made for me fit better than expected, and the blue ribbon accented my waist. My eyes shifted from my figure to Joey and his hands on my shoulders.

"See?"

I nodded. "Yeah."

"Great." He moved his hands from my shoulders and walked back over to the tables. "Now, we need to pick a few before we go, so let's get started."

Before we left the shop, we ended up choosing several wide ribbons and a few thin ribbons for my day dresses. The ribbon for my formal ball gown was a very wide, midnight blue satin one. We even found a shimmery light gold that was wide enough for extra embellishment on the dress (which, surprisingly, was Joey's idea, not mine.)

Happily, we strolled back to the wagon where we loaded the ribbons. Joey sent the driver off with a few pieces of gold.

"The currency here is gold?" I asked as we walked the path to the castle.

"No, we use paper money. The royal family handles the gold in the kingdom. Gold coins aren't common in the villages, but they're worth a lot of money, so a single coin can buy a month's worth of food for a small family of commoners. I try to bring a few whenever I come out here."

"That's very kind of you," I noted.

"It's nothing special," he responded. "I just try to put myself in their position. I am, after all, the only one in the castle who has even an inkling of what it's like to live here and not in a castle. Edward is very kind; don't get me wrong. He's kinder than I, most days, but..."

I frowned. "But?"

He shrugged. "But he doesn't quite understand like I do. When I'm not assisting Ed, I'm roaming the countryside and visiting villages. I even lived out here for a time, when my mother stayed in the cottage on the outskirts."

"How do you manage to find the time?"

He smirked at me. "It's one of the perks of being a bastard."

I laughed. The gates opened silently as we made our way to the front doors, lost in conversation.

"Sadly, I must leave you here," Joseph said when we reached the base of the large staircase. "I believe you're past Margaret's deadline, and I must speak with the nobles of Baile before they threaten to behead me."

"You sound less than happy."

He shot me a look. "You would be too if you knew who I have to deal with."

I grinned. "Have fun."

He let out a breath that had a hint of a laugh in it. "I'll try. I'll be at your door to escort you to dinner at seven o'clock tonight, then?"

I nodded. "I'll be there."

"Good," he nodded. "See you then."

———

Just as he promised, Joey was at my door as the clock stroke seven. After a long evening of being scolded by Margaret for being late and being forced into another fancy dress, I was relieved to see him.

"You look great," he said, eying my dress.

"Thanks," I said.

He nodded before holding out his arm for me. "I have to warn you, before we get into the Great Hall, that the nobles of Aon can be a little… overwhelming."

"The nobles of Aon?" I asked. "I thought we were meeting Baile's nobility?"

"Heavens, no," he said, scoffing. "I wouldn't ask you to suffer that. No, I met them a couple of hours ago. They wanted to have a big meeting, but I met them for an hour or two and rescheduled them. Just having them in the castle puts my teeth on edge."

When we reached the doors of the Great Hall, Joey flashed me a nervous smile. "Good luck."

When he pushed the doors open, I gasped.

This was *nothing* like I expected.

The hall was *filled* with men. All of them yelled and laughed when they spoke, swinging wine glasses and kegs in their hands as they clapped each other on their backs. One particularly large man ate rather quickly, like he'd never seen food in his life. No one seemed to notice us until someone yelled out.

"Joseph's brought a girl!"

The room went dead quiet. Every head turned in our direction.

"Joseph!" a long bearded man exclaimed, standing from his seat. He bowed gracefully, which surprised me; I was pretty sure I had just seen him tip his entire keg over onto the floor.

The men in the room all followed suit, standing up and bowing. I noticed one familiar face, smirking in our direction from his place at the end of the table.

I couldn't help but laugh as none other than Alexander Fell waved at me from the other end of the room. Edward sat across from him with a mischievous grin on his face.

"Gentlemen," Joey said with an amused expression, "this is Elizabeth Knight. She's our guest and the very first Keeper from the Outside."

"Well, I'll be," the bearded man said. "It really is a pleasure, Miss Knight."

I smiled nervously as Joey led me around the table to the end. When we reached it, Joey sat at the head, and I took the only empty seat left—the one at Joey's right hand next to Alec. Edward, seated across the table from me, offered a smile.

The room was quiet until Joey raised the glass in front of him. "To Aon."

"To Aon," everyone repeated. "Long live Prince Edward."

Glasses rose in the air, and the sounds of glass clinking and drinks pouring filled the room. It wasn't even another minute before the room continued on with the same things that were happening when I'd come in.

"This is insane," I said, grinning at Joey. "It's not what I pictured at all."

"What exactly did you picture?" Joey asked, his sly smile growing.

"Posh men in suits and scrutinizing remarks," I said plainly.

"Oh, you're thinking of the Baile nobles. They're bloody ridiculous. None of them have hearts, I swear," Alec said, reaching across me to grab my champagne glass. He filled it with wine before returning it to my spot. "You're old enough to drink, right?"

I laughed nervously. I was only twenty. "Um…"

"She is *here*," Edward interrupted, grabbing his own glass. "Fill me up?"

"Not a chance," Joey said, grabbing the cup from his little brother.

Alec shrugged. "Nice try, bud. Maybe next time."

I laughed, sipping from my glass. The taste was strange, but I liked it more with each sip.

"Is every meeting like this?" I asked Alec.

"Every last one, without fail. It's almost as chaotic as that time that Darren let that dragon loose in the Forum."

I raised an eyebrow. "You were here when that happened?"

"I was small," he said. "My father told me about it."

"Everyone," Joey said loudly, tapping his knife against his glass, "we need to begin the discussions."

The room quieted down to whispers and then silence. Someone cleared his throat, and a man with dark hair and a moustache rose at the opposite end of the table.

"Nobleman Chauncey? You'd like to start us off?"

The nobleman nodded, tucking his hands behind his back before speaking.

"I'd like to thank Miss Knight for joining us this evening." He bowed in my direction. I bowed my head towards him. "I'd also like to start with the topic of the Night Rider."

Joseph sat up in his chair, leaning onto his elbows. "Where would you like to start with the discussion?"

"With the attack on Miss Elizabeth Knight only two months ago, m'lord."

The nobleman next to Alec spoke as Nobleman Chauncey took his seat. "The Night Rider's attacks have grown bolder, have they not?"

"No," Alec interrupted, "they haven't. Attacks like Elizabeth's aren't uncommon on the borders of Baile. This is, however, the closest he's ever been to the royals since the ambush in the forest."

"Joseph technically isn't even a royal," another noble I couldn't see piped up. "The last time he was this close was when Devin Meverel's father worked for him."

"And we'd like to keep it that way," Joey said.

"Devin Meverel?" I asked. "As in, the Devin I met in the Forum today?"

Several gasps broke out among the table.

The bearded nobleman from before stood up and cleared his throat.

"I'd like to start the discussion on the arrest of Devin Meverel."

Immediately, arguments roared around the table. Men were standing up, pointing fingers, and yelling. Alec looked at me and rolled his eyes.

"I swear, something like this happens every time Devin's name is mentioned. I wish they'd come to a decision already."

"I forgot to ask," I said, leaning into Alec's ear so he could hear. "Why are you here?"

"Joseph hasn't told you, has he?" he asked. "How rude. If you must know, I'm a noble myself. I took over for my father when he died a few years back."

"You're a noble?" I asked. "Is the orphanage in the village named after you, then?"

"Indeed, it is," he said proudly. "Designed that one myself."

"I love how the nobles are about to start war

amongst each other and you two are talking about *Alec*," Edward said.

"Hey, I'm an interesting person," Alec said, pretending to be offended.

"Keep telling yourself that," Edward said, waving him off.

"ENOUGH!"

I jumped at the sound of Joey's voice echoing through the room. He was on his feet, leaning with his palms on the table. The room went dead quiet.

"Enough," he said again, looking around. "Everyone, *sit down and shut up*."

The nobles obeyed.

"Devin Meverel has not committed any crime against Aon," Joey said. "His father may have posed as the Night Rider in the past, but there is no proof of the same situation with the son. I advise each and every one of you to hold your tongue unless you have substantial proof against his case."

"What does he mean?" I whispered to Alec. "About Devin's father, what does he mean?"

"His father worked for the Night Rider," he whispered back. "He posed for him when the king was first threatened."

"Why didn't the Night Rider come himself?" I asked. "Why send someone else out?"

"Why risk being caught?" Alec asked. "He needed someone to go to jail for him if need be. He's a huge coward, if you ask me."

"So, Devin's father was a devoted servant of sorts," I figured.

"I don't know, Liz. I'd say he was more afraid of the Night Rider than he was devoted to him."

I looked at him. "Where is his father now?"

"He was in the dungeons. He was caught in service to the Night Rider, and he was there for years... but he's been let out on probation."

So, Devin's father worked for the Night Rider. Is that why he didn't want me speaking to him?

I turned from Alec to listen to Joey speak.

"The Night Rider is planning something. He's being bold. He's burned villages on the outskirts of Baile and he's attacked both Elizabeth and me. There's no doubt in my mind that if we don't stop him, things will take a turn for the worse."

"Miss Elizabeth," someone called, "have you read anything in the Book of Aon? Anything that may help us fight this wretched man?"

I felt the pressure of the eyes watching me as I cleared my throat.

"Nothing, nobleman. Nothing of any importance."

My answer seemed to satisfy a few, but many looked at me with skeptical glances.

"M'lord," a noble said, "has any more evidence been uncovered on the Night Rider's identity?"

Every head turned towards Joey.

"No, there hasn't been any evidence," Joey said solemnly. "And if things keep going the way they are, there won't be any."

twelve

Alec's back hit the mat on the ground with a thud. I smiled triumphantly at him, propping my foot up on his chest.

"I told you I was stronger," I taunted him.

"You did, didn't you?"

In a split second while I enjoyed my glory, his hands shot out, grabbed my ankles and pulled me to the ground. I landed on my back next to him with the wind knocked out of my lungs.

He laughed. "I guess you were wrong. Sorry, Elizabeth. Maybe next time."

"What'll it be?" I asked, my chest heaving as I tried to catch my breath.

"Hmm…" Alec thought for a moment. "How about knife throwing?"

I thought about it a minute, then reached over and shook his hand. "You're on."

Just then, the doors opened. Heavy footsteps echoed in the training hall and stopped right next to my head.

"Am I interrupting something?"

Joey didn't seem happy as he looked down at Alec and me sprawled on the floor.

"Not at all," I said, nudging Alec's shoulder, "I just taught old Alec here a lesson."

Alec scoffed. "Right. How did you end up on the floor again?"

"Well, if you two are done messing around," Joey said, his jaw tense, "Elizabeth, I have to ask you something."

"Oh," Alec said, sitting up with raised eyebrows. He looked at me, a suggestive smirk crossing his lips.

Joey sighed. "Shut up, Alec."

"What did you need?" I asked him, ignoring Alec and sitting up.

"Can you take Ed out riding? He's been asking all day," he asked, holding out a hand to help me up.

I studied his expression. He was tired, worn. I wondered what bothered him.

"Sure," I answered, accepting his hand and jumping up from the mat. "Out of curiosity, though, why aren't *you* taking him?"

He grimaced. "I have to meet with the nobles of Baile."

"Again?" Alec asked, pushing himself up to his feet. "Thanks for no help, by the way."

Joey rolled his eyes. "They want to talk about the treaty."

"The treaty has been fine for hundreds of years. What's new that requires a meeting?"

Sighing, Joey ran a hand through his hair. "I don't know, but I'd love to get out of it as soon as possible.

Elizabeth, Ed is in the downstairs library, if you don't mind taking him out."

"No problem," I waved him off. "I'll head there now."

"Great," he said, seemingly relieved. He turned to Alec. "Is it too much to ask you to suffer the meeting with me?"

"If you weren't my best friend, I'd be threatening to hit you for even asking," Alec stated, "but since you are, I'll go just out of the goodness of my heart."

"Oh, brother," Joey said. I giggled as I skipped towards the door of the training room.

"See you later, boys. Have fun with your posh nobles."

They waved at me as I swung the door open and scampered into the hallway in a fantastic mood.

With no problem, I found the library. Almost as soon as I opened the door, I found the young prince sitting crisscross in front of a shelf.

"Hey, Ed," I said with a grin. "What's up?"

"Hey, Liz," he said, his eyes still trained on his book. "I'm not doing much of anything. What about you?"

"I just finished up training with Alec. Do you want to go riding?"

"I was about to ask you the same thing."

"Guess it's just you and me, then. Are you ready to go right now?"

He snapped his book shut eagerly. "Let's go."

Once we reached the stables, our horses were already ready for us, so we mounted straight away and set off with cloaks wrapped around our shoulders. The cool, fall air sent a chill down my spine. I knew it wouldn't be long before winter was upon us.

"Where do you want to ride today?" I asked him.

"Well, there's a pond not far from here in the countryside," he explained. "I thought we could go look around?"

I nodded, tapping the side of my horse with my boot to urge it to go faster. Riding behind Ed, we followed the main road through the village ,waving at the villagers along the way, and headed towards the fields on the outskirts of the city.

Ed's favorite thing about riding was the speed; the journey to the pond wasn't long because Ed insisted we lope the entire way there. I wasn't complaining, as I'd grown to love horseback riding (and was actually quite good at it, despite what Joey said).

Soon enough, the large pond came into view. It was beautiful, reflecting the sky onto the water. The sun began to set, and the water appeared to be different shades of red, orange, pink, and purple.

I jumped out of my saddle and onto the ground, and Ed followed suit. "I found this place on the way to Baile with Joey, once," he said. "I only saw it out of the window of the carriage, but I've wanted to come here ever since."

"It's really pretty," I said, bending down to run my fingers through the water. It felt as soft as silk.

Just then, a brilliant idea popped into my head, and a grin spread onto my face. "Hey, Ed, do you want to swim?"

It's true the weather had cooled down quite a bit, but the sun provided a little warmth for us. I knew I'd probably get sick again, but making a new memory of this place seemed like a good enough reason.

His eyes went wide. "Right now? In our clothes?"

"Yeah," I said, taking off my boots.

"It's probably freezing! What will Joey say when we

come back soaking wet, hmm?" he asked.

"I don't know, but you can blame me. It was my idea, after all." Setting my boots aside, I waded into the pond. It was a little cold at first, but it only took a few seconds to get used to the sensation.

"Come on, Ed," I urged, grinning as I paddled around in the water. "Be a little adventurous. You *do* know how to swim, don't you?"

"Of course I know how to swim," he said, taking off his shoes and putting them next to mine. "Joey is going to kill me for this."

"Since when are you afraid of Joey?" I asked.

"Since never. I'll just have him lecture you on being responsible." He waded knee deep into the water next to me.

"I've had that lecture once; I think I can handle it again."

Ed jumped the rest of the way into the water, splashing me in the face.

"Hey! What was that for?" I exclaimed, rubbing the water out of my eyes. When I opened them, I couldn't see Ed.

"Ed?" I asked spinning around. "Ed!"

He told me he could swim, I thought frantically, plunging under the water to search for him. *He told me he knew how!*

Breaking the surface of the water for air, I heard hysterical laughing.

"Ed!" I exclaimed, catching sight of him rolling on the grass on the bank. His hair stuck to his forehead. "You scared the crap out of me! That wasn't funny!"

"You should've seen your face," he said through laughing fits.

I didn't laugh with him.

"Oh, come on, Liz. It was just a joke," he said,

sitting up. "I'm sorry."

"Are you?"

"Yes, I am," he said.

I splashed water up at him, laughing. "Good. That's payback."

He grinned, jumping back into the pond with me. I shielded my eyes this time.

The sky grew darker and darker as we swam and splashed around in the pond. Soon, it was so dark we could barely find our shoes when we got out of the water. The only lights we could see were the faint lights from the castle, the identical lights in Baile, and the stars above us.

"Joey will skin us both alive when we get back," I commented as we mounted our horses. "Me more than you because I let you stay out so late."

Ed scoffed. "You aren't my babysitter."

I laughed. "If I'm not, then who is?"

Silence.

I frowned. "Ed?"

"Elizabeth," he spoke quietly, "there's someone over there on a horse."

"What do you mean?"

"To your right," he instructed, "towards the tree line."

My eyes wandered to the tree line where I caught a little glimpse of a light moving up and down.

"Is that a torch?" I asked. "What's he doing?"

"Liz, I think he's coming towards us," Ed said urgently.

"He is," I confirmed, my stare locked on the unknown rider. "Ride, Ed, and don't look back all the way to the castle, understand?"

I heard the snap of the reins in response, and Ed

took off ahead of me. I watched as the one tiny figure started to grow bigger, and the torch he carried grew bigger. I looked from the figure to Ed and back again before snapping the reins and taking off after Ed at full speed, making sure to keep both him and the mysterious rider in view.

The rider grew closer behind me, and the torchlight illuminated more of the unknown figure. I pushed my horse to the limit, desperate to create some distance. Nearing the village, I turned around once more, and my heart dropped to my stomach.

The Night Rider was chasing us, gaining speed with each stride.

My horse caught up to Ed's. The air rushed past us as our speed built up, trying to hold our place ahead of him.

"Ed," I said urgently, "it's him. It's the Night Rider."

"Figures," he said, letting out a short breath. "What do I need to do?"

"As much as I hate to admit it, I think we need to split up in the city," I said, trying to stay calm and keep my head clear. "Do you know another way to the castle other than the main road?"

"I do. I'll take it as fast as I can."

"Good. As soon as you get there, tell Joey what's happened and have them prepare. I'm going to take the longest, most obvious route; maybe it'll buy you a little time and he'll follow me instead of you."

"Be careful, Liz," he said before snapping his reins again. The horse picked up as we entered the city limits, and he was way ahead of me by the time we reached the main road. Just like he said, he turned off the road into a small alley and disappeared just as the Night Rider rounded the corner onto the road behind me.

"All right," I murmured to myself. "Let's send him on a bit of a wild goose chase, shall we?"

I snapped the reins again, and my horse sped up. The Rider dropped his torch, igniting the hay bales that sat against the wall of a house. They blossomed into flames as we galloped through the streets, which were mostly empty and lined with dark houses; however, as we rode on, torches were lit, and the buildings were filled with light as the sounds woke people up.

Glancing behind me, I found that the Night Rider was closer than I'd thought.

"You won't catch me this time," I said, taking a sharp turn down an alley. Just as I thought, he followed, and I knew my plan would to work.

I took random roads, weaving back and forth between neighborhoods and the main street. I didn't bother to look back anymore; I was too afraid of losing focus.

Finally reaching the castle, I leapt from my horse and sprinted up the stairs, leaving the horse with the stable keepers. As soon as I reached the doors, they opened, and Joey and Ed walked out together.

"Thank goodness you're all right." I squeezed Ed into a hug.

"I could say the same for you," he said, hugging me back. "Where's the Rider?"

I turned back to the main road, expecting to see the dark horse charging up the hill.

It was empty.

"I must have lost him," I said. "He must've given up."

"Cyneward," Joey called, speaking for the first time since I'd gotten back.

Cyneward seemed to appear from thin air, coming

up from behind me. "Yes sir?"

"Send out a group to search for the Night Rider. When you find him, follow him as far as you can. Don't get any closer than you have to, understand?"

Cyneward nodded before turning on his heel and heading for the barracks.

Joey looked down at me. "Haven't we had this talk before? About being responsible and trying not to be reckless?" he asked, obviously holding back anger.

"Yes, we have," I answered, "and we weren't being reckless. We were swimming in the pond, and it got dark faster than we expected."

"Well, that explains your appearance," he said, eying me and then turning to Ed. "I expected more from you, Ed. I thought I could depend on you if Elizabeth was being immature, but I suppose not."

"He's thirteen-years-old, Joseph. Cut the kid some slack."

His head whipped in my direction, and he shot me one of those deadly glares I'd grown familiar with. I ignored him.

"Ed, go inside, get dry and get some sleep, okay?" I said. "You'll get sick out here." He glanced uncertainly between Joey and me before disappearing inside.

"You're infuriating, you know that?" Joey asked through gritted teeth once Ed had gone. "You could've gotten Ed killed."

"Oh, thanks for the concern," I remarked snidely. "Good to know you were worried about me too. Ed was my first priority, for your information, and I don't have the energy to argue with you tonight, so I'm going to bed. I've had enough of risking my life for one day."

I left him on the front steps, storming into the castle in a dangerous mood.

"Where have you been?" Margaret caught me by the arm and dragged me up the staircase, down the corridor, and pulled me into my bedroom faster than I had ever seen her move. She slammed the door, continuing to push me into the bathroom, where a bath was already drawn.

"Violet," she said, gesturing to one of the two maids that stood in front of the bath, "ten minutes, that's all. Get her washed up; she smells like dust and sweat. Ten minutes, understand?"

Violet nodded.

"Good. Get a move on!"

Exactly ten minutes later, I was clean and dressed in my nightgown, and Margaret had braided my wet hair. She scolded me for making her worry before patting the top of my head and bidding me goodnight. I fell asleep as soon as my head hit the pillow, exhausted.

thirteen

—three hours earlier—

As soon as the door closed behind Elizabeth, Joey turned to Alec, his hands forming fists at his sides as the anger built up inside him.

"How could you?" Joey asked angrily. "I've told you what I think about Elizabeth, and yet, here you are, alone with her in the training room. What exactly were you two doing?"

"Exactly what this room is meant for," Alec said plainly, raising an eyebrow. "Training. Take a breath. I'm not after Elizabeth."

Joseph blinked. "You're not?"

"No, I'm not. I know you well enough to know that you have a major crush on her."

"It's not a crush, it's just—"

Alec held up a hand. "Save it. I don't like Elizabeth,

not in that way, at least. She's been a great friend while she's been here, but I have no intention of taking it any further."

Joey cast a skeptical glance at his friend but sighed in relief at his words. "Thanks, Alec."

"Don't worry about it. Now, we need to get out there. The nobles won't be happy if we make them wait any longer."

Together, the boys left the training room and jogged the corridors to the Great Hall. Cyneward waited for them at the large, wooden doors.

"They're here, sir," he said, his voice grave. "They aren't happy."

"They're never happy," Joey said. "Thank you, Cyneward."

"Why do I get the feeling that this meeting will end in war?" Alec joked.

"It very well might." Joey cracked his knuckles, taking a breath before nodding at Cyneward. "If I don't come out in two hours, send someone in for me."

"Don't forget me," Alec said, his eyes narrowing as he grimaced. "I don't know how much of these idiots I'll be able to handle before I go insane."

"Good luck," Cyneward said, pulling open the door. "I'll wait for you here."

"See you on the other side," Alec said, slapping Joey's shoulder as he walked forward.

The table in the Great Hall was full of men. One particularly tall, blonde male sat at the head of the table, standing as Joey entered.

"Dauphin," he said, his daunting stance and solemn expression clear from across the room. "We've been expecting you."

fourteen

The next day, I woke up late. It was about eleven o'clock when I finally pulled myself out of bed and got dressed, not even bothering to call Margaret. I left my hair in the braid, glad to keep it out of my face. When I got downstairs, I was met with the busy and bustling foyer. I caught Violet before she could disappear into the Great Hall.

"Violet, what's going on? Why is it so busy around here?"

She raised an eyebrow. "Why, we're getting ready for the ball tonight. What else?"

The ball. I had totally forgotten. It seemed like only yesterday that Ed was telling me about it, but time had passed so fast.

"Thank you," I said, and she curtseyed before hurrying away.

The flow of traffic seemed to be going back and

forth from the hallway on my right, so I followed a couple of footmen down it and into a room with double doors.

"So, this must be the ballroom," I said to myself in awe, looking up at the high ceilings and large windows. People were everywhere, decorating and preparing tables and moving in chairs.

"Elizabeth!" Margaret's voice called. I found her polishing a box of silverware by the window where a string quartet practiced.

"Can I help?"

"Be my guest," she said, handing me a rag. We listened to the strings play happy tunes as we polished.

"Have you seen Edward or Joseph this morning?" I found myself asking.

She shook her head. "I haven't seen Edward, but Joseph's been up and about since early this morning. He's been organizing most of this, poor soul; he shouldn't work as hard as he does at his age. These are the best years of a person's life, and he's spending them running a kingdom for his younger brother."

I looked at my reflection in the silver knife in my hands as I listened to her, agreeing when necessary.

We finished polishing the silverware after a couple hours (Margaret said she wanted to be safe rather than sorry; she didn't know how many villagers would come) and moved on to help decorate. We spread out tablecloths on tables up against the walls and arranged a few chairs here and there. Flowers were brought in and arranged all around us; there were even garlands of flowers that were hung and draped from the ceiling.

Around one o'clock, Margaret said she had to go check on my dress and made me promise to be back in my room to get ready at two o'clock. I promised, and she hurried towards the servants' hallway.

I decided to go to the library on the first floor to pass the time. I said goodbye to the servants I was helping, who thanked me profusely for my help, before making my way to the library.

Though it was quieter than the foyer or the ballroom was, it wasn't as quiet as I'd thought it would be when I stepped in. Several people were on ladders, dusting the shelves from the top down. Stacks of books were being shelved and rearranged. A low hum filled the room—not too loud but enough to know that there was a lot of work being done.

I weaved between shelves and people, waiting for a book to jump out at me from one of the shelves.

"Elizabeth," Joey's voice rang in my ear. I jumped, turning around.

"Don't do that!" I exclaimed, shoving his shoulder.

"I'm sorry. I just need to speak with you."

I crossed my arms. "Are you here to tell me how irresponsible I am? If you are, you can leave. I'm not interested."

I turned away, but he caught my arm.

"I'm here to apologize," he said. "I acted like a jerk last night, and I'm sorry. I know you were just looking out for Ed when you split up."

I raised an eyebrow. "And?"

"And I did worry about you," he explained. "I was just angry."

"Apology accepted."

He seemed surprised. "Really?"

"Yeah." There was no need to prolong it. Joseph knew he needed to control his temper.

"That's a relief," he said, scratching the back of his neck. "I also wanted to talk to you about the Night

Rider. Cyneward took a group out last night, and they found him. They followed him all the way back to the pond and to the edge of the forest where Cyneward says that he disappeared, just on the outskirts of Berkeley."

"We should talk more about this tomorrow," I said. "Right now, I have to get upstairs before Margaret skins me alive. See you at the ball!"

He chuckled. "See you tonight, Elizabeth. I'll be at your door at seven o'clock sharp, okay?"

I nodded, waving before taking off towards the door. I caught a glimpse of the clock on the wall as I ran through the foyer.

Shoot, I'm late!

I burst into my room out of breath.

"Late," Margaret scolded.

"I know," I breathed. "Sorry."

"Violet, go ahead."

Once again, they whisked me away into the bath and scrubbed me from head to toe. Violet managed to get me washed *and* force me into a corset in under fifteen minutes. Margaret combed my dark, wet hair neatly down my back.

"What about my dress?" I asked.

"It's finished," Margaret said, sorting through a shiny box full of jewelry. Violet and the other girl (whose name I had yet to learn) pulled out various items that I assumed were going to be used on my hair. "Our seamstresses are very experienced and *very* quick, not to mention we have a dozen of them."

"It's done?"

Just then, a soft knock came at the door.

"Thank heavens, they're here," Margaret sighed. "Come in!"

The door opened, and in came the most beautiful

gown I had ever laid eyes on. Three servant girls carried it into the room and spread it on the bed next to me.

The dress was ivory, with a few layers underneath, so the skirt flowed out just slightly. It had a low, squared neckline with capped sleeves, and the very bottom of the skirt was decorated with an elegant pale gold pattern. A satin blue sash laid on the bed next to it. My fingers gingerly ran across the smooth fabric.

I could see Margaret grin out of the corner of my eye. "Beautiful, isn't it?"

"It's the most beautiful thing I've ever seen!"

"You exaggerate," she said, standing me up from the bed and untying my robe. "You're more beautiful than the dress is."

The skirt came over my head and dropped down to the floor. My eyes went wide as I took it in.

The three girls who brought in the dress began to work. One tightened the back, one worked with the hem, and the last girl circled us.

"We almost had it exact," she said, propping her chin with her hand. "Just a little smaller on the waist." She motioned to her friend.

The waistline sat right above my waist in a high Victorian style, but it wasn't as high as some I'd seen. Although I could barely breathe in the corset, I was happy with the outcome.

Before I knew it, two of the seamstresses had left, and Violet positioned the wide, midnight blue sash on my high waistline.

"Now that that's done," Margaret said, "take it off."

"Take it off?" I asked incredulously.

"Yes, take it off. You can't have your dress on before you're completely ready otherwise! Besides, would you like to sit in that for the next five hours?"

My mouth dropped open. "*Five hours?*"

"Yes! Now take it off so we can get started." She untied my sash, laying it on the bed.

"Mary," she said, pointing to the girl who stayed behind, standing next to Violet. Violet raised the dress over my head and laid it over the bed once more.

Mary, that's her name.

She pointed to the door. "Go get Elizabeth her lunch. Not much, mind you; she still has to fit into this dress when the time comes."

Mary scampered out the door.

"Not much? But I'm starving," I groaned, falling back onto the bed.

"Oh, quit being dramatic," she said, lightly patting my thigh. "You can eat plenty at the ball tonight. Until then, you only need to snack on a few things."

I sighed. "Fine. So what do we do now?"

"Hair. Violet, if you will?"

Violet wrapped me back in my robe and sat me down in the chair she had moved from the corner. Her hands immediately went to work; she was taking her time, I could tell. She combed through my locks multiple times, spraying something sweet smelling into it before using her fingers to nimbly create braids.

The hours that followed consisted of my hair, makeup, and jewelry being groomed and polished to perfection. I was told to don the dress once more, and to my surprise, we really did need every second of the time we had.

———

The castle buzzed with life by the time the clock tolled seven. The sounds of footsteps as people filed in through the front doors and loud conversations drifted up the stairs and turned into a faint hum of happiness.

I stood in front of the full-length mirror that Margaret had brought in for me, taking in my appearance. The dress was perfect, complementing my light skin tone and my dark hair. Violet had woven an array of intricate braids that pulled up into a bun at the nape of my neck where I wore the teardrop necklace, the one from the night in the dungeon.

Before I forget... I picked up the Book of Aon from my bed, moving it to the desk that sat against the wall. I dipped the quill from the holder into the ink, opened the Book to the last page, and started writing. As I wrote, the necklace glowed a bright white, then faded back to clear.

A knock sounded at the door, dispersing my thoughts. Violet paced to the door and opened it for me.

Joey stood in the doorway, looking as handsome as ever. I tried to keep thoughts like that to a minimum, but when the boy that hates you happens to be utterly attractive, mental rules like that seem to slip away.

His eyes met mine, but he didn't say a word as he let his eyes wander down my figure, taking in my appearance.

"Wow," he said quietly.

"What?" I asked, looking at my dress. *Did I spill something on it? Wait, I haven't had anything in here to spill. Is there a rip? If there's a rip, I'm going to—*

"You're beautiful," he answered, stepping into the room. "Absolutely stunning."

"Um... Thank you," I said, shocked; the compliments seemed to easily flow from Joey these days.

His eyes shifted down to my arm. "Are you bringing that with you?"

Looking down, I realized that the Book hung off my arm by its strap.

Huh. I must've subconsciously picked it up.

"No," I said, shaking my head. I slid it off my arm before putting it on my desk.

"Shall we?" He extended his arm.

I took his arm and followed him into the corridor and towards the staircase. When we reached the bottom, he led me through the swarms of people down the hallway the ballroom was on.

Men and women greeted Joey from across the room, and he would smile politely and wave before moving me along. We finally reached the set of open doors almost as big as the entrance doors and slipped inside the room with the crowd.

"Whoa," I breathed.

Joey grinned as I looked up at the glistening chandelier and the dazzling decorations. "Amazing, isn't it?"

I nodded, taking in the splendor of the grand room. A shiny pianoforte sat against a wall. Several young women lined up to use it after the first. Militia and guards both leaned against walls, drinks in hand, while they conversed with one another. In the center of the room ran two long, parallel lines, one made up of men and one made up of women. They faced each other, and a string quartet played cheerful music at the far end of the room.

Scanning the area, I realized several people were looking towards me.

"People are staring at me," I whispered to Joey, uneasy.

"You've given them reason to," he chuckled. "They're jealous."

"Elizabeth!" a voice called from behind me. I turned, only to see Ed dressed up as nicely as Joey was.

"Ed!" I exclaimed, giving him a hug. "Happy birthday!"

"Thank you." He sported a wide grin. "Are you feeling better? Did you catch up on sleep?"

"I did. Did you?"

He nodded.

"I have your present," I said, reaching behind my neck to unclasp my necklace. I handed it to him, placing it in his open palm.

"I've written more about it in the Book," I explained. "Now, when you look into it, it shows your most precious memory, so you can watch it again and again when you're sad."

"That's amazing," he said, picking it up by the charm and holding it to his eye. I watched as his awestruck expression turned into a full-blown grin.

"Thank you so much, Liz. This is the best present ever," he said, giving me another hug.

"You're welcome."

"Now," he said, pocketing his new found treasure and using a posh voice, "as payment for this fine gift, can I ask you to dance?"

I giggled, holding out my hand for him to take. "You may."

Joey let go of my arm and bowed to Ed before standing up again to ruffle his hair. "I'll catch you later, Ed. Save me a dance, Elizabeth, okay?"

Before I could respond, he disappeared into the crowd.

"Remind me to tell Alec he lost," Edward commented.

I frowned. "What?"

He laughed, shaking his head as we headed to the dance floor. "Never mind."

People danced and clapped and bounced in a pattern that I picked up surprisingly quickly. Ed and I laughed and jumped around like idiots, having the best time. I was glad that he hadn't chosen a slow song to ask me to dance because we would've looked way funnier because of his height compared to mine.

All too soon the dance ended, and we bowed, following the suit of everyone else around us. I laughed, wrapping my arms around Ed's neck before letting him go. He waved at me and cantered off to another part of the ballroom.

"Liz, can I have the next dance?" asked Alec, leaning over my shoulder. "I'm a great dancer; it'd be a shame for you not to experience my skills."

I rolled my eyes but accepted his invitation anyway. Another upbeat dance ensued, and Alec and I spent the entire thing making faces and laughing. I wasn't expecting to have much fun at such a formal party, but I was having a great time. At the end, Alec bowed and thanked me before walking away—but not before I caught his eyes shift to someone behind me.

"Elizabeth!" exclaimed Devin. He approached me, holding his arms out in front of him and gesturing to my dress. "You look amazing!"

"Devin!"

"My, you look splendid! Every man I've seen has glanced your way more than once, you know."

I rolled my eyes. "I doubt that."

As he drew closer, I noticed the dark spots around his eyes. Gasping, I held my hand up to the bruises. "What happened to you?"

"An accident," he said, pulling away. "Nothing important."

I didn't push him. Instead, I let my arm fall to rest at

my side. "So, what brings you here?"

"You, of course. I couldn't pass up the opportunity to see you again."

He watched the couples beside us as they arranged themselves for another dance. "Speaking of which, could I have the next dance?"

"Sure. I must warn you, though, I have two left feet."

"I'm well enough acquainted with you, Miss Elizabeth, that it is no matter to me. Step on my feet a hundred times, if you want."

"You really shouldn't offer things like that. You'll lose your toes by the end of the night."

He shook his head, laughing.

I joined him and we prepared to begin the dance. This one was very similar to the previous one I had danced with Ed. The music was upbeat and fun, and the couples laughed and jumped. The bystanders in the room clapped to the beat.

"How are things here?" he asked. "I heard you had quite a scare last night. The village was buzzing."

"It was nothing, really," I said.

"You know, you could always write something in that book of yours to change everything up," he offered. "You could probably write some way to get rid of this Night Rider."

I frowned. "I don't know if it works like that. Even if it did, I'm not sure I'd want to do that. I don't know who this person is or even what his story is, and I don't want to be the one to stand in front of what should be. Writing in the Book almost feels wrong, like I'm trying to bend things to my will."

"You're an interesting character, Elizabeth," Devin said with a chuckle. "I hope we stay in touch. I haven't found anyone like you in a long time. You're a gem."

"That's kind of you. I'd like to stay in touch."

"May I cut in?" I heard a voice say. I turned to see Joey, his stare hard and cold. I raised an eyebrow.

Rude much?

"Of course," Devin said with a bow. "She's all yours."

"Thanks," Joey bit in a monotone, promptly taking Devin's place. Devin gave me an apologetic smile before bowing.

"Until next time, Elizabeth," he said, winking before disappearing into the crowd. Joey muttered something under his breath that I couldn't quite understand, though I'm not sure that I wanted to know what it was.

As soon as the blond boy was out of sight, Joey's face relaxed and he flashed me a smile.

"Want to dance?"

"Do I have much choice?" I asked, smiling back at him. Dancing sounded like fun, especially with Joey, but I was terrified I would step on his feet and ruin everything.

"Don't worry," he said as the music slowed, "just follow my lead, like before."

He took my hand and the dance began.

I watched the women around me, trying to copy their movements as well as let Joey lead. I was glad that it was an easy dance to remember.

Joey chuckled. "Not so bad, is it?"

"I'll let you know when it's over," I said, my eyes trained on my feet to make sure I did the right steps.

"Look at me," he said, tilting my head up with his fingers, "I promise it makes it easier."

We danced the entire dance in one piece, surprisingly. As much as I hated to admit it, it worked. I did, however, have a permanent blush on my cheeks. The way his eyes pierced mine sent chills down my back, and he smirked at me the entire time, as if he knew something I didn't.

I treaded carefully with my words. "So… Care to tell me why you're acting like a jerk towards Devin?"

He sighed, the cheerful smile disappearing into a thin line. "We've been over this, Elizabeth."

"Your suspicions don't give you an excuse to treat him like you're better than he is," I reasoned.

"I am better than he is. I don't betray my family, or my country for that matter. I may have stood up for him at the meeting with the nobles, but I don't think he's working with us. It would make more sense that he's working against us."

I groaned. "Joey, quit acting like you're superior to him. How would you like it if I treated you like that?"

"It'd be for good reason if you did. I'm sure I'd deserve it."

I remained silent until the dance ended.

We clapped, bowing to one another before the dance floor residents dispersed.

"I'll see you later," I said coldly, backing away from Joey. I caught his expression flash with hurt for a split second before I turned my back on him.

Desperate for a change of atmosphere, I searched for Ed. He wasn't dancing, and he wasn't leaning against a wall. He wasn't running around with the village boys like I thought he'd be, either.

As I circled the room, I noticed a young girl in a pale pink tulle dress standing next to a tall man wearing tails. A crown adorned his head.

He must be the king of the kingdom to the east, I thought. *Baile.*

My gaze shifted to the girl who appeared to be about Ed's age. She had flowing blonde hair, and her dress reached her ankles, revealing her polished flat shoes. Her eyes were a brilliant shade of blue. From where I stood, she seemed absolutely perfect.

That must be Aileen.

My gaze traveled around the room. *Didn't Joey say that Ed was supposed to spend time with her?* Yet, I couldn't seem to find him anywhere.

Making my way back to the entrance of the ballroom, I walked back through the large doors and out into the hallway. People were scattered through the corridor, leaning against walls with drinks in hand. Young women flirted with militia, married couples walked arm in arm, and children skipped together.

Weaving between people, I searched for Ed through the hallways, but he was nowhere to be found.

Maybe he's in the library. He uses that place as an escape on a daily basis.

I climbed the staircases until I got to the third floor that held the library. I heard books being shuffled on the bookcases as I approached the door.

"Ed?"

Ed turned around, a large book in his hand.

"Hey. Come to get away from the party?"

"No, just to find you," I answered. "Why'd you leave?"

"I was bored," he lied.

"Liar. You know Aileen is looking for you downstairs, right?"

He shot me a glare.

"I don't want to dance with her, Liz. I don't see why I have to."

"Because she's here for you. It's your birthday; why

not have a little fun?"

"Dancing with a little girl isn't fun," he grumbled.

"She's not little; she's one year younger than you."

He sighed in aggravation. "Elizabeth, did you seriously come up here just to tell me to go back downstairs?"

I shrugged. "You don't have to. I just thought it'd be nice. She seemed pretty bummed out."

Ed raised an eyebrow. "Bummed out?"

"Yep. Very disappointed."

"She doesn't even know me. We've literally met twice."

"So? Now she has no dance partner."

Putting the book back on the shelf, he stepped around another bookcase out of sight and shifted the books around again.

"Elizabeth, I don't really want to get involved in this. Not yet, at least. I'm too young to be betrothed to anyone."

"I'm glad you realize that," I said, nodding.

"Joey realizes it too. He's just thinking of the kingdom."

I put a comforting hand on his shoulder.

"Well," I said, turning back towards the door, "since you're okay up here, I'll go back down to the party. It's a birthday party, after all; I need a piece of the cake."

He didn't say anything as I left the room.

fifteen

Moments later, after I had returned to the ballroom, I noticed Ed slip back into the room. He hesitantly approached Aileen, weaving through people until he got to her. She turned to face him, offering a nervous but polite smile as he spoke. I couldn't hear what they were saying, but he bowed and offered his hand, and she smiled and nodded.

"What're you smiling at?" a voice asked in my ear.

I jumped, spinning around on my heel. I grimaced, punching Joey on the shoulder as he came into view.

"Would you stop doing that?" I exclaimed. "You scare me every time."

"That's the point," he chuckled, rubbing his arm and looking on at Ed and Aileen who had taken the floor. "So, you convinced him to dance?"

"Maybe," I said in satisfaction. "He's a good kid. I knew that when I told him that Aileen was disappointed, he would come to her rescue."

"He doesn't like to disappoint people in general," Joey said. "We're nothing alike, and I'm so jealous of him."

I raised an eyebrow. "I thought you had no interest in being king, Joey."

"I don't. I'm talking about his character. He's kind to everyone, no matter who they are, and it's amazing. I don't know how he does it."

I chuckled at him before turning back towards the floor. "I think you're more alike than you give yourself credit for."

Out of the corner of my eye, I saw him look at me, but I pretended not to notice.

"Do you want to dance?" he asked suddenly.

"Again?"

"Why not?"

He held out a hand for me, and surprising myself, I took it.

The dance was slow. It was a different kind of dance from the others we'd participated in; this one was a waltz, the kind I'd only seen in movies. Surprisingly, Joey didn't say anything to me the entire dance. He watched me but never said a word.

When he finally spoke against my ear, it sent a chill down my spine. "Come with me." He took my hand in his and led me through the ballroom. I decided not to argue this time.

He took me through the doors at the far end of the room and out onto the balcony. From there, he led me down a set of stone stairs into the gardens. We entered the maze from a different entrance than usual.

"Where are we going?" I asked.

"We need to talk," he answered.

He led me through the maze by the hand, the music fading the farther we got. When we reached a small, round clearing, he stopped, turning to face me. We could still see the balcony and the lights coming from the ballroom over the shrubbery.

"This world you've jumped into..." he started, his eyes traveling down to our hands, "it isn't perfect, you know. We have problems, some worse than what you could imagine."

"I know," I answered quietly, watching him. "I don't want to leave either way."

"We're imperfect. We're in pieces, and we're barely holding on."

"I know what I'm dealing with. If I couldn't handle it, I would've left long ago."

"You don't care that our world isn't all it could be? We're a broken world, Elizabeth. We have as many problems here as your world does."

I shook my head. "No, I don't care. No home is perfect, but this one is as close to perfect than I've ever been in. I'm aware of all the risks of my being here."

"Then I can't deny it anymore," he said, letting go of my hand and taking a few steps away from me. His back was to me, tensed as his arms came up to rub his face. "It's so utterly frustrating. You're driving me insane. You're stubborn, oblivious, annoying, and I *can't stand*—"

"I'm sorry?" I asked, sounding more like a question than an apology. I was confused as to why he brought me all the way out here to complain about how much he didn't like me. "I thought we'd been through how much dislike runs between us already."

"I don't hate you," he said.

"I know." I remembered, thinking about the night I

had gone out into the woods alone. Joey had made it perfectly clear that I wasn't his favorite person in the world.

But so much has changed.

"Elizabeth," he cut me off, finally facing me, "I like you, okay? I more than like you. I've tried my best to keep it to myself, but it isn't working. I understand that you're afraid to get too attached to us because you don't want to be heartbroken if you're forced to leave, but you don't understand that some things are just worth it. You're already horribly attached to Ed, and you don't even realize it. You love it here, admit it."

"I don't understand what you want from me, Joey."

"I love you."

I felt the weight of my heart drop to my stomach where it was surrounded by a strong feeling of butterflies. "*What?*" I asked, shocked. "What did you just say?"

"I love you. I have for a while now. I just couldn't find the courage to tell you."

"That's impossible," I said, the thoughts running frantically through my head. Every possible bad outcome seemed to suddenly become clear to me, and I could feel the anxiety building in my chest. "You can't love me. What happens if something happens to me? To you? We're both going to be in so much pain. I can't put you through that, I can't—"

"Elizabeth?" he interrupted, taking a step closer.

"Yes?" I asked, my voice almost a whisper. He was so close; I had to tilt my chin up at him now.

His hands came up to cup my face. "Shut up," he said.

Before I could even respond with an "okay," Joey's lips were against mine. The butterflies that I had become so used to erupted into flurries in my stomach in a whole new sensation that overtook me. The heat rushed to my face under his fingertips.

He leaned his forehead against mine as he pulled away, after what felt like mere seconds.

"Do you believe me now?" he breathed.

I nodded, my eyes still closed, trying to catch my breath. When I opened them, he had tilted his head up to look at the sky, but he kept a hand on my cheek.

"I don't expect you to feel the same way as I do," he said after a while.

I stayed silent. Sure, I liked Joey more than I could have planned, but was I ready to invest my emotions so much and have my heart ripped out if something went wrong and I was sent back to the real world?

"I don't know what to say."

"You don't have to say anything," he reasoned. "Just think about it."

Should I tell him or not? I know how I feel; there's no doubt in my mind. I know what I want.

But Liz, what happened to not getting hurt?

Just as I opened my mouth to reply, a strangled yell came through the open doors on the balcony.

"Fire! Fire in the Forum!"

sixteen

Gut-wrenching screams emitted from the ballroom and then the sound of hundreds of pairs of feet after. We caught sight of Ed and Alec sprinting down the stone steps of the balcony and down into the maze with us.

"This way!" Ed called, taking my hand and pulling me behind him. Joey and I ran with him down a deserted path towards the village. The smoke was thick, and we could smell it all the way up the hill.

"Alec and I are going this way to make sure no civilians are injured," Joey said, pointing to a road that would take him in front of the Forum. "You go the other way; get people as far away from the damage as possible! Ed, get back in the castle!"

"Not a chance!" Ed yelled. He took off towards the Forum at full speed with me at his heels before Joey could say a word.

Ed and I pushed through the crowd, scrambling to find an open space so that we could get a look at the roaring chaos. We stopped, standing right in front of the burning marketplace. Flames covered everything, licking rooftops and stretching towards the night sky. My jaw dropped open at the intensity of the scene that surrounded us. "Who would do this?"

My question seemed to be answered right away when I caught a glimpse of a dark shadow standing across the Forum from the crowd. He seemed to stare right at us then turned slowly, running off into the night.

Ed and I seemed to be the only ones to notice him.

"I could think of someone. It's an omen," he said. "Something bad is going to happen, and soon."

"I think it already has," I said, gaping at the chaos. A building had collapsed, and the sparks ignited the homes next to it. Within seconds, the fire spread, and massive parts of the village were burning.

"I'm going to help!" Before I could interject, Ed sprinted off into the throng of people.

"Ed!" I pushed past people, trying to catch up with him.

"Elizabeth!" I heard him yell. "Hurry!"

"Ed!"

I couldn't see him anymore, and that worried me. Fire, people, and chaos surrounded me, and I feared for not only my life but Ed's as well.

When I saw him, my stomach dropped.

He stood in front of a young boy and a young girl. The distraught girl cried as her brother held her, trying to shield her from the flames.

While Ed showed them where to step to get out of their burning cottage, I sprinted past everyone, my shoes slipping off in the process. I didn't care; the tight shoes from the palace had been pinching my feet since I put them on, and they were holding me back.

Free to run faster, I made it to Ed just in time for the boy and girl to reach the flaming doorway. I reached across a fallen beam, picking up first the girl and then the boy, pointing towards the lake and yelling at them to run and not to stop until someone came for them. The young boy took his sister's hand and pulled her along through the streets.

"Ed," I breathed, reaching for his hand.

"No!" he yelled, and I flinched, pulling my hand back just in time for another beam to fall, shooting sparks up in between us. The bottom of my dress caught fire, burning my leg—I smothered it as fast as I could, ignoring the tears that fell from the pain.

"Ed!" The beams continued to creak, sliding down farther towards the ground. Hot stones fell and rolled around my feet.

"Run, Liz," he said. "I'll find another way out."

"No. There's no way I'm leaving you."

His voice became tight and angry. "Go!"

I yelled with just as much force. "No, Ed. I'm getting you out of here."

I pulled at the beams, managing to shift one to the side before I slit my hand on a splintered section. I ignored it, the adrenaline pushing me towards the goal—getting Edward out alive.

"Come on," I said, reached once more, straining at the weight. Thankfully, he latched onto my hand, and I pulled him towards me.

"Elizabeth, watch out!"

The roof creaked, and the flames burned all the way through. Just before Ed could climb out, the roof started to fall. Ed dropped my hand, and I stumbled back.

"No!"

The burning wood and hot stones created a wall between us, and I could no longer hear his voice.

"Ed!"

There was no response.

A body ran into me, knocking me to the ground. Joey's familiar voice spoke frantically in my ear. "Elizabeth, where's Ed?"

He held a hand out to help me up.

"He was helping two kids, and then I tried to get him out, and then..." I trailed off, unable to make out a coherent sentence. I pointed towards the pile, my face contorted with pain.

"He's in there?" he asked incredulously. I nodded.

"Help me, quick," he said, reaching down to the fiery wood. Together, we pulled the scorching wooden beams and rolled searing hot stones away, trying to make a path into the house. We moved them, one by one, with blistering hands. The roof creaked at the shifted weight.

"Wait," he said, holding a hand in front of me. "It'll cave in. This hole is big enough for me to crawl in and grab him; do you think you can hold this steady?"

I took a beam from his grasp, causing more creaking sounds to emit from the house. It was so heavy, but the adrenaline running through my veins made it so that I hardly noticed.

"Go," I breathed, "and hurry."

Joey crawled into the hole, disappearing into the hot coals.

I held for as long as I could. The beam started slipping, and now, not only was I afraid for Ed, I was afraid for Joey too.

"Hurry, Joey!"

As soon as I saw Joey's soot-covered hair, I knew I

could let go. The beam fell with a giant thud to the ground and in a pillar of ash. Joey fell to the ground with Ed, limp in his arms.

I fell to my knees in exhaustion, pulling Ed up to me and crying into his shoulder.

"Liz," he said quietly, his hand covering mine. I gasped, trying to see through my tears. He was covered from head to toe in black, and everything smelled like smoke. His face was cut, burned and scraped. Despite the chaos around us, he gave me a weak smile, his eyes closed.

"You're okay."

"Yeah, I'm okay," I told him, sniffling. "You're going to be okay too."

His smile faded.

"Liz?"

I took a deep breath to stop the hiccups. "Yes?"

He opened his eyes. Not much, but it was nice to see those sparkling green eyes again. Tears fell from them, and his face contorted in pain.

"It hurts, Elizabeth." His hand formed a fist and his knuckles turned white as the color drained from his face. I felt something wet under my hand, and I realized that there was a large wood splinter in his side. Blood streamed from his side, soaking his shirt dark red.

"I know," I said, trying to stay calm, "I know it hurts. It's going to be okay. Joey?" Joey moved to my side, doing his best to hold pressure to Edward's side.

"Take care of Joey, please," he whispered. "You're good for him."

I shook my head. "No, you will," I said, almost pleading with him. "You will, Ed." I peered through teary eyes at Joey, silently pleading him to tell me what I should do.

Joey took one look at his brother, mouth open and eyebrows furrowed, like he had no answer.

Ed shook his head, stopping in pain at the sudden movement. His hand stretched towards Joey. Joey moved immediately, taking his brother's hand and holding it with both of his own.

"I love you, Joey," he murmured. Joey gave him a small smile, his eyes glimmering with tears not yet formed.

"I love you too, kiddo."

"Take care of her?"

"If that's what you want. I will, Ed. With everything I have."

"I'll tell Dad you said hello," he said. "He'd be so proud of you."

Joey shook his head. "He'll be more proud of you. You're so brave. Keep fighting, Edward. You'll be okay." Tears fell from Joey's eyes as he squeezed his brother's hand.

Ed smiled. His shaking hand found his waistcoat pocket and pulled out the necklace, which he handed to me. He was in unbearable pain—his jaw tensed as he raised his hand, more tears slipping from his eyes. It was painful to witness; he tried so hard to be strong.

I forced a smile at him, letting the tears roll down my cheeks and I held him close. He cried with me, gripping my arm with his weak hands before I felt his grip loosen. I pulled away with a gasp, trying to figure out what to do.

Joey pulled Edward from me, holding his brother's limp body as he struggled to breath. When Edward's head fell against Joey, I knew it was over.

Edward had given up.

Joey let out a strangled breath, falling back off of his knees. He stared at the ground, the emotion and color drained from his face.

I sat, closing my eyes as the fires raged around us, until they burned down to dying embers, one by one. The Forum became deserted, and I stayed on the ground, refusing to acknowledge the tears sliding down my face or the unbearable, deafening silence.

We sat in the quiet as the smoke rose into the air and disappeared, along with every ounce of hope left in me.

seventeen

The sun had broken through the horizon, and a heavy rainfall had long since put out the fires. A mixture of smoke and vapor filled the air and drifted up from piles of debris that used to be homes. My dress, soaked with rain, tears, and blood, looked like a battlefield.

I didn't feel the cold. I didn't feel anything.

Edward was back in my arms. I'd pulled him back to me after Joey fell to the ground next to his brother, refusing to look at him.

Refusing to accept it.

Right then and there, the realization hit me.

The family I'd depended on, the only one I'd ever had—it was gone, ripped from my life.

I didn't dare move. I knew as soon as I got up, someone would take him from us, and the next time I saw him would be in a casket surrounded by the ghosts of people wearing black. All of these people would send their mind elsewhere for the entire ceremony; they'd forget him for hours until they could deal with the grief.

I couldn't do that to him.

He deserved more than that, more than a few words of solace to ease the minds of a few bothered citizens and his illegitimate brother and a pretty casket to be piled with dirt.

"Elizabeth." Joey's soft voice rang out from behind me.

His cold hand rested on my shoulder. His voice was tighter, more controlled than it had been hours ago.

I didn't look at him.

"Liz, we need to take him to the castle. You're freezing, and it wouldn't do him any good for you to die of hypothermia."

He was silent, waiting for some sort of reaction from me.

"He died by fire, I'll die by ice," I murmured, sniffling and holding him closer to me. Joey sighed and sat down next to me, opening his cloak and wrapping it around the both of us. He took Ed's head in his lap as we held the small boy together in silence.

"When we go back there," I whispered, "it'll all be over. He'll really be gone. Here, I can pretend that he's asleep, that we're just resting before we have to get up and run again."

"You can't be afraid of going back, Elizabeth."

I scoffed through angry tears. "I'm not afraid of going back. I'm afraid of being alone."

It was true. Being alone did the worst things to me, gave me the worst thoughts, scared me more than anything else ever could. All I had ever known was being alone... until I'd found Ed. Now that I'd had a taste of what family felt like, I wasn't sure I could bear going back.

This was so much worse than being alone.

Joey's hand came to my face, turning me towards him. When I took the time to step back and look, I realized that he was just as much affected by this as I was.

Yes, I loved Ed, but Joey was *his brother.* He could have a million friends in the world to try to fill the void, but Joey would only ever have one brother.

"You aren't alone, Elizabeth. I'm here, and I'm not going anywhere."

His eyes were red when he looked at me, trying to give me some sort of comfort I knew that he didn't even have himself. My eyes filled with tears. I reached over to hug him around the neck. Joey gave me a strange feeling, one that was almost comforting and protective. I felt safe.

He rubbed my arms, trying to create some warmth. I felt the cold pierce my arms then—it was almost as if Joey had made me remember and brought me back to reality.

In the silence, I heard Joey begin to weep. I rubbed his back with my hand, the only thing I could think of to do. We stayed in the empty Forum for another few minutes while he let everything out. When at last he pulled away, he dried his eyes and stood up, offering a hand to me.

I sniffled, looking down at Ed one last time before standing and handing him over to Joseph. He took Edward up in his arms. Covered in Joey's cloak, I walked beside him, looping my arm through his and leaning against his shoulder. The silence was cold and empty, nothing but our footsteps echoing among the almost deserted Forum.

Step after step, we gradually made it to the front gates. The guards opened the iron-barred gates without a word, and Cyneward gave me a solemn glance before straightening his back and resuming his post. I noticed the pity and remorse in his eyes but chose to ignore it. It made me feel so helpless.

"Cyneward," I rasped, "send out a horseman to ride the perimeter of Devereux. I sent a boy and girl out to avoid the fire, and they'll be out towards the lake until someone decides to get them."

He nodded. We continued to the castle.

The castle was long empty; all of the guests had left when the fires broke out. I was glad that we wouldn't have to deal with questions I wouldn't know how to answer or see the hundreds dressed in pristine gowns while ours were covered in soot.

A servant met us at the castle doors, crying out when she saw Ed's body. She gasped, running back towards the kitchen, her hand over her mouth. I hugged Joey's cloak around my body tighter as I heard a shrill, ear-piercing scream.

Just like that, the news was out. Servants rushed to the foyer from every part of the castle to see the truth for themselves. The women fell to their knees in tears, and the men bowed their heads in respect. Joey paid no attention to them.

Alec rushed into the room, covered in soot. He looked relieved to see us, but his face fell as he noticed Ed's limp body in Joey's arms.

"*Bloody hell*," he said under his breath, eyes wide. "What happened?" His gaze was fixed on Ed. "He's not—is he…?"

Joey didn't answer. He just shook his head, looking at the ground and leading me down the corridor and away from the crowd. I looked over my shoulder finding Alec on his knees, still facing the door we came through.

The warmth from the fire in the dark parlor should have made me feel better, but in all honesty, it made everything worse. Joey laid Ed on a sofa directly in front of the fireplace and plopped down in front of it, facing the hot coals. He turned and looked at me, moving the coffee table and patting the spot next to him on the floor.

Hesitantly, I obliged, slowly approaching the couch. I tried not to look at Ed because I knew that the second I did, I would disappear into a puddle of tears. I saw him out of the corner of my eye, but resisted the temptation. Sitting down next to Joey, I took the cloak off my back and handed it back to him.

"Keep it," he said, shaking his head. "You need it more than I do."

I wrapped it back around my body, moving the fabric so that it covered the bloodstains—Edward's bloodstains—on my dress. I didn't want to look at them.

The fire taunted me. I couldn't keep my eyes away from it; it was almost as if I was afraid it would jump out and consume me. I had never been afraid of fire before, but it seemed that now it terrified me. I squirmed in my spot, terribly uncomfortable.

"It's bothering you too, isn't it?" Joey asked without looking at me, his eyes trained on the flames.

I forced myself to speak. "Yeah, it is."

Sadly, everything that used to be comforting was now a bother; Joey's breathing didn't help because it reminded me of Ed's shallow breaths. The warmth of the fire did nothing to soothe my nerves and my chapped skin when fire was the very cause of Ed's demise.

In the silence, the bell tolled once. I pulled away from Joey, putting my head in my hands.

"Bloody hell," he whispered, his breathing ragged as the loud ringing resonated in our ears.

This could have all been prevented, my conscience hissed at me. *If you'd kept reading the journal, you would've known this would happen.*

I opened my eyes, shaking my head and trying to dry the tears forming in my eyes.

"Elizabeth?" Joey's hand found mine and held it.

I looked at him once more, seeing my reflection in his eyes and feeling more guilt pile on my shoulders. I didn't even try to stop the tears now, ignoring them as they rolled down my cheeks and onto my lap.

"He could be alive right now," I said with a quivering voice. "He could be alive if it weren't for me."

"What do you mean?"

"I mean exactly what it sounds like," I said, my angry voice raising. I was a mess, drowning in my own guilt.

"Elizabeth, enough," Joey said sternly. "This isn't your fault, and you know it. You didn't start the fire. You didn't make that house fall in on him. You read the Book, El, and nothing was there. Some things just… happen. Don't blame yourself, please."

I didn't answer.

"Elizabeth," he said my full name again, "you read the Book. Right?"

The realization in his eyes was painful to watch.

"You didn't read it."

Once again, I didn't answer.

He ran his hand through his hair in frustration, cursing under his breath. When his fist came down on the short coffee table, I jumped, burying my face in my hands and sobbing. When I peered through my fingers,

Joey had stood up and walked to the door.

"Joseph, wait!" I called, trying to think of some excuse to get him to stay.

His back tensed.

"I asked *so little* of you, Elizabeth," he said. I cringed, the tone in his voice angry and hurt but somehow dead at the same time. "All I asked was that you read the Book and tell me anything that happened. I wanted us to be *prepared* for something like this, and now look what you've done... My little brother is dead, and it's *your fault.*"

His image was blurry through the tears that flowed down my cheeks. I knew everything he was saying was right, and that's what hurt the most—taking in the reality that it was all my fault.

His hands were clenched into tight fists at his sides. His knuckles turned white. "You're a *murderer.* Stay away from me."

He left without another look back.

eighteen

I lay in bed the entire day, not finding the will to sleep. Three times a maid came in, trying to force me to eat, and three times I sent her away, stating simply that I wasn't hungry. The sun went into hiding during the day, a thick layer of gray clouds covering it as if even the sky went into mourning over the loss of the boy.

When the clock struck eight, Margaret, teary eyed and worn, came in. She did not speak at all, and I gave her no help in changing out of the once beautiful dress, now tattered, dirty, and covered in soot. Burn marks were scattered along the skirt.

She folded it up along with Joey's cloak before placing them on the chair. A nightgown slid down my arms and over my head, and she disappeared into the bathroom only to return moments later with a wet cloth. The water washed the dirt off my face, legs, and arms until there wasn't a spot left on my skin. Bandages were drawn out from a drawer, and my hands were cleaned and wrapped as well as the various burns, scrapes, and cuts scattered on my body. Then she left, as silently as she came, but not before I made her take the Book of Aon with her.

"I don't want it," I said, my gaze fixed on the ceiling. "I don't want it in here. I want it gone. Take it to Yula."

She looked like she wanted to protest but decided against it and took it from my room, relieving me of the horrible paranoia it had created in my brain. It taunted me with what could've been and what I could've done.

I crawled back into bed to try to sleep, but I knew very well that my attempts were futile. I eyed Joey's cloak that laid across the chair in the corner, waiting to be returned to him. I never got up the nerve to even take it to his door.

––––

For the first time in ten years, my nightmare was different.

I don't know how much time passed before the fiery images of burning buildings flooded my mind. The fire grew big, surrounding me. On one side, Ed stood, encircled by the flames. On the other, Joey stood with the journal clutched in his hand.

I'm sorry, Ed, I tried to say. *I'm sorry this happened.*

Ed only shook his head.

I'll never forgive you for what you've done, Joey said. *You've taken my brother from me, and nothing you can do will fix it.*

I didn't mean for any of this to happen, I reasoned.

Doesn't matter, he argued. *It did. Now there's nothing you can do but watch.*

Joey pointed over to Ed, still standing silent in the circle. The flames advanced on him, the circle growing smaller and smaller.

Ed! I called, but it was too late. Right as the fire reached him, fire flooded my vision.

I woke up screaming that night.

The next few days after the incident didn't come any easier. Slowly, the villagers trickled into the palace, some asking for food, some for money, and some just asking to step inside for a minute or two of warmth. Many came for help, but all came to pay respects to the fallen prince. The cold air pierced the skin of any who walked the steep path to the palace. *Seasons changed very rapidly here*, I noted, remembering how it was summer when I had arrived.

Right foot, left foot, right foot again. I felt nothing, heard nothing.

Those nights, I didn't go back to sleep after waking up from the nightmares. Deathly afraid of the same scenario reappearing in my dreams, I wandered the hallways in my nightgown, not even bothering to change. My hair was in a mangled braid on my shoulder, and my arms were wrapped around my body, trying to hold all of the pieces together.

Shadows hit the walls from the moonlight and made me feel confined, and the rain hit the windows harshly. The seemingly never-ending corridors gave me plenty of places to walk without being bothered by anyone. Part of me hoped to see Joey somewhere, maybe doing just what I was doing, but part of me didn't want to see him at all. The latter part was pleased when I didn't find him roaming the corridors like me.

One night, I leaned against the wall, wearing Joey's cloak in the chilled air of the castle, staring out at the rain that seemed to have taken permanent residence in Aon. It seemed as though the world was in mourning. All the doors in the hallway were closed tightly, not a single speck of light escaping from the cracks. Only one door sat slightly ajar, but the sliver of space that barely separated the door from the frame only held more darkness that I could not see through. I ignored it, my gaze staying straight ahead of me.

As I moved my feet once again to continue my walk, the door behind me closed. I turned, expecting to see someone coming out of the room, but I had no such luck. I was relieved to not have to face anyone.

I rubbed the fabric of Joey's cloak between my fingers. It still smelled like smoke. As I remembered the night it was given to me, scenes of fire and destruction flashed before my eyes. The cloak suddenly weighed heavily on my shoulders, as if it held all of my guilt. It threatened to drag me to the ground.

I decided enough was enough. I dropped it in the hallway and kept walking. My walks continued without interruption after that.

When I finally got up the courage to appear downstairs at mealtimes, I didn't eat anything. I walked back to the room where I had sat with Joey before.

Ed was gone.

I didn't expect him to still be there—honestly, I didn't. Seeing the room empty, however... It only tugged at my mind and threatened to drag me back to reality.

Where he had laid was a white sheet, covering the sofa, and a black rose. In front of his portrait on the wall was a small table with a candle and more black roses like the first.

If I were normal, I would've at least reacted, but I didn't. I looked at the boy on the wall as if I didn't know him; I pretended I had never seen his face before. It didn't seem to make a difference.

My bare feet ached and felt even colder than my body, but I kept walking. Anything to keep me from falling asleep somewhere and seeing those images all over again. I returned to my room, but sat on the floor, studying the drops of dew and rain on the glass of the window.

Eventually, I did fall asleep, and when I did, the nightmare was worse than the first.

This time, I watched the entire thing happen over again. I followed Ed through the crowd, seeing him help the little boy and girl. I helped them out, told them to run, and when I looked back at Ed, I couldn't move. I was paralyzed, and I could only watch the house cave and the stones roll in the burning coals. Ed cried my name, but I was helpless.

Joey knocked me over, just like before. This time he didn't help me up.

You get to watch, he said, holding up the journal. *You should've known this would happen.*

Please, don't make me watch, I pleaded. *This isn't you, Joey.*

But there was no answer.

The beams fell in front of the doorway, and I watched as the flames consumed everything.

The entire week was a repeat of each dream, walking around like a zombie, not feeling anything. Margaret managed to force a little food down my throat, but I didn't eat willingly.

At midnight, there was a soft knock on my door. Not even acknowledging the fact that it was very late at night, I called, "I'm not hungry," to the unwanted visitor. My eyes burned from lack of sleep and nightmare-induced tears, and I didn't have the energy to speak to anyone.

"Good," said Joey's quiet voice as he stepped in and

softly shut the door behind him. "I don't have anything for you."

I sat up, eyes wide. I couldn't find any words.

He lingered awkwardly at the door. There was a moment of quiet, and then he spoke, his voice hoarse and low. "I'm sorry."

I looked down, conflicted on whether or not I should tell him to leave.

He took a step towards me. "It wasn't your fault."

I shook my head, feeling the tears spring to my eyes as soon as he spoke. "You had every right to be angry," I reasoned, "because if I hadn't lied about reading the entire journal then I could've prevented this."

Joey took another step forward, shaking his head back at me. "You're wrong, El."

I frowned. "But I—"

"You can't change what's written in the Book," he explained. "When have we ever been able to change what's already there in ink?"

I thought for a moment, shrugging my shoulders when I came up with no answer. The tears threatened to spill, but I held them back as best I could.

"That's right," he said, taking another step, "because we haven't. It's impossible. You can ask Yula; even if we had known, there would've been nothing you could've done about it. Quite honestly, I've thought about it, and it was probably better that we didn't know. Would you have wanted Ed to worry about it until it actually happened?"

I had to say I agreed with him. It would've been horrible to watch Ed obsess over what was yet to come instead of enjoy the time he had left.

"Don't blame yourself," he breathed, closing the gap. It seemed that I had cried enough for a year in the last week, but right then, I didn't care. I let the tears slip through, crying for Ed and the guilt that Joey had seemed to wash away within a few sentences.

His hands dried the tears from my cheeks, ignoring his own that spilled down his face. My arms wrapped around his neck, and he pulled me to my feet.

Once again, I felt comfort in Joey's arms.

"I miss him," I cried, holding him tightly.

"Me too, El," he said, stroking my hair. "I miss him too."

I relaxed at the sound of my name. It was so familiar, so comforting, almost like the feeling you get when you go home after a long time. That was it—I was home. This was home.

He pulled back to look at me, wiping the tears from my cheeks.

"You have no reason to feel guilty. It wasn't your fault." His own tears rolled down his cheeks as he spoke his next words, his voice coming out broken and tired. "You aren't a murderer. I never should have said that to you."

I offered him what little of a smile I could muster up, taking my turn to wipe the tears from his face. His eyes closed, and he leaned into my hand.

With a burst of confidence, I leaned in and kissed Joey. It surprised him, but he only hugged me tighter and kissed me back. I was so comfortable with him—I felt safe. I didn't feel alone.

He pulled away, hugging me and burying his head into my shoulder. "Are you okay?"

I rested my chin on his shoulder. "Are you?"

"I will be." His grip on me loosened, and he pressed a kiss to my forehead before letting go.

"Go to sleep." His hand pushed my loose hair back

behind my ear. "You look like a zombie."

"I might as well be," I said. "I feel like one."

"I'll let you sleep, then," he said. "I'll see you tomorrow."

My hand reached out and grabbed his before he could leave. He looked down at our hands, then up at me.

Normally, I'd be blushing like crazy, but I wasn't surprised that I didn't. I had been so cold and felt no emotion for so long that my body had almost forgotten what embarrassment felt like.

"Don't leave. Please," I said, "not again."

He seemed to hesitate, thinking it over.

"I'll sleep on the floor," he stated, turning back towards me. Without question, he made a place to sleep with a couple pillows and the extra blankets in the corner of my room. He kissed me on the forehead, as if it were something routine, before lying down to sleep.

I felt better after that. I lay down and closed my eyes, sleep finally taking over after almost a week of horror, sorrow, and terrifying loneliness. None of that seemed to bother me as I fell asleep with Joey on the floor next to me.

The nightmares that night were intense. I woke up screaming again, scaring Joey. He shot up. When he caught sight of me, his shoulders sagged, and he let out a sigh of relief before sitting on the edge of the bed and holding my shaking hands.

"I- I'm s- sorry," I said between crying hiccups, pulling my knees closer to my body. "I didn't mean to w-wake you."

He shook his head and gave me that sad, crooked smile. "It's okay," he reasoned, wrapping his arms around me. I closed my eyes and took a deep breath, trying to calm myself down. His hand stroked my hair.

"Are you okay?" he asked.

I nodded, still trying to stifle the hiccups and sobs that wouldn't go away.

He picked up a blanket off of the floor and sat on top of my comforter, using the blanket as a cover. His arm came around me, and he held me close to his chest.

Joey was a gentleman through and through.

I leaned my head against his shoulder and tried to find sleep again, fighting back the flames of the fire that pierced my mind before. His voice came softly through the dark.

"Go to sleep, Liz. I'm here."

———

The next morning, sunshine streamed through the windows. I felt better than I had in days, and my mood instantly improved when I realized that I had made it through the rest of the night without dreaming.

Joey stirred next to me, his hand adjusting so our fingers were interlocked. "Morning," he said, rubbing his eyes.

"Morning," I said, looking at him. I didn't bother slipping the word *good* in there.

He sighed, rubbing the back of my hand with his thumb, his eyes still closed. "His funeral is today, you know."

Actually, I didn't know. I'd been so selfishly trapped in my own bubble that I hadn't heard when—or if—anyone had tried to mention it to me.

"Are you going?" I questioned softly. He scoffed.

"Did you just ask me if I'm going to *my little brother's* funeral?"

"I'm sorry," I said, shifting my gaze to the window. "I guess I'm just selfish. I don't think I'll be able to handle seeing him... you know."

"Hey," he said, his hand turning my face back to look at him, "it'll be okay. Besides, I need you there with me. I can't do this without you."

I nodded.

"After all," he continued, slightly quieter, "we aren't the only ones who can't cope. The village needs to be comforted. We can't let them lose hope, or Aon will crumble."

I had to agree with him, even though I hadn't seen anyone besides Joey since before Ed's death. Devereux adored the little prince, and I was almost afraid to see what it was like outside the walls of the castle.

"I promised myself that I wouldn't shut him out," I said, leaning into his hand, "but I looked at his portrait and pretended that I'd never seen him in my life."

"That was a tricky promise to make," he said, looking down at the hands we'd intertwined. "You know, most people handle loss by trying to forget it at some point or another. They may not care to admit it, but everyone has to have a second to pretend none of it is happening and to think of a way to control themselves."

"I promised I wouldn't be one of those people," I murmured, closing my eyes. "It seems horrible."

"Ed wouldn't have wanted you to mope the rest of your life, would he?" he reasoned. I shook my head, opening my eyes.

"How were you?" I asked curiously, switching the topic to him, "after it happened, I mean." It was true that Joseph had been upset when it had happened, and who knows what he did the entire week while I was holed up and miserable, but right then, he seemed to be... okay.

"I was a mess," he said, not bothering to look up. "You should see my room. After I left you alone, I threw everything off the walls, sat in the piles of rubbish and cried. The staff sent Alec in to calm me down—they were all too scared to come near me."

I cringed. I couldn't stand to see someone like Joey cry; he was usually so level-headed and collected that it was hard to imagine him upset. When I saw him on the night of Ed's death, it was a hard pill to swallow.

"After sitting in my room for a couple days without food and moping around, I decided that I was being selfish and there were other people who needed a shoulder to lean on. I went down to the kitchens the next day to help out and fill the spaces of the people who left to be with their families. Margaret was in rough shape, so I sat her down with a box of tissues and told her to tell me what to do."

"How are your cooking skills?" I asked curiously.

"Terrible," he remarked casually. "I burned two apple pies before Margaret made me leave, insisting that she could handle the work. After that, I went outside the gates to help the remaining staff pass out soup. The villagers aren't taking it well at all." He ran his free hand through his hair, eventually resting his chin in his palm. "I did a lot of crying that day. So many people lost their homes, families, and children. Some are still out there today looking for missing loved ones, hoping someone survived the fires and is lying under the rubble."

Ed was so well known among the villagers that it was no surprise when the entire kingdom went into mourning. No doubt, a black rose was placed on every doorstep as a sign of respect for the dead just like after Rose's death.

"When I went back to my room that day, I started to

think. I was in there for hours, sleeping on and off and doing more thinking when I woke up. I guess that's when I cleared my head, thought about it, and figured you couldn't be blamed for Ed's death, and I couldn't hold back in coming to tell you. I couldn't let you sit in here and beat yourself up any longer."

I pressed my forehead against his. I missed Ed so much; every time I heard his name, I felt a pang in my chest. Joey protectively wrapped both arms around me, resting his chin on the top of my head. Butterflies erupted in my stomach at the way he held me, and I couldn't get them under control.

I sat up, jumping out of bed and throwing on my robe. He looked at me, the slightly hurt expression on his face changing quickly back into the serene, content one he had moments earlier.

"I guess we should get ready…" I said, looking down, "for the funeral, I mean."

His face fell. He stood up and ran a hand through his hair. "You're probably right."

With a subtly longing—and slightly awkward—glance at me, he strode to the door and pulled it open. "I'll come to escort you in an hour?"

I nodded, hugging the robe tighter around me. My mood deflated as reality sunk into the morning, and Joey left my room without another word.

I sighed in relief when he was gone, sitting down on my bed. All of this felt wrong. I wasn't a romantic, I never had been; I certainly wasn't going to turn into one at a time like this. I understood that Joey needed some source of comfort, and I did too, but the way he made me feel—I wasn't sure whether the feeling was good or bad. I couldn't decide whether we wanted each other or *needed* each other. Would I slip back into lonely depression without him? Would he?

Either way, I had to think of Ed. I couldn't get distracted and forget him. I knew that Joey hadn't forgotten him, and probably never would, but I didn't want to be in the way of a brother paying respects to a brother. I could worry about my love life—or what little existed of it—later.

Padding into the bathroom, I brushed my teeth and combed my hair through thoughtfully, taking my time. Luckily, I had the hour to myself to get ready as most of the staff had been sent off to be with their families. I was alone.

I stepped into my long-sleeve, floor-length black dress, buttoning up the back. It didn't take me long to get ready at all; just the dress, a braid, and a pair of flat shoes, and I was done. Checking my reflection one more time in the mirror, I swung open the door.

Joey looked great. As great as it gets for a funeral, I mean.

He sported a black jacket and pants over a gray vest and a shirt, with a solemn expression to match. He held out his arm, waiting. I cleared my throat, making a mental note not to stare for too long before I wrapped my arm around his, closing the door behind me. He straightened up and escorted me down the hall without a word.

When we reached the grand staircase, everyone buzzing around downstairs seemed to stop and look. They bowed graciously before returning to their work.

"That's the first time I've seen them bow to you," I murmured to Joey.

"I'm supposedly the next heir," he said, his eyes dead. "I'm all they have."

"Supposedly?"

"I don't want to be king," he said. "I never did."

His words took me by surprise; I thought after Ed's death that he'd want to do the job for his brother. I didn't question him, though. He was already in a terrible mood, and being bombarded by questions would only make the situation worse. We carefully descended the stairs, me clumsily trying not to trip over my dress.

I felt Joey tense up beside me. Curious, I looked at him and then followed his gaze to find a very tall, blonde-haired man in a dark coat and boots standing by the door to the Great Hall. He looked less than happy, his expectant gaze locked on Joey.

"Excuse me a moment," he said, his voice strained.

I curtsied politely before he paced away.

I tried not to worry too much about Joey, but the way he tensed up when he caught sight of that man unnerved me. My thoughts were silenced as I spotted Joey talking animatedly with someone. He was outside, and I could see him through the huge window in the foyer; the other person was behind the wall where I couldn't see, but my bet was on it being the tall gentleman.

Joey threw his hands up angrily and then ran his hand through his hair, a gesture that was expected when he was on edge. Taking a step back, he shook his head, eventually turning away and walking back towards the door to come inside.

I realized how awkward I felt standing in the middle of the corridor alone with so many people bustling around me. I tucked my hands behind my back and pretended to be admiring the paintings on the tall ceiling when he stepped into the room.

"Are you ready?" he asked, holding his arm out once more. I nodded.

"Who was that?" I asked. "You seemed angry."

"The nobles of Baile want a meeting right now," he said through gritted teeth.

"Right now?" I asked. "As in, right *now?*"

"Sometimes I wonder if any of those men have a heart," he growled. He was livid, his hand balling into a fist as he spoke. "The nobles are corrupt, that's for sure, and poor King James either doesn't see it or doesn't have a choice but to ignore it."

My arm looped through his, and he led me to the door and down the marble steps. The sides of the carriage were draped in black fabric, and shades were pulled down over the windows. The coachman opened the door without a word and stared straight ahead, not even blinking.

That was the first thing that made me uncomfortable.

Joey offered his hand as I lifted one foot to the step, then the other, praying that I didn't fall forward on my dress. When I was safely inside, Joey followed, sliding in opposite me. The door shut, and the carriage became dark.

The silence between us was deafening. I listened, trying to find a sound to focus on. The faint beats of the horses' hooves against cobblestone faded as a shower of rain pattered around us. I lifted the shade to allow the gray light to shine in.

Riding through the forum, I noticed that it was almost empty in the section that had the worst damage. A few women in gray dresses could be seen scavenging through what used to be their homes for belongings.

As we progressed, I expected things to get better, but they didn't.

Although the homes in this part of the city were

almost untouched, every shop was closing its doors. Men placed *closed* signs in the windows and locked up for the day. Women carried empty baskets around as they followed their husbands, picking up scraps and collecting their things to take home. The children, who had once flooded the Forum with happiness and excitement, were nowhere to be seen. Every doorstep had a black rose. I felt sick to my stomach.

———

The funeral went smoothly.

It was the first I'd seen of Alec since the night that Ed died. He looked rough, and I had to remind myself that Alec had known Edward since he was a baby. Alec watched him grow up and then he watched him die.

I was taken aback when I assessed the crowd. Everyone stood at full attention. Every last person. I'd expected people to zone out, to pay no mind, but my thoughts were far from the truth. Women cried, dabbing at their eyes with tissues. Men stood with straight backs in a salute to the fallen prince.

The people of Aon took the hit when we lost Ed, and they took it at full force.

No matter how hard I had tried to put myself back into my bubble before, I couldn't do it. It was so much easier to just not feel. Now that I'd come back into the real world, it was almost impossible to get out, to escape back to my bubble.

But you're not in the real world, my conscience whispered.

The funeral seemed to last forever, though I know it had to be only an hour or two. Joey went up to speak, and so did a number of other people. One by one, villagers rose to place a black rose on the end of the casket.

Joey struggled to keep his composure throughout the ceremony. I slid my hand down into his, squeezing it reassuringly before letting it drop.

At last, Joey was presented with a flag. He stood tall, shoulders back between Alec and me, staring into the distance as the flag was placed into his arms and a small, golden crown was balanced on the top. His breathing was quiet, but as I listened, I realized it was ragged, almost like he was struggling. Silent tears fell from his eyes and down his cheeks, soaking into the flag in his arms. He didn't acknowledge them. Alec put a hand on his shoulder.

When the service concluded and it was all over, Joey took my hand and led me to the casket where his little brother rested. Alec followed.

My heart sank to my stomach as I caught sight of Edward lying in the casket. His skin was pale, his eyes sunken, and his face sported several cuts from that night. Ed lay on the velvet material, looking serene, almost as if he was asleep. I held his cold hand in mine.

Here was this boy—this young, innocent boy that brought me to this world, protected me, loved me, and had a heart the size of the galaxy—and he was gone. Just like that.

He deserved a long life. He deserved a chance to grow up, to find love, to take risks, to go on adventures.

He didn't deserve to die.

Joey tried as hard as he could to hold his emotions back, and I could tell when his hands shook that he was failing. Alec stood at his side, hugging him tightly when the tears came rolling down his cheeks. Joey cried into his best friend's shoulder, and we exchanged a look before I couldn't take it anymore. I quit fighting it; I let the tears fall without a care. When I looked back up at

Alec and Joey, I found that Alec was crying too.

The villagers around us all bowed their heads as Joey mourned the loss of his little brother.

nineteen

That afternoon after the funeral, we all sat in the study in the floor in front of the fireplace. I had asked that the fire be put out; today was not the day to try to conquer our fears.

Joey sat forward on his elbows, not even trying to hold back. He let out everything he had been bottling up for the past week in tears. I just wrapped my arms around him, pressed my face against his shoulder, and held him. His hands came up to cover my arm, and he leaned into me for comfort. Alec sat on his other side, arm stretched out behind us.

It hurt me to see Joey like this.

The three of us sat together like that while Joey poured it all out. Alec and I didn't say anything.

When he calmed down, he stared into the empty fireplace for a long time, his expression pained and exhausted.

"I'm going to go to my room," he finally spoke, his voice hoarse.

I nodded, wrapping my arms around his waist. "Get some sleep."

I felt him kiss the top of my head before he pulled away. He clapped Alec's shoulder before he rose and left the room, running his hands through his hair. Following him, Alec and I watched him walk up the staircase and out of sight.

"I have an idea, Alec," I said once he was gone.

He raised an eyebrow. "What did you have in mind?"

Luckily, Cyneward happened to stroll through the main foyer, and I caught him.

"Cyneward," I said, beckoning him to me, "just the person I needed to see. I need both of your help."

———

That night, Joey sat on the stone balcony of the castle, overlooking Aon.

"It's quiet," I said, closing the door behind me as I approached him.

He didn't turn his head. "Yeah, it is."

I climbed the stone railing to sit next to him. Our legs dangled down over the edge.

"All of the lights are out in the Forum," he said. "In fact, it looks like all of the lights in Devereux are out."

"Looks like it," I agreed. This was no surprise to me. "It almost looks like the entire country is in mourning. I can't see any light past the city walls."

"They've never mourned like this," he murmured. "The entire kingdom going dark isn't typical of Aon during mourning."

I didn't answer.

We were both silent for a few minutes before Joey spoke.

"Do you see that?" he asked, pointing below us. "Who is that? It looks a bit like Cyneward. And is that Alec?"

I looked down, following his direction. "You're right. That's them."

He furrowed his brow. "What's in his hand?"

Leaning back, I shifted my gaze to Joey. "It looks like a paper lantern."

"What is he doing?"

"You ask a lot of questions," I said, turning to gaze out over the land.

"Do you know something about this?"

I shushed him, swinging my legs back and forth. He glanced at me suspiciously.

"The Forum," he murmured.

"What was that?"

"The Forum is lighting up. It looks like more paper lanterns."

"Does it really?"

"Elizabeth," he said, turning his body to face me, "what is all this?"

I offered him a partial smile. "Just watch."

And so he did.

Joey watched intently as first the Forum lit up with lanterns, then the entire village, then the countryside, all the way to the next village, to the major cities, and to the roads in a chain reaction until the entire country was lit up before our eyes.

"Whoa," he breathed.

"I know."

"Why aren't they sending the lanterns off? Those aren't the type that you just hold."

"They're awaiting orders," I explained, sliding off the railing and back onto the balcony.

"Orders…?"

I hopped off the ledge and walked back towards the door. My hands easily found the two lanterns I had hid behind the potted plants earlier in the day, as well as the matchstick. I tapped his back when I was behind him.

His eyes grew wide when he realized what I held.

"It's for Ed," I explained, shrugging my shoulders. "He wouldn't want us all to be depressed for so long, so I thought, why not do something beautiful to remember him instead of being sad?"

Joey didn't respond. He just pulled me into a hug, almost crushing the lantern.

"Thank you," he spoke into my ear.

Pulling away, I handed him a lantern and the matchstick. He took them, striking the match against the stone and lighting his lantern and then mine. They grew lighter, filling with hot air and floating in our palms.

"On three?" he asked. I nodded.

"One, two, three."

The lanterns lifted from our hands, floating high into the air. We observed the chain reaction as Cyneward sent his off, and then the Forum, the village, and the rest of the kingdom followed suit.

"He told me that he loved the stars the first night I was here," I said quietly. "This was as close as I could get."

"He would've loved it," Joey said. "You did all of this?"

"Cyneward organized it. I just told him what I wanted to do, and he took care of the rest."

"It's amazing," he breathed, his eyes fixed on the bright lights that surrounded us.

A warm yellow glow engulfed everything as the lanterns rose, first lower than us on the balcony and then higher as they filled the night sky. Looking up, it was nothing but stars and lanterns as far as the eye could see.

Out of the corner of my eye, I saw him look at me, then back up at the sky.

The lanterns melted in with the stars until I couldn't tell which was which. My eyes focused on two stars straight above us, seemingly the two brightest stars in the entire sky.

I couldn't help but smile.

"Hello, Ed," I whispered.

My eyes must've been playing tricks on me because I could've sworn that the smaller star twinkled before my eyes.

twenty

The weeks that followed the funeral were the hardest to endure.

For me, my newfound fear of fire sent me into a sort of paranoia. The fiery dreams of the Forum and Edward haunted my thoughts during the night. I never seemed to have enough sleep. Margaret wasn't allowed to light my fireplace anymore; instead, she had to resort to heating hot pans, putting them between my sheets, and praying I didn't burn myself during the night.

Joseph was worse off than me, and I did my best to be there for him. He pretended he was fine, but it was too easy a facade to see through. It was as if every ounce of drive or energy was gone from his body. Sometimes I'd walk into a room to find him gripping the back of a chair for support with his eyes closed or sitting on the floor against a wall, staring off into space.

Though things were hard at first, they gradually grew

easier. By the second week, Joseph and I were both back into a normal routine. Our appetites were still smaller than they should have been (Margaret made sure we were aware of that), but we at least mustered up a smile to put the staff's mind at ease.

"Join me for breakfast this morning?" Joseph asked politely, holding out his arm. It was a gesture that I'd seen a million times by now, but it still reminded me of how different Aon was from the real world.

"Sure thing," I answered. I started towards him, but he stopped me.

"I hoped we could take a walk through the gardens afterwards," he said sheepishly. "It's rather cold, so you might want to bring a cloak."

I raised an eyebrow. "A walk? This early?"

He shrugged. "Why not? I'd like to show you something."

I didn't question him anymore. After grabbing my cloak, we set off down the stairs to the grand dining room. It was strange, two people sitting alone at a table that could easily fit twenty, but it was also nice. The food was amazing, as usual.

Usual. A strange word for the situation. I wouldn't have thought a month ago that the meaning of *usual* would ever mean eating delicacies in a storybook world.

Weird.

The morning air was frigid when we stepped outside. I was glad I brought my cloak. The fur on the inside kept me from turning into a human popsicle. It also helped that Joey walked with his arm around me.

"He died a heroic death, don't you think?" he asked quietly. I looked over at him.

"I guess he did," I replied after a moment.

"Saved those kids and everything. They would be

dead now if he hadn't saved them."

I didn't respond, my mind wandering.

"Hey, Joey?"

"Yeah?"

"Why did Ed leave Aon at the start?"

He looked at me briefly then back at the fog-covered lake.

"Ed didn't much like doing things that royals were supposed to do," he recalled. "He absolutely hated studying the histories and learning how to fence. He always found a way to sneak around the guards and maids and take off somewhere. His charades wouldn't have been dangerous were Father still alive, but since his death, the Night Rider's banishment has been lifted. He can pass through any part of the kingdom now or at least until someone sits on the throne again. It was incredibly dangerous for Ed to leave."

"So, you're telling me that Ed left because he didn't want to study?" I looked at him in disbelief.

"No, that's not why. I wasn't finished," Joey said, shaking his head. "Ed liked to run away, but that's not why he left in the first place."

"Then why did he leave?" I demanded.

"I don't know, but my guess is to save us," said he. "The Night Rider followed him; everyone knew that. If the Night Rider assassinated him, then all of the struggle would've been for nothing. Ed left for a reason, and that was to pull the Rider on a wild goose chase away from our world."

"He was a smart kid," I murmured. "Smarter than I gave him credit for at first."

"Cunning, that one," he remarked in admiration. "Smarter than any war chief I've ever heard of."

Ed was *incredibly smart*. The gears started turning in

my head.

"Joey," I said slowly, "how did Ed get out of Aon?"

He frowned. "What do you mean?"

I paced, thinking it through. "If people from my world come by reading and leave by writing their death, how would someone from your world leave?"

His eyes widened in realization.

"I see what you're thinking, El, but that can't be. It's impossible, it—he, he—."

"Just like traveling to another world in your sleep is impossible?" I pointed out.

He scratched the back of his neck, thinking it through.

"But the Night Rider...? He obviously didn't do anything himself to the Book to leave."

"Ed could've done something to the Book to make sure he followed him," I realized. "He must've added to the story! It's the only logical answer!"

"That's impossible," he scoffed.

"Think about it," I urged. "Put it all together. What's the only solution?"

His eyes went wide. "You don't mean..."

"That's exactly what I mean," I said. "Ed wrote his own death."

twenty-one

He gaped at me, trying to find words. "It all fits," he breathed. "But I don't think my brother wanted to die. Why would he write his own death?" He raised his head, looking right at me.

"He must not have meant to come back," I realized. "Maybe he was going to trap the Night Rider in my world with him!"

"And then he met you and followed you back into the world where he knew that what he had written had come true," Joey pieced together, his eyes widening. He let out a short breath, his eyes wide as he tried to make sense of everything. "How clever."

"That means he had to have some sort of back-up plan in case the Night Rider found the Book. He would've thought of that—something to stop the Night Rider if he got back into Aon."

"What if he wrote it down?" Joey suggested.

I knew what that meant. We were going to have to read the Book, and I didn't know if I was ready for that.

"We need to get to Yula's," he said, pacing back in the direction of the castle. "We need to get there *now.*"

We wasted no time in taking the carriage to Yula's.

"What do we have here?" Yula's warm voice greeted us at her doorstep. "It's been a while. How are you?"

"Hello," I murmured, shifting my weight. "We need to talk."

"Straight to the point," she noted, looking at the pair of us skeptically. "I get it. Come on in; I'll make some tea."

Together we followed her into her cozy cottage, and she set a kettle of water over the stove. Pulling back a chair, we each sat down. Joey eased back into his seat; I was on edge.

"Now," she said, dusting her hands off as she prepared a tray, "what's on your mind?"

"We think Ed left something in the Book," I said. Joey beat her to the kettle when it whistled, placing it down next to her tray.

She perked up. "I see." She turned and gave a thankful smile at Joey, grabbing the tray and offering us cups. She then placed the Book down on the table in front of me.

The tea felt nice running down my throat after spending all morning in the cold outside air. Unlike Joey's straight black tea, mine was a light brown color, the milk and sugar changing the color.

I had always loved hot tea back home. The sweet, familiar taste was a comfort.

Joey moved his chair closer to mine as I hunched over the table, laying the Book flat and opening the cover.

"It'd be at the end," he murmured in my ear. "Unless someone else has found it." Yula just looked at us skeptically.

"Wait," she said, putting a hand on the pages so I couldn't turn any more. "Before you go looking… well, what exactly are you looking for?"

Joey and I exchanged a look.

"We think that Edward might have written his own death," he explained.

"Why would he do that?" Yula asked, her tone suspicious. "I don't necessarily think your little brother had a death wish, Joseph."

"He didn't," I stated. "We were just thinking; how do you think he left Aon with the Book in the first place?"

She sat down in front of us, crossing her arms. "I don't have an explanation. I've never had any of my characters leave the story before him and the Night Rider when he followed."

"I don't think Ed would be an exception to any of the Book's rules," I explained. "I think Ed wrote his own death to leave the story and draw the Night Rider out of the story with him. Maybe he never meant to come back, and he was going to trap himself and the Night Rider in the real world."

She seemed to think for a moment. "It would make sense. There must not be any loopholes; the Book still found a way to draw him back in." She nodded towards the Book of Aon, looking up at me. "Go ahead and open it up—let's settle this."

I stared at the leather cover of the Book, almost scared to open it. The room grew silent.

"Elizabeth?" Joey asked, his hand resting on my arm.

"I'm fine," I said. "It's just, now that it's in front of

me… I don't know if I want to know."

Honestly, I was scared of what I would find. I didn't want to read anything that brought back unwanted memories.

"Why don't you step outside," he suggested. "I'll read it, and then we can be on our way."

Hesitantly, I nodded. I was better off not knowing.

I rose from my seat and stepped outside onto the front porch. It was cold outside; winter grew closer by the day. I noticed a few snowflakes falling from the sky. I caught one in my hand, and it melted.

Minutes passed, and the door opened. Joey came out with the Book in hand.

"Let's go," he said, nodding towards the carriage. "Let's get you warm."

He offered the Book to me, and I shook my head. "I don't want it."

He looked like he wanted to say something or to ask me why, but he decided against it. Instead, he pulled me into his side to keep me warm.

The ride back to the castle was painfully quiet. I was dying to know what Joey found, but at the same time, I felt like I already knew.

That night, I sat next to Joey in the library. I couldn't help but think about my suspicions of Delia, the ones I'd forged months ago; we hadn't heard from her, and Joey hadn't contacted her, keeping his grief to himself. My mind kept drifting to the Night Rider and the night I was attacked in her house.

If she was the Night Rider like my conscience kept telling me, then so many questions could be answered. I knew getting Joey to believe me would be tough, but I had to try. If I was right, not taking action could be dangerous.

"Joey," I said, closing my book, "can I talk to you about something without you getting angry?"

"That depends on what it is, Elizabeth," he said, "but go ahead."

I took a deep breath.

"The day we left your sister's house all those months ago, she said something to me," I said, treading carefully. "She told me that if I hurt you, she'd make sure I would pay."

He chuckled, as if it were a joke. "I doubt she said that, Liz."

"I'm serious," I said. "Joey, I don't think it was any accident that she left that lamp on in the window. She knew from the beginning that I wasn't reading the Book of Aon."

"My sister wouldn't try to kill you," Joey protested, waving me off. "You're insane."

"You're not listening, Joseph," I muttered through gritted teeth. "Delia hated Edward, remember? She didn't like that he had power. She doesn't like me because I loved Edward, and she doesn't like me because I'm a threat."

"Elizabeth, that's enough. My sister isn't a murderer."

"You don't know that. You haven't seen her in months. I'll bet the only way her men found us in the forest was because you told her we would train up and go scouting. She had this planned from the beginning, and with her power, she'll be nearly impossible to defeat on our own."

"*Enough*, Elizabeth!"

Joseph was standing now, his chest heaving as he breathed heavily. He glared at me, his eyes hard and unforgiving.

"My sister is *not* a murderer, and she *never* will be. I don't know what your problem is, but leave Delia out of this."

He paced to the door, not even slowing down as he stormed from the room. Alec stepped into the doorway as Joey pushed past him. He pointed at his friend once he was down the hallway.

"Geez, Liz. You couldn't have been a little gentler?"

"You heard all of that?" I asked.

"Every word."

"And what do you think?" I questioned. "Am I overreacting?"

He shook his head. "No. Frankly, I think you're right, but I think you could've broken the news to him a little more subtly."

"You believe me?"

Nodding, he leaned into the doorway and crossed his arms. "You missed something, though. If Delia *is* the Night Rider, who attacked you when you stayed with her? She was in the house, wasn't she?"

I frowned. "I didn't think of that. Do you think it was one of her followers?"

He smirked, winking at me. "Lucky for you, I know for a fact that it was. For the past two weeks I've been keeping busy, hunting down the little runts that ambushed us in the forest. I found them, and they happen to be in the dungeons right now."

My mouth opened in shock. "*Right now?*"

He nodded. "Would you like to come ask them some questions?"

I stood up from my seat. "Take me to them. I'd love to give them a piece of my mind."

———

The last time I had been in the dungeons was a day

or two after I'd arrived in Aon. I never had the need to go back down there, nor did I want to; that place was a living nightmare. As I followed Alec down the stone staircase into the dark, musty cellar, I wondered if going back down there was a good idea.

"This way," Alec said, gesturing ahead of him. "Watch your step."

I followed silently when we reached the cellblocks. There weren't many people in the dungeons, I realized, because it was reserved for the worst of the worst—the murderers, the assassins, the plotters, and worst of all, the allies of the Night Rider.

I stuck close to Alec's side as we walked between cells. Several men spit, women taunted, and a few said some rather crude things as we passed by.

"Quiet, all of you!" Alec yelled, throwing a nasty glare behind us.

We rounded the corner of the first row of cells, and Alec stopped, stepping in front me.

"I know you wanted to think the best of him," he said, looking slightly guilty. "I'm sorry that he isn't all that you hoped he was."

I blinked. "What are you talking about?"

He didn't say anything. He simply stepped to the side to reveal the cells behind him.

My jaw dropped as the man came into view. "Devin?"

twenty-two

Devin looked up at me through the bars of his cell. His face was heavily bruised.

"Hello, Elizabeth," he greeted quietly.

"Did you do that to him?" I asked Alec. He shrugged, the keys jingling in his hand as he unlocked the door for me.

"I couldn't let him get away with shooting my best friend and dragging you from a house. You weren't even armed. It was totally unfair." Alec pocketed the keys when he was done and then leaned against the wall and pretended to inspect his fingernails. "He also committed arson twice, so I think he deserved it."

"Good job," I murmured, looking the bruises that decorated Devin's face. Alec seemed proud.

"Hey, thanks."

I walked closer to Devin's cell. My jaw tensed as I stopped in front of him. He made no move except to lift his head to look at me.

"You've been working for her the entire time, haven't you?"

He didn't answer.

"I *trusted* you."

"That was a poor decision on your part."

Fury built up inside of me, and I realized how utterly *angry* I was. My elbow swung back, and my hand made contact with his cheek. The sharp sound echoed through the dungeons.

"Nice shot," I heard Alec murmur behind me.

Devin flinched but only hung his head in response. He made no move against me.

"How can you live with this?" I asked him. "How can you live knowing that you caused the death of an *innocent child?*"

At that, his head snapped up, and his eyes narrowed at me.

"Because *I didn't cause it,*" he bit back, his tone gravely serious. "I wasn't the one who set fire to the Forum. How could I have been? I was at the ball myself. You saw me. You *danced* with me."

I blinked. "Who set the fires, then?"

He laughed a humorless chuckle. "Who do you think?" He scoffed, his eyes locking on me. "She was angry with me. She threatened to *behead* me, so I told her she could do the work on her own, and that's exactly what she did."

"So, it *is* Delia," I said, clenching my fists at my sides.

"I was supposed to be aiming for the horse when I shot at you in forest," he recalled, holding his head up to look at me. "I misfired and hit her brother instead. She almost killed me for that one."

"You shot him twice," I said.

"I shot him *once*," he clarified. "*He* shot him the second time, though I don't believe it was an accident." He nodded towards the cell to his right.

I looked at the person in the cell next to him. I didn't recognize the face, but he looked like he was considerably older than all of us.

"This is Devin's father," Alec said, walking to stand in front of the cell. "He was put on probation a while back, and well… you can guess why he's back."

The man sneered. "Like father, like son."

Devin pushed himself against his cell bars. "I am *nothing* like you."

"You're *just* like me. If you weren't, you wouldn't be in a cell next to me, son."

"*Don't call me son*," Devin scoffed. "You're *not* my father."

"Devin," I said, stepping closer to him, "what can you tell me about the Night Rider? About Delia?"

"She ordered me to kill you, several different times," he admitted, looking from his father to me. "I couldn't do it. That's what got me here."

"No, you're here because you were really bad at hide and seek," Alec scoffed. "You didn't make it hard to be traced, you know."

"She's expecting you to come for her," Devin warned. "She knows you've figured it out."

"Where do I find her?" I asked.

He looked at me warily before answering.

"In the woods beyond Wilmington Place. It takes forever to get there. You'll know when you've found it, though; trust me. You won't miss it."

"Thank you, Devin," I said, stepping away. "I'm going to end this."

"Elizabeth, one more thing," he called. "Her powers are *very much* real. She can and will use them against you. Be careful."

"I will."

Turning to Alec, I motioned for him to lead the way, and we jogged from the dungeons back to the entrance.

"You aren't seriously thinking of going by yourself, are you?" Alec asked, stopping me before I could climb the staircase.

"Do you have a better idea?" I asked. "Joey is in denial. There's no way he'd show up of his own accord."

"Talk to him about it one more time," he suggested. "If he doesn't believe you after that, go ahead and go. I'll send reinforcements after you to back you up in case her followers are with her."

"Will you try to talk to him? Do you think he'd listen to you better than me?"

He shook his head. "Not a chance."

I let out an exasperated sigh. "Where do I find him?"

"Try the throne room. That's usually where I find him when he's upset."

I frowned. "The throne room?"

He shrugged. "Yeah. Lots of room for him to pace like he does."

"Can you show me where it is?" I asked. "Ed showed me at one point, but I can't remember ever seeing it."

"Well, sure," Alec said, starting up the stairs. When we reached the top, he pointed down one of the hallways. "See the two really tall double doors at the end of the hall? That's it, right there. Oh, and, uh…" He patted my shoulder. "Use caution."

Gulping, I thanked him and then trekked down the impossibly long hallway in front of me.

"Don't let him have a sword," Alec called jokingly down the corridor after me. "I'm kidding… kind of."

"Thanks, Alec," I called sarcastically over my shoulder.

I walked as slowly as I could manage. All I could hear was the sound of my footsteps echoing on the floor. Turning around, I expected to see Alec watching me, but he was gone.

Too soon, I reached the double doors. My fingers traced the handle until I got the courage to pull the door open and slip inside.

Alec was right about Joey and his pacing. When I found him, he paced back and forth in front of the thrones that sat at the far end of the long room. Silently, I watched; he still hadn't noticed that I was there.

Suddenly, he dropped to his knees. I looked on as he fell back; he sat down on the open floor. I expected him to cry, scream, do *something* to get the frustration out— but he didn't. He just looked at the thrones and didn't say a word.

Deciding that it was safe to approach him, I slowly made my way down the deep red carpet towards his limp figure.

"Are you okay?" I asked, standing behind him. He didn't turn around.

"I'm fine," he said.

"Really?" I wondered, sitting next to him. We stared at the thrones together.

"No," he admitted. "No, I'm not."

"Do you want to talk about it?"

Joey shook his head no but changed his mind and nodded instead.

"It's just… He'll never get to sit there," he said, his stare still trained on the extravagant seats. "He'll never get to sit there with someone he loves at this side. He'll never get married, he'll never have kids, and he'll never get to see them grow up. He'll never accomplish anything he dreamed of doing."

I looked at him just in time to see a single tear escape his eye. He ignored it.

"It's hard to take in," I said, turning back to the thrones. "I get it."

"Do you think he's happier now?"

"No doubt that he is," I answered.

"How could someone cause the death of a child and still live with himself?" he wondered aloud. "I'd live in agony until I died."

"If that person didn't have a heart, then he or she wouldn't feel it," I answered solemnly. "Joey, Alec caught the Rider's men."

His head whipped towards me. "Who are they?"

Grimacing, I replied, "Devin and his father."

Joey cursed under his breath. "I never trusted him."

"I know you didn't, but I did," I said, "and it saved both of our lives."

"What do you mean?" he asked, turning towards me.

"He was ordered to kill me," I said. "He couldn't do it. And he was ordered not to touch you—the arrow he shot was an accident. He was beaten for it."

"Good. That hurt like hell." His hands balled into fists at the thought. "But why would he be ordered not to kill me?" Joey questioned.

"For the same reason I told you before you started yelling at me."

"Elizabeth, I just find it incredibly hard to believe that *my sister* would try to have you killed."

"Is it easier to believe that she killed your half brother?" I asked. "She never liked him."

"She wouldn't murder him, Elizabeth. I thought you were better than this."

"Why would I lie to you?" I asked him.

"You had no trouble lying to me before," he mumbled.

I watched him with wide eyes. "You really want to bring that up now?"

"I'm sorry. You have to understand that it's a little harder for me to trust you now."

"Whatever," I scoffed, standing up and dusting myself off.

"Where are you going?"

"To find Alec. At least he believes me."

"Now hold on a minute," he said, springing to his feet next to me. "What is Alec going to do to help?"

"I don't know. Maybe he'll help me find the Night Rider so we can end this. I'm sick of arguing with you over who it is; at this point, it doesn't even matter. What matters is that we find a way to stop this."

"You'll need the Book for that," Joey reminded me. "I have it."

"I would ask you for it, but I know you won't give it to me."

"How can you be sure?"

"Would you?"

"No."

I scoffed, throwing my hands up and moving towards the door. I felt his hand wrap around my wrist and pull me back.

"You can't go alone, Elizabeth. You need my help."

"I don't want your help. You don't believe me," I spat. "You still don't believe me."

"Whether it's Delia or not, we still need to figure out if Ed wrote anything about the Night Rider that can help us," Joey said. "I didn't read far enough to see, but do you think Ed wrote about how the Night Rider would be defeated?"

"There's only one way to find out. Where is it?"

He grimaced, seemingly conflicted about whether or not he should tell me.

"Joey, where is the Book of Aon?"

Sighing, he gave in. "It's in a drawer in my desk."

I pulled my wrist from his grasp and ran to the door, wasting no time in finding the staircase and skipping steps until I made it to the top. When I reached his room, I swung the door open and frantically looked around until my eyes spotted the desk pushed up against the wall.

Heaving and out of breath, I approached the wooden table, picking a drawer and pulling it open. I found nothing inside. Confused, I pulled open two more drawers to find nothing, like the first. My hand rested on the last drawer—the only one with a keyhole—and I tried to pull it open.

It was locked.

"You'll need this if you want to see it," Joey called from the doorway, holding a key between his forefinger and his thumb.

"You could've mentioned that a bit sooner," I huffed, trying to catch my breath.

Without a word, he walked in front of me and slid the key into the keyhole, turned it, and pulled the drawer open before reaching inside and retrieving the Book.

Hesitantly, he put the Book on the top of the desk.

"Are you okay to read it?" he asked, looking at me skeptically.

"Open it."

He flipped the Book open to Ed's page, and we both

peered at the writing. It was messy, like it had been written by someone who was in a rush. At the very end of the page, one sentence was underlined.

The fight ended at the hands of the one who started it.

"The one who started it? What does it mean?" Joey asked.

"I don't know," I said. "Started what?"

"Maybe it's talking about when the Night Rider started attacking Aon," he offered.

"No," I said, shaking my head. "Could Ed have known about anything that long ago?"

"Maybe he meant coming back from your world," Joey said.

I was the one who forced Ed back into Aon and made him return to the castle. I started it all.

It can't be me.

"That would mean…" he trailed off, looking at me.

"It can't be," I breathed. "I—"

"No," Joey shook his head.

"Is it? Did I start all of this?"

"It doesn't matter," he said, snapping the Book shut. "You aren't going."

"But I have to," I argued. "I have no choice."

"You don't have to do that," Joey said, turning towards me. "We don't even know if it's for sure talking about you."

"Who else could it be?" I asked.

"I don't know," he said, "but Ed wrote it this way for a reason. If he didn't put down a name, he probably wanted us to think about it before we acted on it."

Be brave, Liz. He has to let you go.

"Please don't go," he said. "I don't want you facing him alone."

"Joseph, stop. I have no choice. We can't let the

Night Rider terrorize any longer." I paced toward the door.

"Elizabeth," Joey pleaded, taking a step towards me, "please."

"Let it go, Joey." I avoided his reach. "*Let me go.*"

I took off, running out of the room and back into the castle corridors, apologizing to Margaret for bumping her. She called after me, but I ignored her.

I burst into my room in tears. My vision was so blurred by the tears that I slammed my shoulder against the wall, causing my mirror to fall to the floor and shatter. My back hit the door as I slammed it closed and locked it, and I slid to the ground.

What if I die? I thought, burying my head in my hands. *What happens to Joey? What happens to me? How will I survive the only stability I've ever had being ripped out from under me?*

Why did Ed pick me?

I dried my eyes, looking down at the few shards that came loose and were spread across the ground. My hands reached for a shard.

My red-rimmed eyes peered back at me in the reflection. I winced, another tear dripping down my cheek and hitting the glass when the sharp edge pierced my skin. Blood flowed from the cuts on my hand as I dropped the shard back onto the ground.

Turning the frame over, I saw my reflection in a sheet of cracked glass.

Shattered, but not broken. Unfinished.

No matter what happened, I wasn't going to let everything fall apart. The story was still left unfinished, and it was my job to create an ending for myself that helped more people than just me.

Slowly, I rose to my feet, drying my face.

I could do this. No matter what happened to me, I was going to make a better ending for Aon.

No matter what it took, I was going to end this.

I straightened myself up. I swiftly changed into the pair of pants I'd taken from the training room and a plain white shirt. The shirt was Joey's—I'd stolen it from his room just in case I needed it—and was too big on me, but I tied the strings at the collar as tight as they would go to keep it on my shoulders. My boots slid onto my feet, and my backpack was pulled from the top shelf as I darted out of my room and into the corridor, making a beeline for the maid's quarters to find Margaret.

I ran into her halfway there. After explaining what I was doing, she grabbed my hand and pulled me along behind her towards the first floor. She led me into the room where Rose had trained me. The sound of scraping metal filled the room, and I was surprised something like this was allowed in the castle—I'd never seen anything like this in the training room before.

"Stewart," she said as we entered, "I need help. It's urgent."

A man appeared around an anvil, lifting his facemask to look at us. "What can I do for you?"

"I'm going to find the Night Rider," I said immediately. "I need weapons and armor."

"No one finds the Night Rider," he said with a laugh as he hammered out a piece of metal, "the Night Rider finds you. And what makes you think I'm going to help you?"

"She's ending this, Stewart," Margaret cut in. "She's the Keeper."

He looked from her to me before nodding. "All right. Give me a moment."

"Thank you," she called. He waved at her before he strode towards the back of the room to a rack of weapons.

"Over here, girl," he said, waving me over. I went to stand next to him. "Try this." He offered me a knife. It was lightweight with a scroll pattern engraved on the handle. He pointed me towards a target across the room.

Carefully, I squared up, aligning my aim.

Seconds later, the point of the knife pierced a spot a few inches away from the bull's eye.

"Maybe another," I suggested. He handed me a smaller, heavier version of the same knife.

This time, the knife hit the target dead center.

"Excellent," he said, handing me two more of the same kind, each with a leather sheath. I put them in my bag.

"You'll need a sword, too," he said, walking to another rack with me close behind. "Pick one up and see how it feels."

I eyed the varied selection before choosing a heavy sword with the same scroll on the handle. It was heavy, but it was accurate.

"Are you sure?" He eyed me with an unsure expression.

"Positive."

He gave me a wary glance before handing me a sheath for that as well. I tied the sheath to my belt, adjusting it so it would stay put.

"What about armor?" I asked.

"I can't give you that here. It will just slow you down, and you won't be able to run."

"I can't fight the Night Rider with no armor," I argued. "I'll get slaughtered."

"Hold on," he said. "Where are you going to begin

the search?"

"The countryside near Berkeley where the search party followed him before Edward's birthday," I answered. "Why?"

"I have a brother who lives there," he stated. "Tell him that Stewart asked a favor, and he'll get you what you need. This way, you'll have less weight on you while you ride and run."

"Thank you for everything."

"Don't mention it. Just don't get yourself killed, okay?"

I nodded before leaving the room with Margaret.

"I'll have the horses readied and the staff out in the courtyard to say goodbye in fifteen minutes," she said. "I've packed food for you as well."

"*Horses*, Margaret?" I asked, confused. "Whose horse is the other?"

"Why, Joseph's, of course. Who else?"

I shook my head. "Joseph isn't coming. Only one horse needs to be prepared."

"But—"

"Margaret," I said with a look. "One horse."

She closed her mouth unwillingly and nodded before bustling off in the direction of the front doors.

Taking a deep breath, I started back up the staircase towards my room. I had fifteen minutes to write everything down and find the footman before Margaret would drag me out and scold me for being late.

The ink couldn't seem to dry fast enough as I scribbled on the parchment. I cursed under my breath for not remembering to sprinkle sand over it to dry the ink last time I wrote a letter; I usually stole some from Joey who did a much better job of remembering things, but it seemed unlikely in this situation. I blew on the ink, hoping it wouldn't run.

On my way down the stairs, I ran into Joey's footman.

"Thomas!" I called, relieved that I caught him. He turned towards me with an eyebrow raised.

"Can I get you anything, Lady Elizabeth?"

"Yes, you can do something for me," I said, handing him the envelope that contained my letter. "This must be delivered to Joseph immediately."

"But m'lady," he said, "he's requested not to be bothered. He's hasn't left his quarters."

"I am aware," I said, "but this is a matter of urgency. Slide it under his door if you have to, but make sure he gets it *today*."

He nodded. "Understood, ma'am."

"Thank you, Thomas."

He bowed before continuing up the staircase towards the residential rooms.

I knew my fifteen minutes was well past up, so I sprinted down the corridor and towards the front doors. They opened as I approached, and I didn't waste time in climbing on my horse and preparing to leave.

"Elizabeth!" Margaret called, a brown bag in hand. I mentally slapped myself; I had forgotten the food, exactly what she had warned me not to forget.

"What would I do without you?" I asked. I put away the food in my saddlebag.

"Starve," she said simply. "Now be off. You need to camp before night falls, and by the looks of it, you only have a few hours. Stay safe."

"I'll try."

I looked around, hoping to see Joey, but was disappointed to realize he wasn't there. Whether he didn't know I was leaving or just didn't care, I didn't know, but I tried my best to erase it from my mind and focus on the task at hand.

With one last look at Devereux Castle, I tapped the sides of my horse and galloped down the path towards the city.

twenty-three

Joey sat down at his desk, huffing in frustration. His fist hit the wood, and the stack of books and papers on the edge fell to the ground.

"Idiot," he murmured to himself, getting up for the third time to pace his room. "You should've gone with her."

His hand ran over his face and through his hair as he tried to think of a plan.

"Sir," a voice called at the door.

"What is it, Thomas?"

The door swung open, and Joey's footman appeared, holding an envelope.

"A letter for you, sir. It's from Lady Elizabeth."

"I don't want it," he immediately answered. He was angry with her, and he didn't want her written apologies.

"She requested that you receive it today," he pushed. "She just left for the countryside."

"She *what?*"

"She left, sir. She's gone to search for the Night Rider."

"*Already?*"

Joey's fist came down on the desk once again, this time knocking a glass vase and a picture frame onto the floor. The glass shattered, sending shards everywhere.

Joey picked up the picture frame that contained the portrait of his brother in it. Carefully, he set it back up on the desk, minding the sharp pieces of glass poking out of the edges.

"Where do you want this letter?" Thomas asked.

"I'll take it," he grudgingly said. "She's gone, so I almost have no choice in whether or not to read it. Who knows what other things she's gone to do. We'll be lucky if she makes it out of this alive."

The seal of the letter was broken, and the contents were spilled onto the desk. The letter, along with the necklace Elizabeth had made for Ed, fell onto the wood.

The clear stone that hung from the thin silver chain was held between Joey's thumb and forefinger as he examined it. When he brought it closer to his eye, an image flashed before his eyes.

"Elizabeth," Joey said, steering her back to the bed, "go to sleep. You aren't going outside to play in the rain again today."

"But this is so boring," she complained, her bare feet padding against the floor.

Wow, she's like a toddler, *he thought.*

"Not my fault."

"You're no help."

"I don't try to be." Joey pulled the covers back for her and walked around the bed, settling with his arms behind his head.

"You're really frustrating, you know that?"

"I've been told."

"*Aren't you going to argue back? Come on, say something infuriating.*"

Joey chuckled to himself, glancing at her out of the corner of his eye.

"*Then you'd be satisfied. Plus, I think I've done a good job so far, you seem pretty annoyed at the moment.*"

She groaned. "At least hand me that book before I beat my head through a wall."

He handed her the book before leaning back again and closing his eyes.

The sound of the book opening and pages turning reached Joey's ears until the sounds stopped. The room stayed silent for a long time.

It doesn't take her that long to read two pages, *he mentally laughed.*

"*You know, staring at me isn't reading.*"

Joey could picture a blush covering her cheeks under his eyelids. Elizabeth was almost too easy for him to predict.

"*I wasn't even looking at you, big head.*"

He opened his eyes, covering his heart with his hand. "Big head? I'm hurt."

She rolled her eyes at him. "Whatever."

Joey laughed, closing his eyes once more and resting his hands on his chest.

"*I thought you were supposed to be keeping me company,*" *she complained.*

"*I am.*"

"*You're sleeping!*"

"*I'm enjoying the silence. Oh wait, there isn't any, because you keep talking. Do me a favor and shut your mouth, Liz.*"

That was a lie, and Joey new it. He didn't want her to stop talking; he found their little talks quite amusing. He also knew that telling her to shut her mouth was a sure fire way to get her to keep talking so she could annoy him.

Oh, how he wished he could hear her now.

A knock sounded at the door, and he opened an eye to see his little brother standing in the doorway. At Elizabeth's word, he jumped on the bed, sitting down next to her.

This is the best, *he thought.* We're all together.

Like a family.

"Sir!" Thomas said, rushing to Joey's side as he fell back against the foot of the bed and slid to the floor. A headache pounded against his skull, and he realized he had hit his head against the desk when he fell.

"I'm fine," he calmed his footman, holding a hand to his head. The necklace was on the floor by his foot.

Hesitantly, his hand reached for the silver chain.

"How in the world?" he muttered to himself.

"Sir?"

Joseph shook his head. "Nothing. I'm fine."

"Are you sure?"

"I can manage, Thomas. Thank you for delivering the letter."

Thomas bowed. "My pleasure, sir. Is there anything else I can do for you?"

"No, you can go," he answered, "but give me the letter as you leave, please."

The footman found the paper on the desk, handing the letter to the hands of his master.

"Thank you." His footman bowed and left the room.

Alone in his room, Joey's shaky hands unfolded the message. The letters were written in a crooked slant, as if she rushed her writing. He wasn't sure why he felt nervous as he read, but he couldn't seem to get his breathing under control.

Joseph,
I've gone to find the Night Rider. I know that you didn't want

me to go alone, but I won't take you away from the duty you have to your kingdom. I know I can be selfish, but I won't be so selfish as to risk your life for my own needs. This is something I need to do alone.

The truth is, before now, I would've been terrified to go by myself. I wouldn't have willingly walked out of the palace doors the day I arrived and said, "I'll do this myself." I was terrified of being alone in my own world. I was deathly afraid of having no one left to care for me. I depended on my job and things I never wanted to change for comfort.

I wasn't strong then. I don't pretend to be the mightiest person now because I know I'm not. I have, however, gained strength here that I couldn't have gained anywhere else.

The love you and Edward have showed me since I have been here with you has been amazing, and I can't thank you enough. You showed me that change can be a good thing, and you showed me that I'm never really alone.

When Ed died, I felt like my world was crashing down around me. I've never felt a loss like that before. When we spent those days in solitude, I thought that it was all over. I was terribly selfish, and I apologize for that. I considered writing in the Book during that time; I wondered if it would be best to die of heartbreak and try to move on with my life. I didn't, however, because somewhere through the sorrow I knew that I wasn't the only one feeling broken down and lost. The day we finally saw each other again gave me hope that it wasn't over. I knew this story wasn't finished, and I know it won't be for a long time.

Now, it's my job to end this chapter. The Night Rider's story is about to come to a close, and a new beginning will emerge for Aon. I hope that you take the new kingdom and run with it to new heights, and I know you'll be a great king.

The journal wasn't clear, Joseph. It didn't say whether or not I would go down with the Night Rider when the time comes. You and I both know that. It's very possible that I could be going home *soon. If that happens before I see you again, just know that I'm sorry for any problems or pain I've caused since I got here. I turned everything upside down.*

I did quite a few things I didn't expect to do during my time here, too. I learned how to fight and how to horseback ride, I played a children's game in the pouring rain, attended a ball, climbed trees. Most of all, I didn't expect to develop such strong feelings for you.

I have to admit, at the beginning, you infuriated me. You teased me and argued with me. I told myself that I hated you, when in reality, I was a little lonely when you weren't there to nag me. As time wore on, I realized that I did feel something for you, and it definitely wasn't hate. *It wasn't* like, *either, but I was too afraid to tell you. Honestly, I was afraid to tell myself.*

Now that there's a possibility my time is limited, it seems I have no choice but to muster up the courage to admit it to both of us.

I love you, Joseph. I think I have for a while now, I just wasn't sure of myself. Facing death does sort of wake a person up, though, and I'm positive now.

Unfortunately, when I added 'love' to the vocabulary concerning you, I also took 'goodbye' out. That means that saying farewell isn't allowed just yet. 'Until I see you again' seems more appropriate.

Until I see you again,

El

"She loves me," Joseph said aloud. His fingers rubbed the paper back and forth. "And she went anyway."

His right hand gripped the paper, crinkling it in his palm and releasing his frustration on the letter. He realized what he was doing and let it fall to the floor.

She did it for Ed, he reasoned with himself. *Don't be*

selfish, Joey. She did it for the both of you to keep your kingdom safe. Isn't an entire kingdom more important than a girl?

He could no longer sit still, and he rose to his feet, pacing the floor. His hands ran through his hair in frustration as he battled with himself.

The precious letter was picked up off the floor and carefully laid on the desk. His hands came up to smooth out the wrinkles.

She wants me to stay, his thoughts reasoned. *She wants me to take care of the kingdom. I could die if I went after her, and she knows there is no other heir. I could ruin everything if I showed up, and she could be killed because of it.*

The memory of Elizabeth flashed into his mind once more, and he was left even more confused than before. Thoughts ran through his mind continuously as he struggled over what to do.

Do I go after her?

I can't go now; I'd ruin her cover. That, or I'd never find her in those woods.

———

Joey awoke slumped against the wall, the white parchment crumpled and creased at his feet. His hand came up to rub his face as he looked around the room.

It was a mess. The desk was the only clean thing in the room. Its contents lay on the floor, spread out in the walkway. The sheets of the bed were rumpled and in a ball at the foot where he had tried to sleep but failed. A tray sat in the floor by the door where Thomas had offered him dinner, but he refused.

His hand instinctively ran through his hair, and he moved to his feet, picking up the letter and carefully setting it on the desk before leaving his bedroom. He didn't know what time it was, but he guessed it was early; there were no maids or butlers bustling about the hallways, and the sun hadn't broken the horizon.

The thick carpet that covered the floor muffled the sounds of Joseph's footsteps. He let his mind wander; he didn't know where he was going, only that he was desperate for a different atmosphere. Window after window passed by, only showing him more darkness.

What if it isn't her fault? he dared to think. *What if she didn't start all of this chaos? Would this mission be any less dangerous?*

His thoughts were interrupted as he realized he had wandered into the hallway that held Elizabeth's room. His feet took one hesitant step in the direction of her door before his conscience stopped him.

Keep moving, Joseph.

Joey's heart won over his mind, and he approached her room anyway. His hand slowly turned the doorknob.

Her room was just like he remembered it. He hadn't entered it since Edward's death, but nothing was out of place.

Except the broken mirror in pieces on the floor.

Shards of glass were everywhere. He was careful not to step on any with his bare feet as he tried to piece together what happened. His eye caught a shard of reflective glass with a bright red stain on it. Had she cut herself?

His fingers grazed the blanket of fragments when he reached for the painted shard. He caught the reflection of his own eyes in the glass.

Shaking his head, he threw it back to the ground and left her room in a hurry. It was painful, being in there, especially when he knew very well that she might not come back.

With no sense of where to go or what to do, he went back to his room. As he trudged back past the desk, the leather binding of the journal caught his eye. It was lifted from the pile and brought into his hands, settling on the last written page.

The fight ended at the hands of the one who started it.

Of course it's El, he thought. *She's the one who brought Ed back from her world.*

But if Elizabeth hadn't come here, then Ed would have been in her world forever. I had no way of winning, he realized. *I would have never seen him again, or he would've died here.*

Quit being selfish, Joseph. Ed being alive in another world is better than him being dead in this one. And Elizabeth didn't know what would happen when she read our story, so don't blame her either.

Why would she blame Delia? he wondered. *Did Delia really say those things to her?*

Joseph's mind wandered back to his visits with his sister after Elizabeth had arrived. When he had left Ed and Elizabeth outside of the city to go see her, she was just returning when he arrived at her chateau. She claimed that she had professional business, but she was wearing her boots and spare cloak, not her formal attire.

When he journeyed from the capital city to see her a second time, she claimed to know nothing of the Night Rider, yet she spouted gossip like she'd heard everything herself.

Delia never liked Ed, he remembered. *She never wanted to hear anything about him, never wanted to see him. She always complained that the kingdom was being ruled by a young boy and not a man.*

She was so mad at me when I stayed in the kingdom with Ed and our father. It took her forever to get over it.

Or maybe she never really got over it.

His breath caught in his throat as he realized that the Night Rider wasn't a man after all.

It was a girl. His sister. Elizabeth was right; there was no other explanation. The timelines matched.

Joey remembered when his sister was sent off to school and how long it was before he saw her again. She certainly could've bent a few men to her will with her talents when she was younger and used them to terrorize Aon until she could do it herself.

The Book slammed shut in Joey's hands. He cursed, running from the room in a mix of emotions. "If Elizabeth is right, that means…"

He shook his head. *This could be disastrous,* he thought.

And yet, it was the only thing that made sense to him.

"Thomas!" he called, sprinting down the hallway. "Alec! Find Cyneward!"

twenty-four

When I woke up the next morning, I found a dagger clutched in my fist like it was a lifeline. I knew where it had come from—I had fallen asleep with it just in case I'd been ambushed again—but why did I even feel the need to have it?

I was no assassin, but it felt like I was being forced to turn into one. This world was far more brutal than I had thought. Defense was one of the first things I learned, and quite frankly, I wasn't sure how I felt about that.

This is for Ed, my conscience reminded me. *He wrote this. There's no way I can lose.*

I hope.

I mounted my horse quickly, swinging my leg over the saddle and tightening my weapons into my belt. My cloak was still wrapped around my shoulders, and the cold air crept around my body. I shivered; the snowflakes fell more rapidly now than they had before.

Instead of riding through the fields like Joey and I had done before, I guided my horse through the trees and stayed close to the border of the forest. I knew Delia would have eyes watching from all directions; if she knew I would be coming like Devin said she did, I had to be extra careful.

My breath made a mist in the air as I rode, and I directed my hot breath onto my hands so they wouldn't freeze. I wasn't far from Berkeley or Wilmington Place now; I'd done most of my riding the night before, only stopping when it became so dark I couldn't see anything in front of me.

Now, in the early morning, I rode slowly, careful to look for any sign of a forest dweller. Hopefully, it wouldn't be long before I'd find Stewart's brother.

The woods were quiet except for the sound of frozen leaves crunching and wind blowing. I was all too aware of the silence that surrounded me, terrified that someone I couldn't see was watching me. I tapped my horse's side, urging it to go faster.

A rush of relief flowed through me when I spotted a clearing in the trees.

In the clearing sat a quaint little cottage. It showed a striking resemblance to the one Joey's mother had, with the same windows and steps in the front. Carefully, I slid from the saddle of my horse and tied it down before approaching the little house.

The snow-covered leaves crunched under my boots. I hoped that this was Stewart's brother's cottage and not one that belonged to someone devoted to Delia.

It would be just my luck if it was one of Delia's minions.

Before I could reach the steps, the front door swung

open, and a man appeared on the staircase.

"Can I help you?" he asked, brandishing his knife. Obviously, he didn't want me here.

"I'm sorry," I said, holding my hands up. Hopefully, he wouldn't throw the blade in his hand. "I came for help."

"I don't help people," he grunted. "Get off my land."

"I was sent by Stewart," I offered, taking a step back. "He told me his brother could help me and told me where to find him."

The man relaxed. "Stewart sent you?"

I nodded.

The blade in his hand was sheathed, and he motioned for me to follow him. Warily, I walked towards the house.

"What kind of help did my brother promise you?" he asked as I closed the front door behind us. The room was small; a bed sat on one end of the room and a table at the other. A shield and several swords decorated the walls.

"Weapons and armor." He certainly had plenty of both.

"I see. And what exactly does a girl like you need weapons and armor for?"

He sat down at the table, taking out his dagger and beginning to polish it. I swallowed.

"I'm hunting the Night Rider."

The blade fell from his hands and made a low thud against the wood.

"You're *what?*"

"You heard me," I said, sitting down across from him. "The Rider has taken a lot from me, and I'd love to return the favor."

"Wouldn't we all," he mumbled, picking the blade back up. "Listen here, missy; I don't know what makes you think you can just go out and hunt down this bastard by yourself, but—"

"I'll tell you why I think it," I said, leaning forward onto my elbows, "it's because I'm the Keeper."

"The Keeper?" he asked. "Yeah, right. Prove it."

I almost told him that I could prove it, but then I remembered that I didn't have the Book. Joey did.

"Whether or not you believe me is your problem. Your brother promised me help. I'd really appreciate it."

"Breathe, kid. I'd help you either way. I just wanted to make sure you knew you were headed into a slaughter."

I grimaced. "Believe me, I know."

He held out his hand across the table. "I'm Gilroy, by the way."

I accepted his gesture. "Elizabeth."

"Well, Elizabeth," Gilroy said, "what exactly do you know about the Night Rider?"

"I know that his followers meet him near Berkeley," I said, intentionally leaving out the part about Delia. "That's all I know."

"Well, you have that part right. You should be prepared for what you'll find, however."

I raised an eyebrow, and he continued.

"He operates out of an old castle, deep in the woods beyond the village. It's been abandoned for centuries; I think it was the original castle of Aon before Devereux Castle was built. It may be worn, broken down, and in ruins, but it's still large. It'll be easy to get lost in it, so be careful."

"How do you know all of this?" I cut in, furrowing my brow.

"I've seen it." He grimaced. "Curiosity is a dangerous thing. Don't underestimate how much trouble your curiosity can get you into." His tone was warning. "His followers are constantly moving in and out of the building. You'll have to sneak in or risk being overpowered."

"Thank you, Gilroy," I said, "for helping me."

"Don't mention it," he answered. "Now, about your weapons and armor…"

Gilroy started to speak but was cut off by the sound of hoofbeats.

He cursed under his breath as he pulled a sword, several daggers, and the shield off of the wall.

"This way, before they see us. Keep quiet." He nodded his head towards the bed. I followed him skeptically.

What is hiding under a bed going to do?

Without warning, he slid the bed out of the way, revealing a trap door underneath. He threw open the lid and gestured for me to go first.

Never mind. Maybe it will.

I cast a glance at the window before sitting at the edge and swinging my legs down first into the hole. My feet found a ladder, and I stabilized myself on it before climbing down. When I reached the bottom, I moved to the side to let Gilroy down.

"Who is that?" I whispered once his feet had hit the floor. He pulled the hatch down and locked it, and now we were in complete darkness.

"Who do you think?" he muttered. I heard a faint noise as he fumbled with something, then a match struck, illuminating a small portion of his face. "Riders. They know why you're here." He handed me the sword and daggers to hold.

"They must have followed me here," I realized. Gilroy searched around the room until he found a candle. He lit it and blew out the match, tossing it to the floor.

"This way," he said, motioning to me. He walked quietly into the darkness, and I made out the stone walls of a corridor as my eyes adjusted to the darkness.

"What is this?"

"This is where I keep the armor," he answered. "It's also an escape route for when those bumbling *idiots* come knocking at my door."

The chilling air of the cellar caused me to pull my cloak around my body tighter, and the edges of the fabric made soft brushing noises against my boots as I walked.

Gilroy stopped, leaning over something I couldn't see. A moment later, light flooded the room, and he handed me a lantern after swapping his candle out for one himself.

My first thought: *Wow, this guy really does have a lot of armor.*

The stone walls were covered with chest plates, shields, and swords. Several training mannequins sat in the center of the room, torn up and worn. The room narrowed off into another dark corridor at the far end.

I put the sword and blades he'd handed me on the table to my left as I admired the large collection.

"Impressive," I breathed, raising the lantern up and tracing a blade on the wall with my finger.

"Thanks," he said, putting down the shield. "We don't have much time, so grab a chest plate over there and let's get you suited up."

I did as he said, pulling a chest plate off a rack against the wall and another shield. He met me in the center of the room with leg armor and a shirt made of tiny chains.

"Why do you have this?" I asked, holding up the chest plate. It was smaller than the rest—made for a woman.

"A woman on the royal guard asked me to make it," he said, taking it from me. "You're lucky I still have it. She was supposed to come get it from me last month."

Rose?

"She's dead," I said solemnly.

"I'm sorry to hear that," he answered. "What happened?"

"Riders."

"Of course it was." He sighed. "Raise your arms."

I did as he said, and he slid the chain shirt over my head. After the shirt was in place, he helped me into the chest plate and secured the leg armor onto my legs. I slid gloves onto my hands, and he latched them onto the armor. Everything felt heavy on my body, but I didn't complain.

This could very well save my life.

When all of the pieces were secure and in place, he handed me a silver shield, a helmet, and a heavy sword.

"I have a sword."

"This one's better," he answered, taking mine from the sheath and replacing it with his. "It's heavier. That dainty sword of yours won't do any amount of damage to the Night Rider."

Nodding, I moved my arms around. The metal made me move a little slower, but I could still move.

"All right," he said, stepping back to look at me, "we need to get moving. I have no doubt they're still looking for you up there."

He picked up both lanterns, handing one off to me

before leading me further into the room and down the dark, narrow corridor. We didn't walk for long before we came to another ladder.

"This opens up just a little ways behind my cottage where my stables are," he explained, putting a foot on one of the rungs. "If they're still there, they'll come after you. You can take one of my horses, but I can't say whether or not it'll be fast enough."

"Let them come," I said. "I'm not afraid of them."

It was true. There were several things that I was afraid of, but after facing them time after time, the Riders weren't one of them—especially Delia.

Delia didn't scare me. Her powers didn't scare me. Her hatred towards Aon didn't scare me. I wasn't afraid of her anymore; I was angry.

He chuckled, shaking his head. He turned towards the ladder. "Brave girl. *Stupid*, but brave."

I chose to ignore his remark. We climbed the ladder, and he slowly opened the hatch. He climbed out, helping me up out of the cellar when he was steady on his feet. When I finally got onto the dirt, I realized that we were in a stable stall with a sleek, black horse.

He raised a finger to his lips and pointed to the door of the stall. I moved to the horse, throwing a saddle over its back and trying to keep it calm as I fastened the straps of leather.

I held my breath, pressing my back against a wall as one of the Riders drew closer, dismounting and stepping into the stables. Gilroy pulled me back behind the horse to block us from view.

"This one's got a saddle on it!" the man called. "Should I take it?"

"Leave it!" someone else answered. "She doesn't need it!"

The Rider scanned the stall again before stepping out of sight.

"*She?*" Gilroy hissed. "A *woman?*"

"Don't worry about it," I whispered back. "Get the door, and stay safe. I'm sorry I brought them here."

"I've been through worse, kid. Be careful."

I pulled my helmet over my head. I had to admit that it was beautiful; it only covered the top of my head and the sides of my face, but it was strong. An intricate pattern had been molded into the metal.

After getting back into position, Gilroy nodded, holding up three fingers and counting down. When he held up one finger, I sprang up, throwing a leg over the saddle and settling into my seat. The horse reared, and the door swung open, allowing me to take off at full speed.

Snapping the reins, the horse reached full speed. I guided it straight out of the stable and blew past the Rider that had investigated the barn, knocking him off his feet.

"There she is!" he called, scrambling to mount his horse. The other Riders spotted me, and soon they were on my tail. Looking behind me, I caught sight of Gilroy who was waving.

I barely felt the cold;the adrenaline pulsing in my veins prevented me from feeling much of anything except a temporary sense of bravery. The horse was smooth, dodging trees with ease and jumping logs. The Riders were almost as skilled as me, but not quite; of the four that were following me, one fell off his horse, and a low branch knocked off another.

Two more, I thought, guiding the horse to the left. Without warning, I moved sharply to the right, causing another to fall from his horse.

Delia needs to do a better job of training her followers.

The last one was harder to get rid of. I kept dodging trees until I spotted a huge one right in front of me. I drove the horse straight at it, only moving away at the very last second. The Rider's horse reared up, knocking him off and running along without him.

My ride in the woods grew quiet. My horse slowed down, and I let him; I knew that if Delia was expecting me, she wouldn't send anyone else out after me.

At least that's what I hoped.

The journey wasn't as long as I thought it would be. It wasn't long before I spotted another clearing ahead. Taking precautions, I dismounted from my horse and walked the rest of the way so I wouldn't be caught.

Once I reached the clearing, I noticed that the ruins of the castle were big, just like Gilroy had told me.

Contrary to what he had thought, though, there wasn't a single Rider in sight.

"Okay, Ed," I mumbled as I left the cover of the trees. "I'm ready."

twenty-five

"How far ahead do you think she's gotten?" Joey asked his best friend as he paced the office that had once belonged to his father. "She can't have gone far."

"Margaret told me that she sent her to Gilroy's. If she left last night, then she'll be at or close to his cottage in about an hour," Alec answered. "We have to leave now if we want to get there in time."

"How are we going to defeat them all? Who knows how many Delia has on her side?"

"We're going to be tactful," Alec said. "We're going to send them in waves, take them down line by line if need be. You and I need to be the first ones in, though; we don't know where Elizabeth will be when we get there, and we need to be the first to get to her."

"Cyneward," Joey said, turning to the guard, "have you gathered the militia?"

"I have, sir," he answered. "They're ready for the

word."

"Joey, Delia is going to be stronger than one hundred militiamen on her own," Alec reminded him. "You know that, don't you?"

"The men aren't for Delia. They're for her Riders."

"Then how do you expect to defeat her?"

"I was the one who started this feud," Joseph stated. "When I told her I wouldn't live with her, away from our father and Edward and the new kingdom, she got jealous and started all of this chaos. Edward wrote that I must be the one to do it, and that's what we have to trust."

"Are our horses ready?" Alec asked.

"The fastest we could find, sir. We've also mapped out the quickest route; it's dangerous but fast. We should get there in half the time if we don't run into any complications," Cyneward said.

"Notify your men of the plan," Alec ordered. "They can't all rush in at once; it could ruin everything."

"Let's go, then," Joseph said. "It won't be long before Delia decides to unleash her wrath on Elizabeth, and I want to get there before it's too late to stop her."

twenty-six

I could feel someone watching me the minute I broke through the tree line. It was too quiet.

I could feel the pressure of eyes on me as I slowly reached the ruins and touched the large door with my fingers. The door opened before I could pull, forcing me to step back.

There was no one on the other side.

She knows you're here, remember? Calm down and keep your mind clear.

My steps echoed in the empty hall as I walked down the center of the ruined room. Stone and marble were lying in rocks and boulders around the room, and the wind breached the room through holes in the walls. The doors closed of their own accord behind me, and I kept my hand hovering above my sword's handle.

The room was all marble and stone. At the far end, remnants of what must've been a throne were scattered along a platform. Rigid, faded edges of what used to be stained glass bordered the hole in the wall above the throne.

This used to be Aon's capital then. It must've been Yula's rough draft.

Treading further into the room, I noticed doors on either wall. Before I could even begin to wonder which door to take, the one on my left swung open by itself.

She's leading me to her, I realized.

Cautiously, I stepped into the hallway beyond the open doors, quickening my pace. I wanted her to stop with the preliminaries, with the games; she made me nervous, and she knew it.

Another door opened on my right. Without any thought or hesitation, I plunged into the room at full speed. It became mechanical; I blocked out my thoughts and followed the open doors, one after another. Now deep into the castle, I knew that it would be near impossible to get out of the labyrinth she'd just led me through. As I passed through another door, it slammed shut behind me.

The last room was the biggest yet. The ceiling was almost completely gone, allowing the light snow to fall onto the wet stone below my feet. Icicles hung from what was left of the stone frame.

I only noticed that I wasn't alone when she cleared her throat. My stomach dropped when her sickening, twisted smile came into view.

"Elizabeth, darling," Delia called, "how nice of you to join us."

My hand gripped my sword handle, but I didn't draw my sword.

"I'm so glad Devin gave you my message," she said, taking a few steps towards me. "I was afraid you wouldn't get to hear it from him."

"I heard it," I answered. I did my best to keep my face straight as I counted the number of Riders in the room behind her, forcefully slowing my breathing when I hit the number fifty.

Fear will only make her more confident.

"And you still came?" she asked, beginning to circle me. "Silly girl."

"I absolutely *love* your choice of location. Are you immune to the cold or something?"

"Elizabeth, unless I'm mistaken, you aren't here to talk about the weather. I assume you're here for revenge."

"Revenge?" I scoffed. "Yeah, I'm here for revenge—the same kind of revenge that sent you off on a tour of terrorism. *No*, this isn't about revenge. This is about putting an end to a monster."

"We aren't here to talk about me," Delia spat. "I have everything I need, now that the *little prince* is dead. All I'm missing is the throne which you will happily hand over if you value your life."

"Do you realize what you've done?" I asked, gritting my teeth and drawing my sword. "Do you realize the people who have been lost? The damage you've caused? The lives you've ruined?"

She chuckled, as if everything I'd said was amusing. "It's a small price to pay for power, dear girl. Put the sword away; we both know you don't have the courage to use it."

"Power?" I laughed a humorless laugh. "You don't mean to tell me all of this is just over power? You have some other reason behind this, and we both know it. You hide behind denial like a child." My sword was already growing heavy in my hands, and my body grew weary.

This heavier sword was a bad idea. It's only been a couple of minutes, and I can barely hold it.

"And you hide behind the sword. Hand over the throne, and I'll let you live. Or better yet, I could kill you. You could go home and forget that Aon ever existed."

"Over my dead body," I growled.

She smiled wickedly. "That can be arranged."

Delia stepped back, waving her hand in the air. Instantly, I hovered right above the ground. With another flick of her wrist, I slammed against the stone floor.

"It took you long enough to figure out my true identity," she mocked, waving her hand so that I was dragged behind her walking figure. "I thought you'd never put the pieces together."

"You're a murderer," I spat, blood dribbling down my chin. I was left still on the stone floor when she turned.

"Call it what you like, but I've learned to live with the blood on my hands. Edward was just another obstacle that had to be pushed aside."

"You're a heartless monster."

"Yes, and you're a scared, pathetic little girl in a suit of armor. Truth is, neither of us are what we want to be, are we?"

I stayed silent. *Don't let her get into your head,* my conscience told me. *She's trying to make you weak.*

You're already weak.

"Elizabeth, you're no hero. You aren't strong enough to conquer my powers. Why not give in now and save yourself the pain? This kingdom was failing anyway."

I pushed myself off of the ground, gripping the

sword tightly. "I won't give in, Delia."

"Pity," she said with a devilish smirk. "You would've made a nice addition to the collection of traitors I have."

"I'm not a traitor," I said through gritted teeth.

"Aren't you?" she asked, coming closer to my face. "You hid the Book from everyone. It told of Edward's death before it came to be, and you chose not to read into the future. They all think you're a fraud," she hissed.

"No," I murmured.

"Yes," she laughed. "You were bound to be killed sooner or later. They hate you. Want to know the only reason you're alive?" she taunted. "You're only alive because you're at the mercy of my brother. If it weren't for him, you'd be burned for treason."

"No!" I screamed angrily, lunging forward. I swung my weapon, narrowly missing her neck. She easily waved her hand, and the sword flew out of my hand onto the floor.

"Anger makes people irrational, don't you think?" she taunted. "Anger and fear together is even more dangerous, and my dear, I could smell the fear on you as soon as you walked in the door."

I ignored her, pulling two daggers from my waist and throwing them at Delia. With another wave of her hand, she deflected them as if they were nothing.

Before I knew it, Delia raised her hand. I felt my throat grow tight, and within seconds, I was ten feet above the ground, struggling to breath as all of her followers watched from the sidelines.

"No!" someone yelled across the room. Just as my vision started to go black, I was dropped from the air. I hit the floor on my side, curling up in pain from the metal armor that dug into my torso. Forcing my eyes open, I caught sight of Delia on the floor. Joey was on top of her, holding her down.

"Joey!" I called. He whipped his head around, catching sight of me.

The distraction gave Delia the leverage she needed to loosen her arm and to throw him off. His back hit the stone wall as she forced him away with her powers, and he slid to the floor in pain.

A loud roar sounded behind me. I turned around to find what appeared to be almost one hundred people, half dressed in black, and half dressed in silver.

Aon's militia, I realized. *They've come to fight.*

Catching sight of Joey, I realized that Delia was closing in. Instinctively, I sprinted towards her, aiming to knock her to the ground. She caught me before I even came close, holding her hand in front of her and hovering me above the ground for a second time. Instead of dropping me, though, she swung her hand to the left and sent me ramming into the wall.

"I'm tired of your interferences," she said, eyes blazing as she swung me towards the opposite wall. "You're a waste of time, Elizabeth Knight. A waste of time and a waste of space."

Pain shot through my body as I came in contact with the wall again. My head rolled back and I cried out; my helmet fell from my head and hit the ground with a loud clang.

She flicked her wrist, sending me hurtling at the ground. I felt a sickening pop in my right leg and a crack that rattled my body. I cried in agony.

It was as if every footstep she took towards me shook the earth. I watched her feet draw closer, and then I was raised again from the ground, her invisible hands wrapped around my throat.

"Farewell, Elizabeth," she spat in my face. "Sweet

dreams."

I was slammed against the floor once more, and my vision faded into dark nothingness.

twenty-seven

Using every ounce of strength he had, Joey pulled himself up from the rubble. He blinked, wiping the blood from his head and trying to clear his vision as he witnessed Elizabeth's body slam brutally against one wall then another. Her helmet fell from her head, and she fell back to the ground.

"No!" he yelled, scrambling to reach her. He was too late; Delia held the girl up, and with one final motion, Elizabeth slumped to the ground, unconscious.

He found a sword lying on the ground and gripped it before sprinting to Delia.

"Enough, Delia!" He threw himself between Elizabeth and his sister. "When did you lose your heart?"

"When you chose the little *runt* over me," she sneered.

"Edward wasn't a runt," he bit back. "He was going to be a great ruler."

"Little brother," Delia called, ignoring his remark, "why deny me of what I want? We could be better rulers together, you and I. Edward couldn't compare to the power we would have over Aon."

Her sly smile turned into a smirk as she glanced over his shoulder to the girl he was protecting. "She isn't worth it, Joseph." She held out a hand to him. "Join me."

"You're right," he breathed, surprising his sister. "She's not worth the fighting."

His sword drifted down towards his side.

"That's right, Joseph. Lay down your weapon." She reached out her hand towards him.

"She isn't worth the fighting," he repeated, strength in his voice. "She's worth *more*."

Joey swung the sword with all his might at his sister. Instead of pushing him back, like she had with Elizabeth, she merely deflected his blade.

"I won't fight you, Joseph," she said, flicking her wrist to avoid his blade again.

"Pity," he spat, "because I have *every intention* of *ending* you."

Delia's expression faltered as she continued to deflect his swings, one after the other. She expected him to grow tired, but his hits just kept coming. Her arms grew tired and her head started to ache; she couldn't keep it up for much longer.

Without warning, the butt of Joey's sword came up to his sister's head before she could deflect it. She fell to the ground with a loud cry.

Joey towered over his sister as her eyes narrowed at him.

"Joseph," she breathed, a laugh still playing in her voice, "you wouldn't kill your own sister, would you?"

Joseph cast a look down at his sister, defenseless on the ground, and the sword at her throat. His gaze shifted back to Elizabeth's motionless body as Alec ran to her side. Her eyes were closed, and blood ran down the side of her face.

Alec caught Joey's eye and nodded.

Joey turned back to Delia. All of the anger and hurt he had stored up over the years bubbled to the surface, and he felt *nothing* for the girl on the ground in front of him.

He grimaced. "*You are no sister of mine.*"

Joey couldn't feel anything. He couldn't even look as he plunged the sword into the girl's chest. He could hear her coughing, could feel the resistance against the blade, could see the blood seep onto the floor and under his shoes, but still, he didn't look. He squeezed his eyes shut as hard as he could.

"She's dead!" someone yelled from behind him. "The Night Rider is dead!"

Instantly, the room grew quiet, and every head turned in Joey's direction.

Alec rose from his place next to Elizabeth and stood in front of Joey who dropped the sword from his hands with eyes closed. He didn't say a word; his chest heaved from lack of air, and he struggled to find oxygen.

"Riders," Alec called loudly, "your time is up. Surrender now, or face death row."

He watched with a triumphant stare as every Rider dropped his weapon and held his hands up. The remaining militiamen held up swords, threatening anyone who stepped out of line. They were filed out of the ruined castle, one by one.

Alec turned to his friend who was shaking. He pulled him away from Delia's limp body, turning him away from the scene and kicking the bloody sword out of the way.

"Joey, look at me," he said, shaking his friend's shoulders. "Joseph, we have to leave."

Joey shook his head, his eyes still firmly shut. "I can't look at her."

"Can you look at Elizabeth?" he asked. "She's alive, but she doesn't have long. We have to get her out of here, *now*. I can't do anything for her here."

Hesitantly, Joey opened his eyes. "I'll get Elizabeth. Please... just make sure I can't see Delia."

Alec moved back over to Elizabeth, scooping her limp body up in his arms. He then handed her off to Joey who furrowed his brow.

"Is she going to be okay?"

"As long as she's here, she won't be," Alec answered. "Get her out of here right now. I'll handle everything else. And be careful—her leg is fractured."

Joseph followed Alec's orders, staggering towards the exit with Elizabeth in his arms. He kept his eyes trained forward and tried his best to ignore the sounds of sloshing blood at the feet of the militia.

twenty-eight

I woke up in a bright white room. Light streamed from a big glass window onto the floor.

My head ached. When I reached up to rub my temple, I realized that my arms were wrapped in thick, white gauze and my head in the same material. Moving my arms hurt, so I rested them back down at my sides.

I tried to move my legs to help me sit up, but as I moved my right leg, pain shot through my entire body. Throwing back the covers, I realized that it too was wrapped in a stiff cloth. My skin was a horrible blue, black, and purple color.

I took in my surroundings, trying to get my mind off the sickening sight of my discolored leg.

I was in the castle infirmary, in the hospital wing, I decided. A row of empty beds decorated with plain white sheets lined both walls. I knew the room was bigger than what I could see, so I guessed that I was somewhere around the center. My head felt so heavy that I couldn't be bothered to move it to see.

"You're awake," a raspy voice called.

A soft pitter-patter of feet could be heard, and then a figure came into view.

"Joey," I whispered, trying to find my voice. It hurt, like I hadn't talked in days.

"Hey, sunshine," he said softly, smiling as he sat down on the bed parallel to mine. "How're you feeling?"

"Everything hurts," I said, "but I'm okay. What about you?"

Joey's bottom lip was scarred, and his hands were blistered and rough. He was still in his dirt and blood stained clothes, and his own dried blood was still on his face, arms, and hands. I wondered if he had been in the infirmary with me since we returned.

"I'll make it," he assured me.

"What happened?" I asked. "Where is Delia?"

"I took care of her," he said simply. "You're safe. The Night Rider is gone for good. You don't have to worry about her anymore."

"I'm sorry," I said. Delia may have been a monster, but she was still his sister.

"I'm not," Joey said, shaking his head. "I barely knew her."

"Are you okay?"

He didn't seem confident in his answer. "Fine."

"I love you," I said suddenly. Surprisingly, I didn't feel any embarrassment by it; it felt good to say the words out loud.

"I love you, too," he answered, squeezing my hand. He gave me a reassuring smile before standing up. "Get some sleep. You'll feel better." He pressed a kiss to my forehead.

I did as Joey said, allowing myself to fall back into a dreamless sleep when he had left the infirmary.

The sound of hushed argument woke me up, and I didn't open my eyes.

"What are you going to do without her?" someone asked. The voice resembled Alec's. "You've committed too much to her; it's going to hurt you both when she leaves."

"That's exactly why she has to leave," Joey's voice responded. "Do you understand how much worse it will be for her down the road? She'd live long enough to watch me die, Alec. I don't want that for her."

"If she chooses to stay, she'll stay for you," Alec answered. "I hope you know that."

"She has a life away from here. She'd be giving it up."

"You don't know that. Her life could go back to normal the minute she leaves Aon, whether it's now or years from now."

"That's a risk she shouldn't have to take. She shouldn't have to choose."

"You shouldn't choose for her," Alec retaliated.

The yawn that had built up in my throat slipped from my mouth, and the two grew silent. Now that my cover was blown, I turned my head, pretending that I had just woken up.

"Go," Joey hissed to Alec. His footsteps drew closer to me, and as I opened my eyes, I found him standing at the bedside.

He was cleaner than before; he'd bathed, changed his shirt, and combed through his hair. He sported dark shadows under his eyes. I was relieved that he was no longer covered in dirt or blood; instead, his hands and head were bandaged like mine.

"You're awake." Dimples poked at his cheeks.

"How long have I been asleep?" I asked.

"About five hours. It's nearly four in the afternoon; you've been asleep all day."

"Have I really?" I asked, spotting the window on the far wall. A soft, warm evening light poured in through the glass into the room. "Why didn't you wake me up?"

Joey moved to sit down on the edge of my bed, taking one of my hands into his. "I thought about it, but I decided that Sleeping Beauty needed her rest. I didn't think you'd take kindly to being woken up with a kiss in this state."

"Hopeless romantic," I teased him.

"I wouldn't say hopeless," he said. "I have you here, don't I?"

"Didn't I tell you? I'm leaving. I'm sure there's another illegitimate child around here somewhere that's more my type."

Instead of laughing, like I'd hoped, his smile fell from his face, and his hand fell from mine as he stood up.

"You *are* leaving, Elizabeth."

I frowned. "What? I was joking, Joey, I—"

"Elizabeth," he said, cutting me off, "it's time for you to go home."

Scoffing, I rolled my eyes. "Very funny. I'm not going anywhere."

"I'm serious. Your time here is up. You've been put in enough danger in just a few months here; I can't put you through any more of it."

"But I'm happier here than I ever was there," I retaliated. "Would you like to see me die?"

He flinched, turning away. "You know I wouldn't."

"Then why? If you wanted me gone, you should've

let Delia finish me off when she had the chance."

He didn't answer.

"Is this your way of telling me that you're done with me? That you're done with whatever this is?" I asked almost angrily. I'd been through too much to throw it all away.

"Of course not, Elizabeth," he said, whipping his head around. "You know that I love you."

"It seems like that doesn't matter, now. What if I love you too? Is that enough to change your mind?"

"*Do* you love me?" he asked. "If you do, you'll do as I ask. You have a life to live, and I don't want to take the risk of either one of us getting hurt. If you stay, we have to worry about who's going to leave first; if it's of old age, we both know it will be me. If you leave right now, you can move on with your life, marry someone else worthwhile."

"You are worthwhile," I answered.

"Am I worth a war?" he asked. "Did you know that the nobles are considering making me the legitimate heir to the throne? When they do, it's going to give the kingdoms across the Leathan Sea reasons to start conflicts. They're already restless, and this will open the door for them to ruin everything. I can't put you through that."

I shook my head. Aon was too important to me.

"Joey, I'd put myself through anything. I don't want to—"

Joey's voice came sharp, quick, and worst of all, emotionless.

"I don't want you here, Elizabeth. Go home."

He stared me in the eye. I desperately searched for something that would tell me he wanted me to stay, but I found nothing. His eyes were empty, like he had put up a shield around his thoughts, blocking me out from his emotions.

He doesn't want me here? That changes things.

I looked away from him, unable to keep my thoughts straight any longer. Tears threatened to spill from my eyes, but I forced them back.

"This is what you want, is it?" I asked bitterly.

His voice came bluntly. "Yes, it is."

"If you're sure." I pointed towards the door, not bothering to give him a second glance. *"Get out."*

End of Book One

Acknowledgements

A writer cannot finish a book on her own. Sure, she puts the pen to the paper (or rapidly presses buttons on a keyboard, in my case), but she can't finish her story without motivation and support. She can't write the thoughts in her head if she doesn't have a goal. If there are no people to help her reach that goal, well... Let's just say that the job gets a little harder. And that's what this page is for—to point out and embarrass the people who helped get your dreams one step closer to the finish line.

I'm only joking. I don't *just* want to embarrass them (though that's a lovely bonus). I want to thank them.

First, I'd like to thank my parents. They were constantly supportive of the hobby I chose to obsess over and were respectful of my decision not to let them read the story until it was in print. Handing them the book in print with my name printed across the top was better than finishing the book itself. I love them very, very much (even you, dad, but I doubt you'll see this because you don't read, right?).

Next, I'd like to thank Haley, my go-to on all things writing and my endless support. She read everything before it was even constructed into an actual story—meaning that she read jumbled up scenes that were out of order and a plot that wasn't developed before it was all one piece. And she *still* managed to tell me it was a good story. That's amazing. Someone who can do all that is a superhero. Thank you, Haley, for putting up with the endless changes in the drafts and sticking by me when I wrote over the rough patches.

Another person who deserves to be recognized is my fellow author and friend Terry Maggert. I met him at a literary festival when I asked him about the beautiful book covers he'd created for his Fearless series. Instantly, he was happy to answer my questions and even kept in touch with me throughout the process of getting my book from the screen and into paper form. I'm forever grateful for the tips and advice he's given me. I hope he understands how helpful he was to me and is proud of how the project turned out.

I can't express enough gratitude towards my tenth-grade English teacher, Mrs. Willis. She agreed to proof-read through my entire manuscript (all 320 pages, mind you) in the final stages of the editing process. She gave me constructive criticism and was extremely kind. Who else has the time or patience to read a story written by a sixteen-year-old? I'm extremely grateful for everything she did for me. I hope she's proud of how the final product turned out, too.

I'd also like to thank all of my beta-readers, who so diligently helped me comb through my story and put the pieces of the puzzle together. They were supportive, constructive, and very kind to me throughout the long process of reading an unedited book. It isn't easy, that's for sure. You guys are rock stars.

I'd like to thank my editor, my formatter, and my book cover designer. If it weren't for them, my book would still be in a lonely file on my laptop.

I'm so thankful to God for everything He's blessed me with in my life. Without Him, I wouldn't have anything I have today. I'm thankful for the people He has placed in my life and the motivation He's given me. I know that when no one else is around, He always has my back and I'm thankful for the opportunities and doors He has opened in my life that made this possible.

Lastly, I'd like to thank anyone who picked up this book and stuck with it until the end. Thank you for making a young author's dreams come true. It can be hard for a self-published author to pick up readers, and even harder if you're still a teenager, praying that you'll be taken seriously. Thankfully, I have you all. You're all lovely people for giving Elizabeth's story a chance. I can't wait for you to read the next book; hopefully, we'll all stick around together to see it.

About the Author

K. M. Higginbotham is a young writer from a small town in North Alabama. When she's not writing, she's enjoying a hot cup of black tea, reading, longingly planning her future trips across the world, or making music with her family.

Kate finished her first fantasy novel, *Keeper: The Book of Aon*, when she was fifteen. She plans to extend the series and is currently writing a stand-alone teen fiction book entitled *September*.

For news and information on upcoming books, go to **kmhigginbotham.com** or like the Facebook page at **https://www.facebook.com/kmhigginbothambooks/**

Made in the USA
Charleston, SC
22 August 2016